# LAST CALL

## LIBBY KIRSCH

*Sunnyside* Press

Sunnyside Press
PO Box 2476
Ann Arbor, MI. 48106
www.LibbyKirschBooks.com

Publisher's Note: This is a work of fiction. Names, characters, places, and incidents are a product of the author's imagination. Locales and public names are sometimes used for atmospheric purposes. Any resemblance to actual people, living or dead, or to businesses, companies, events, institutions, or locales is completely coincidental.

Last Call/ Libby Kirsch -- 1st ed.

ISBN 978-0-9969350-8-1

*Thank you, Tom.*
*You're so supportive, and I'm so lucky.*

# CHAPTER ONE

Janet slammed the drawer of the cash register. By the time Cindy Lou jumped at the noise, Janet had her phone out to make a call.

"Hey, darlin'," Jason said when he picked up the line. "I was hoping I'd hear from you."

Janet smiled, in spite of her foul mood, and pushed wisps of light brown hair off her face. Her hand came away damp. She'd been sweating in the Knoxville summer heat since before she even rolled out of bed, and the ancient air-conditioning unit behind the bar couldn't seem to keep up with the soaring temperature. Then she remembered the reason she was calling and frowned. "I just counted—and then I re-counted. Money's missing again." She walked toward the back of the room, away from Cindy Lou and Frank, her bouncer, who'd just arrived for his shift. "This time we're short eighty-two dollars." She couldn't stop herself from turning back to look at her employees suspiciously.

"And?" her boyfriend asked.

"*And* Elizabeth was working last night." She watched Cindy Lou disappear into the back cooler with an empty bucket.

"Anyone else?" Jason asked.

Her lips puckered. Why did he always sound so irritatingly reasonable? "Well, yeah, but I don't think—"

"I'm just saying. Don't fly off the—"

"I can keep my cool, okay?" she snapped, then flushed. She hadn't meant to shout. She lowered her voice to a whisper. "Jason, can you please just check the video? I gotta go." They disconnected, but before she could shove her phone back into her pocket, the screen lit up with a delayed notification telling her she'd missed two calls overnight from the very employee she suspected of theft. She glared at the walls, then realized it wasn't the poor reception *here* that was the problem. She'd been home all night with Jason, and for some reason the incoming calls from Elizabeth were only now showing up.

She tapped a few icons and shook her head. Her youngest staff member hadn't left a message, but the timing seemed suspicious. Janet had learned just days ago that money was disappearing from the register, and now Elizabeth was trying to call her on her cell phone for the first time ever? Did she know, somehow, that Janet knew about the missing money?

Cindy Lou hobbled out from the walk-in cooler, her gait awkward as she wrestled a full bucket of ice behind the bar. As usual, she was dressed to kill—or at least maim. She had poured herself into a bright pink tube top that ended just above a shiny green belly-button ring. Her tight jeans rode so low that her hip bones jutted out, and Cindy Lou had tied her bleach-blond hair back with a teal bandanna. Body parts were spilling from every piece of her outfit.

"You gained a set there." Janet motioned to Cindy Lou's chest. Something had happened when she dumped the ice bucket into the freezer drawer, and her two boobs had turned into four.

"Oh my gosh! They musta come unstuck!" Her twang made the words musical. She bent over and reached into her tube top to rearrange things.

"Come on!" Frank turned away from the bar in disgust and headed for the far side of the room.

Janet watched him walk off before asking Cindy Lou, "What's under there?"

"It's a silicone push-up thingamajig. Sticks right to my skin and pushes the girls up—but I'm sweating so much, they must've slipped down." She wiped beads of sweat from her brow and then smoothed the fabric of her tube top over her restored figure. "You know, I didn't used to need all this business under here, but after Chip, everything just kind of . . . fell."

Chip, Chip, Chip. It was all Cindy Lou ever wanted to talk about. Janet plastered on a smile when her bartender looked up. "Kids, huh? How old is he now?"

"Seventeen, going on forty." She smiled indulgently. "He leaves for college soon." She turned back to the bar, a towel and spray bottle in her hands, the goofy grin still on her face.

Frank slammed two chairs down from the table in the corner, still scowling. He might not have liked Cindy Lou's methods, but he took his share from the tip jar every night without complaint. Janet only paid minimum wage, but they all cleared more than thirty dollars an hour on a good night, thanks in some part, perhaps, to Cindy Lou's ramped-up double Ds. Their nice pay made it even more frustrating to discover someone had been stealing money from the register, and if Janet's new accounting program was right, it had been going on for weeks. That's why she'd had Jason install a state-of-the-art surveillance system. She was ready to catch a thief.

"Damn gum," Frank muttered, scraping the tabletop with a razor blade.

He fit the job description for a bouncer—tall and strong—but his light brown hair was smashed flat on one side, as if he'd fallen asleep while it was wet, and his eyes were red and puffy.

Was he the sticky-fingered employee? Though Elizabeth, Janet's other full-time bartender, was her prime suspect, Frank was no prize, so if Jason saw him stealing in the surveillance video from the night before she wouldn't be shocked.

But Elizabeth still seemed the most likely culprit, although

Janet couldn't articulate why to Jason. She just had a feeling the other woman was hiding something.

"Anything unusual last night?" she asked lightly as she walked back behind the bar.

"Oh, you know," Cindy Lou said without taking her eyes off the two bottles of top-shelf vodka she was combining, "same old, same old. We had to throw poor Ike out just before midnight, bless his heart. Other than that, it was the usual."

"Did he make a fuss?" Janet already knew the answer, since she hadn't been called.

"Nah." Cindy Lou placed the full bottle of vodka back on the shelf and dropped the empty one in the recycling bin.

Frank cleared his throat. "No fuss?" He hefted two more chairs off a table and dropped them to the ground with a bang. "He shouted the whole way out the door, 'The man will always find you—he knows,' not to mention the hail of curse words he spewed at Elizabeth."

Cindy Lou shrugged as she took two bottles of well vodka from the bin and unscrewed the caps.

Janet looked shrewdly at her bartender. "Did we call him a taxi?"

"Yes, ma'am, we sure did, and didn't kick him out until it arrived," Cindy Lou said, unconcerned.

"Well, shit," Janet nodded and shrugged. Really, you couldn't ask for a better outcome.

Cindy Lou raised her eyebrows and looked pointedly at a jar on the counter.

Janet grinned. "Aw, hell, Cindy Lou," she drawled, making a show of pulling not two but three dollar bills out of her back pocket and pushing them into the oversized, washed pickle jar. The swear jar already had five bucks in it from the last hour alone. "I keep forgetting to watch my damn mouth."

Her good humor was tested, however, by Frank, muttering in the corner.

"That's not how you'd have handled it on the force?" she asked.

"It's not a police issue. I just don't know why he's welcomed back time and again." Frank turned away from the women and kept working.

Janet had hired him a few weeks ago, desperate for a bouncer and impressed by his pedigree. She figured a former cop would surely know how to handle the door of her small bar. So far, however, he'd been a disappointment, always ready to escalate a situation and challenge the status quo.

"I suppose you think that kind of behavior is fine?" he asked over his shoulder.

"No, but this is a bar, not a bookstore. It's going to happen." Janet crossed to the back cooler and emerged minutes later with a white plastic bin full of lemons and limes. She looked up at a sudden clattering at the front door. A gray and grizzled man with greasy hair and dirty clothes pulled at the handle. She could practically smell his days-old sweat through the glass.

"Door's broken!" he called, cupping a hand over his eyes so he could see into the bar. "Ma'am? It won't open." He jiggled the handle again, and then, as if he'd expended too much effort, he leaned in, leaving a streak on the glass with his forehead. Janet and Cindy Lou exchanged amused looks, but Frank crossed his arms and stared daggers at him.

"We're not open," Frank said, looking at the man like he was the leftover foam at the bottom of a pint glass.

"Not open?" The man smiled, revealing several missing teeth. "How'd you get in?"

Janet chuckled and looked at Frank. "Take care of it." She pointed to the number for the taxi company nailed to the wall behind her, then waited until Frank picked up his cell phone before she took the empty fruit bin to the back room.

There, Janet caught a glimpse of herself in the mirror on the back of the door. She turned to the side to check her boobs. She was thirty-one years old and had no kids, so they were right where they were supposed to be. She smoothed her black T-shirt with the bar's logo on it and tucked it into her jeans before heading to the desk.

She spent a few minutes going over the books. It was Thursday, which meant they could expect a big college crowd thirsty for deals. She squinted through the window into the back parking lot. If the beer truck didn't show, she'd have to change her happy-hour special, as her inventory of cheap, crappy beer was low.

Janet looked at the clock on the wall and blew out a sigh. She'd check the cooler to see what would make a good replacement.

But first, she decided to call Elizabeth. The call went straight to voicemail, so she left a message, telling her bartender to call in; she wanted to ask directly about the missing money. Her phone chirped—the battery was low—so she laid it on the desk and called Jason on the landline, leaving him a long, detailed message about her plan for Elizabeth.

Despite the missing money, she liked being in charge. It was freeing to think that if there was a problem with an employee, she could fix it.

Buying the Spot a year ago had made her a boss for the first time ever, and she was on a mission to be unlike any crappy boss she'd ever had. She wanted to be calm, be unflappable, and stay the hell out of her employees' personal lives. With a final nod to herself, she logged out of her computer and left the office.

As she cut through the main room, however, her step stuttered and her heart slammed into her chest. What was it about seeing cops that made you feel instantly guilty?

The man and woman in uniform were chatting with Frank by the front door. Cindy Lou was behind the bar, not making eye contact, but Frank looked up defiantly when she cleared her throat.

"Hello, Officers," Janet said. "What's going on?"

# CHAPTER TWO

"I'm telling you for the last time, Frank, you either get on board or you get out. Your ninety-day probationary period isn't over, so there won't even be any paperwork to file." Janet spoke low and fast to her bouncer. She'd pulled him aside after gleaning that he'd dialed 911 instead of the taxi company.

"Why do you care if that homeless guy has to spend the night in jail?" Frank's superior smile was almost enough to make her snap.

With a supreme effort, and ignoring the roar of blood rushing in her ears, Janet turned on her heel and marched over to the officers. "More sweet tea?" She attempted to cover her anger with acute kindness. After all, it wasn't the police officers' fault she'd hired an idiot.

The woman shook her head, but the man smiled and held out his glass. After she topped it off from the pitcher on the bar she said, "What are you booking him in on?"

"We got a call for a drunk and disorderly person, but now I'm thinking public intox is a better fit."

Janet shot a disbelieving look at Frank. "Disorderly? He called me 'ma'am' when he tried to open the door. He really just needs a ride home . . . or—or a meal, maybe." She looked out the glass door and saw the person in question huddled in the backseat of the cruiser. "Cindy Lou," she added, "get him a sweet tea to go." She watched her bartender pull a large Styrofoam cup from an upper shelf. "Y'all don't mind, do you?" she asked the woman cop, purposefully bringing out a little Southern flair.

The officer smiled and held out her hand for the drink, but her partner said, "He *is* getting a ride . . . just not home."

Janet bristled at his attitude. Business would plummet if her bar got a reputation for calling the cops on people who were minding their own business. She shot Frank another dirty look.

"Frank here did the right thing." The male officer nodded with approval. "Public intoxication is a class-C misdemeanor." The two men fist-bumped.

"You two know each other?" Janet asked, looking at the pair shrewdly.

"Frank worked under me for a bit," he answered, then turned to Frank and said, "I still think you got a raw deal, man."

"Thanks, brother," Frank said. He walked the cops to the door.

"He'll spend a few hours in jail, sleep it off, and be on his way," the woman said over her shoulder to Janet as they left.

Janet's expression darkened. She'd have liked nothing more than to fire Frank right then and there, but she couldn't. He'd been the only one to apply for the job when she posted it at the start of summer, so for now, she was stuck.

She had gone over her policy with all the employees many times: if someone was drunk, she would pay for their ride home. The steps were outlined in the employee handbook Jason had insisted she write up when they bought the bar. A bartender took away a customer's car keys and called a cab if they'd had too much to drink. The customer could get their keys back the next day after reimbursing Janet for the cab ride. Sure, they'd had complaints from some customers, but usually only on the night in question. The next day, most were not only apologizing but also thanking Janet for saving them from themselves.

She even had a deal with the local taxi company for a discounted rate for her customers—a system that should have worked seamlessly.

Unfortunately, her newest hire seemed determined to forge his own path at her bar, and it was starting to piss her off.

She spotted a lone lemon lying forgotten next to the cutting board and angrily grabbed the knife.

*Thwack.*

The blade slammed through the lemon and she shook her head, thinking about Frank's attitude. He was a self-serving, sanctimonious—

"Ouch!" All the air squeezed out of her lungs as the knife sliced right into her finger.

Cindy Lou jumped at the sound and then rushed to the cabinet for the first-aid kit.

After Janet caught her breath, she went to the sink and held her hand under cold running water. The red-tinged water swirled down the drain as Janet's anger swirled up inside of her.

"Am I unclear, Cindy Lou?" she asked under her breath. "Am I not articulating the rules well?" She took the bandage the other woman held out and clumsily unwrapped it with one hand.

"No, you're clear, boss. Clear as a bright, sunny day. He just wants to do it his way."

"When he gets his own bar, he can do that. It can be like the goddamn OK Corral if he wants, with cops there every night. But that's not how we are going to do business *here*." She shrugged off Cindy Lou's offer of help, finally freed the bandage from the wrapper, and then wound the small strip around her left index finger. Cindy Lou lowered her head and looked at Janet through her eyelashes, then put a dollar in the swear jar from her own pocket.

Was she paying for Janet's swear word or swearing at Janet in her head? Janet was surprised enough that she had to fight off a smile. But her good humor faded when she tossed the bloody towel into a trash can. The bin was overflowing—no one had bothered to empty it after closing the night before. Janet pulled the black trash bag out of the waist-high trash can, groaned when her finger pulsed with pain, then tied off the bag and headed for the alley door.

"I sure wish people would share the work around here, instead of their opinions on every damn decision I make," she called to Frank as she pushed through the heavy metal door to the side alley. Within seconds, her tank top stuck uncomfortably to her skin and her jeans felt heavy. The heat of the day was already oppressive.

She took a bracing breath, then heaved the bag up into the Dumpster. Her mouth fell open when she saw several more trash bags on the ground around the other side of the bin. The sound of rushing blood was back, roaring past her ears

"Trash bags go in the Dumpster, not by it!" she shouted toward the bar.

"I put them *in* the Dumpster," Frank replied mulishly at the door, making no effort to come out and help.

"Then why are they on the ground?" Janet glowered at her bouncer. She gestured to the abandoned building next door. "We look like we're competing with old Ben Corker's restaurant!" Foreclosure signs and trash littered the lot, which blended in seamlessly with hers.

When Frank didn't answer, she stalked over and hefted the closest bag up into the Dumpster, then froze when she bent down to get the second bag, her mouth suddenly dry. "What the . . ."

She reached down and gently lifted the lower corner. Nestled underneath the black plastic were what looked like toes. "Whoo," she breathed, and her heart skipped a beat. She took an involuntary step back before recovering her wits. She nudged the bag out of the way with her foot and then swore under her breath when it became clear the toes were attached to a foot and the foot to a man, lying alongside the Dumpster. The exposed skin was bluish white, smudged with dirt that looked as dark as the trash bags.

"Well, shit," she said, staring at the body. "This day can't get any worse."

# CHAPTER THREE

A slow, gigantic fly buzzed overhead, and Janet swatted it away. It lumbered toward the Dumpster, joining dozens of others swarming around the body.

"Officers!" she called when she heard a crunch of gravel. But her throat was dry and the word was barely more than a croak. The cruiser was finally pulling away from the bar. Janet waved her arms and called again. "Hey! Over here!"

The woman cop glanced over and seconds later the cruiser stopped with a jerk. She climbed out and headed along the building toward Janet.

"Yes, ma'am?"

As she got closer, Janet turned and pointed to the toes.

"Oh!" The officer hurried forward and moved the final two bags of trash away before pressing her fingers into the neck. "Cold to the touch," she said. "No pulse."

The other cop had honked twice since she walked over, and he finally climbed out of the cruiser and shouted, "Davis, let's go! I don't have all day, here."

Officer Davis muttered under her breath, "We literally have all day—our shift started an hour ago." Louder, she said, "Got a dead body over here, Gale! Our day just changed." She reached up to press a button on the radio clipped at her shoulder. "I've got a ten twenty-nine at the Spot. Body out back." Davis turned back to Janet with a squint. "Do you know this guy?"

Janet shrugged and took a few slow steps toward the Dumpster, ignoring the tightness in her chest. Her eyes moved from the feet, over the light-wash jeans with a belt buckle the size of Tennessee, to a bright, construction-sign-orange tank top. Her eyes finally settled on the face and she pressed her lips together.

"That's Ike Freeman—he's a regular. He—ah . . . he was here last night."

"Was?" Officer Davis said, her eyebrows raised. "Still is." She took out her notebook. "Did you have any trouble with him?"

"Oh no—nothing like—" Janet's throat constricted. The reality of the situation left her momentarily speechless. "Well, I mean, I heard we had to kick him out, but nothing like . . . *that*." She gestured toward the body. When Davis's chin shifted to the left, she added, "We called a taxi. He didn't want to leave at first, but he did."

"No." The officer shook her head and stepped closer to Janet. "He didn't. Do you have any idea why he's here, behind your bar?"

"No." Janet crossed her arms. "I have no idea at all. Like I said, we called a cab."

Officer Davis narrowed her eyes but took a step back. "I'll need to speak to everyone who was working last night."

"Of course."

"EMTs and homicide are on the way," Officer Gale said. He stopped walking when he got to his partner, but his eyes kept traveling until they landed on the dead body. "We need to rope off the area."

Before his partner could reach her hand out for the crime scene tape, a car pulled into the lot. Officer Gale sprang forward, waving his arms as he moved toward it. "You can't park here! This is a crime scene!"

Jason leaned forward over the steering wheel, his eyebrows

drawn together, lips pursed. Janet raised a hand in a weak wave, and he backed up a fraction and then parked near the entrance to the bar. Officer Gale shook his head. "I said it's a crime scene! Back out of the dang lot!"

Jason climbed out of the car, and the cop hurried forward. "Sir, you need to move this car and vacate the premises. This is an active crime scene."

"I'm the co-owner," Jason said through clenched teeth.

Janet felt the weight pressing against her chest release. Jason was here. It would be okay.

He brushed past Officer Gale, and her heart flip-flopped against her ribs, as if she were seeing him for the first time.

Everything about Jason was a study in contrasts. His preppy, short-sleeve, navy blue polo showed off part of the sleeves of colorful tattoos that went from his wrists, over his shoulders, and down onto his back and chest. His dark hair and all-star smile made him a perfect candidate for a lead role in a rom-com, but when Jason turned on his intense, focused gaze, heartbeats accelerated—including hers.

Was Officer Davis panting?

Jason's lips, usually curving up at the corners with a ready smile, were flat and white as he headed for Janet. "What's going on?"

"Homicide's on the way," Gale said, motioning toward the Dumpster. "Until they get here and clear the scene, I'll need everyone—employees and owners—to wait inside the bar."

Janet glanced at the guy in the cruiser and asked, "Does that include him?"

Officer Davis sighed. "I guess it does."

Her partner turned and motioned to Janet. But instead of following him inside, she raised her eyebrows at Jason. His lips hitched up unhappily on one side and he shook his head; her eyes opened wide and she threw her hands on her hips before turning to the cop anyway. "I think we have something that might help."

"What's that?" Officer Gale asked.

"Jason owns a security company. He recently wired the bar from top to bottom with cameras."

"Inside and outside?"

"Mmm-hmm." She turned to Jason for confirmation, but he was rubbing his face. She knew he didn't like the police, but this was a dead customer; he needed to step up.

"I can't."

"Jason!"

"I came here to tell you my whole system is down. I've been hit with some kind of malware attack." But when his gaze swept the outside of the building, his frustration gave way to a new emotion.

"What is it?" she asked, unable to read his expression.

Now squinting, he walked slowly toward the building. "We have four cameras outside and one of them monitors this part of the alleyway."

"We'll definitely need a copy of that surveillance video for our investigation," Gale said before relaying the information into his radio for whoever was arriving.

"I already told you the system is down, but I don't think it matters, anyway." Jason folded his arms over his chest.

Officer Gale took two steps toward Jason and stopped with a wide stance, his chest puffed out importantly. "It wasn't a question, Mr.—what was your last name?"

"Brooks," Jason answered, still distracted.

The officer scribbled that information into his notebook before speaking. "Well, Mr. Brooks, we'll take what we need when there's a dead body to investigate."

Jason's eyes narrowed as he finally turned to face the cop full-on. "It's not a question of whether I want to share it with you." He closed the gap to the building, shook out a folding ladder that had been leaning against the wall, and climbed up until his face was inches from the exit sign hanging over the rear door. After studying the device for several moments, he said, "It's a question of why I can't share it with you."

Janet was relieved to find that Officer Gale looked as perplexed as she felt.

"I'm sure I'll get to the bottom of the malware attack, but it won't matter: it looks like somebody tampered with the camera."

"Don't touch anything!" Gale said as he took a step closer. "Ah . . . what camera?"

"I have a security camera hidden in this sign, and right now, the lens is covered with a strip of electrical tape."

"Why would somebody do that?" Janet asked.

"One guess," he said, turning to look at the body.

"How many people knew about the camera?" Officer Gale's eyes narrowed as he looked between the co-owners.

"Not many," Jason answered after a pause. He jumped off the ladder. "In fact, I thought it was just me."

The words floated in the air and landed heavily at Janet's feet. Officer Gale's look as he stared at her boyfriend was unsettling. Had Jason just become a murder suspect?

# CHAPTER FOUR

An hour later, Janet added ice to a glass and filled it with sweet tea from the huge metal urn on the bar. The cubes clinked and settled under the liquid, and the outside of the glass was cold and wet by the time she raised it to her lips to drink. She almost sighed at the perfect blend of sweet and savory flavors. Cindy Lou was a lifelong Southerner and had named herself Chief Tea Brewer after watching in shock one day as Janet scooped iced tea powder into a glass of water.

So far, the beat officers had given them a wide berth, but Janet had a feeling that was about to change. Two homicide detectives who'd been outside by the Dumpster for the last forty-five minutes had just walked into the bar.

Detective Mark Finch, older, grayer, and heavyset, moved moodily through the space, lifting things with the tip of a pen and looking suspiciously at her staff and her furniture in equal turns.

"He likes to look around first and then ask questions," Detective Patrick O'Dell said, walking up from the opposite side. He was just over six feet tall with broad shoulders, slim hips, disarmingly bright green eyes, and a slight accent. Janet heard a trace of New York just at the end of his sentences.

He gestured to the gunmetal-gray, bottle-shaped refrigerator that sat in the exact center of the bartender's space behind the counter. "Is that a Beerador?"

"Yeah." She looked at the detective in surprise. "You know about them?"

"My granddad had one in his shop back in the day. You don't usually see them this far south."

"It came with the bar when we bought it a year ago, and I know why. It's heavier than a car—I couldn't get rid of it if I wanted to!"

"Still chugging along, though, huh? That's saying something. It must be nearly seventy years old." He eyed the room. "You've got an interesting setup here. Doesn't seem very efficient, ya know?" She squinted back at the man standing in front of her. She'd heard of the good cop/bad cop routine, but this seemed a bit much. He was looking at her pleasantly, as if he didn't have a dead man to deal with. "The square bar top should be good—ya know, more seats for customers on all sides—but then you've got that Beerador blocking vision down the middle, so one bartender can't see the whole room. It doesn't make any sense."

"You're not breaking any news here, Detective. It came like this. We have a plan to make some changes, but we just don't have the funds, yet."

They stared at each other for a moment before he said, "Mrs. Black, have a seat. I have a few questions about last night."

"It's Ms. Black, and please, ask away, but I wasn't here, so I don't know how much help I'll be."

"Where were you?"

"At home."

"Was anyone with you?" He asked the question pleasantly, but her mouth went dry just the same.

"My boyfriend."

"Did you know the victim?"

"Sure. He was a regular here—a pain in the ass, but usually sorry the next day."

"Any idea what happened?"

"Nope."

He leaned back against the seat, his expression unreadable. "Did he have any problems with anyone?"

"Only everyone who got in his line of sight when he was drunk. Like I said, he wasn't a model customer. He drank too much, and we had to call him a taxi to take him home more than once a week."

"So, what happened last night?" O'Dell's eyes were bright, curious, and lightly suspicious as they locked onto Janet.

"I don't know—I wasn't here." Her nostrils flared. Why was he wasting his time with her?

O'Dell nodded and stood, placing his card on the table. "Call me if you think of . . . anything worth saying." He smirked and started to move away.

"Detective, are you sure this was a murder? I mean, couldn't Ike have just hit his head or had a heart attack?"

O'Dell looked down his nose at her. "You don't often die of natural causes and then cover yourself up with garbage bags."

She frowned. "Yes, I know that, but he could have . . . I don't know, decided to cover himself up first . . . maybe for warmth?" Even as the words left her mouth, O'Dell shook his head.

"Sure. The low was eighty-four overnight with ninety percent humidity. It's a possibility, I guess. Also, there was . . . trauma to the body. We'll have to wait on the coroner's report to be certain on the cause of death."

"I'd just rather—" She turned at a clunk of noise coming from the back and looked suspiciously at the office door. Was someone in there? She got up and tried the handle. It was locked, just like it should have been. She reached into her pocket for her key ring when O'Dell cleared his throat.

She heard the clunk again and instinctively turned toward Detective Finch, interviewing Frank nearby. He banged on the jukebox with his fist and the music cut off. He grinned and did it again, and the music started back up.

She blew out a breath and frowned at her own jumpiness.

O'Dell was staring at her intently. "You'd just rather what?"

"I'd just rather it not be a murder," she answered truthfully.

O'Dell tilted his head to one side and finally said, "Yeah. I know." He turned and walked away.

Finch moved behind the bar, picking things up with his gloved hands, searching under shelves and across surfaces.

Jason made his way to her table and slid into the seat next to her. "I hate this," he said, watching as Finch opened the cabinet that held the first-aid kit and the extra dish soap. "What's he looking for, anyway?"

"No idea," she replied.

He took her hands in his. "Are you okay? You found Ike, are you . . . okay?" he repeated.

"Yeah, I'm fine." She started to pull her hands away but he didn't let her.

"Janet, it's a big deal. Some people go their whole lives without seeing that. It's okay to feel shaky or scared, or sad." Jason's eyes were trained on hers and her heart *lub-dub*bed at his gentle touch.

"I promise, I'm fine."

With a sigh that meant he didn't believe her, he squeezed her hands once before letting go. He leaned back and something fell out of his pants pocket with a tiny clink. Janet reached down and picked up his pen from the floor.

"That is the ugliest pen I've ever seen," she said, watching him tuck the neon blue and yellow pen back into his pocket.

He grinned. "I special-ordered it that way. Ain't nobody gonna steal that!" He looked across the bar. "Speaking of special orders, it wouldn't hurt to have everyone wear a uniform." He nodded at Janet's shirt and said, "Even those old bar T-shirts would be better than *that*." His eyes darted across the room. "It would at least look less . . . or, I mean, more . . . hmm."

She scanned the room and found Cindy Lou, sitting alone at a corner booth, stirring a glass of ice water with a small black straw. With the table covering most of her lower half, she looked PG-13 versus the R rating when her full body was on display. If not for the circumstances, Janet might have laughed.

"I don't want to hurt her feelings," she said. "I think she spends a lot of time getting her look just the way she wants it."

"These damn cops rub me the wrong way," Jason said in a low voice. O'Dell had just sat down across from Cindy Lou, his notebook out, pen poised. When Janet looked over at her boyfriend, she expected to see anger. Instead, his eyebrows were drawn together, concern—sliding toward disappointment. He glanced at her and added, "I mean, they're just dying to be suspicious of regular people. I hate that."

Now it was Janet's turn to cover Jason's hands. She squeezed until the tiny creases around his eyes smoothed a fraction.

"Jason—"

"I'd rather you don't talk to each other until we talk to each of you." Finch had apparently finished his work behind the bar. He planted his feet wide, and folded his arms across his chest as he looked between Janet and Jason.

Jason peered up at him but didn't move. "Ask away." He steepled his fingers in front of his face and waited.

"You first." Finch pointed at Janet. "I'll come for you after."

Jason rubbed at his eyelid and shook his head. Janet felt a rising wave of emotion churning inside of him, which was the last thing they needed with cops everywhere and a dead body outside.

She turned so that her lips were a scant inch away from his ear and whispered, "Looks like you're sloppy seconds."

He snorted, then pushed himself up from the table. "I'll be over there if you need me," he said to Janet, pointing to a nearby booth.

"Thanks," Finch said. "I'll be right over."

Jason frowned but moved across the room.

Fifteen minutes later, Janet was appreciating Detective O'Dell's brevity.

Finch was apparently determined to break her by discussing

everything about the bar except Ike. Just then, he was honing in on how inappropriately her employee was dressed.

"All I'm saying," he eyed Cindy Lou, "is that nobody wants to see belly button anymore—especially not before dinner."

Janet looked down at her own midriff. Her belly button was completely hidden, but with Finch's attitude, she'd never wanted to show it off more. She'd just opened her mouth, ready to defend her staff, when O'Dell spoke from across the room.

"Finch, leave her alone. Don't you know who her dad is?"

"Brass is going to come down hard on this one—first murder in five weeks. The mayor was just about to hold a press conference about how safe our streets are, and now this?" Finch snapped. "I couldn't care less who her dad is. I'm only interested in solving this murder." He shot Janet a disgruntled look but got up from the table and walked away.

"And belly buttons," Janet muttered, but she couldn't help agreeing with the jerk. She didn't care that her dad was a federal judge, either, and she also wanted to get to the bottom of Ike's murder. The killer was someone who knew about their security system—that much was clear—which meant it was probably someone associated with her bar.

Her eyes swept the room. Someone had gone out of their way to cover their tracks—and the outside camera. The truth was, somebody in this room knew something.

# CHAPTER FIVE

By four o'clock, Janet had resigned herself to the fact that she wouldn't be able to open the bar for business. Homicide had only just begun their investigation, crime scene techs were still dusting every available surface for fingerprints, and Ike was still lying next to the Dumpster—although his body was now covered with a black tarp.

Elizabeth's shift had started a half hour earlier, but so far, she was a no-show.

"All I'm saying is it doesn't look good," Frank said to Cindy Lou, unable to contain his glee. "She's not here, and there's a dead body outside?"

Janet turned away from the bouncer; leave it to Frank to be excited about the crime. She stared thoughtfully out the window. She couldn't deny that it was odd Elizabeth wasn't here, though. Her absence was either worrisome or suspicious, and the homicide detectives appeared to be leaning toward the latter, based on the questions they were asking. She tried Elizabeth's cell phone, but the call went straight to voicemail—again.

She disconnected, her finger throbbing in time with her heart-beat. Although Janet had changed the bandage three times, blood seeped through again, and her pain level increased with each passing minute.

"You think she's an intern?" she asked Jason. They sat at the bar, watching an evidence tech use packing tape to lift fingerprints from the section of counter across from them. What the woman was hoping to find was beyond Janet—there had to be sixty different sets of prints from the last night alone. "Are you guys going to be here all night?" she called.

The crime scene investigator didn't answer.

Jason groaned. "What a day. My system is attacked by some malware program, and I'm stuck here, waiting on a detective to tell me I can go back to work. It's just so frustrating!" He grabbed her hand and she moaned, the pain in her wound seared straight up through her elbow. He flinched and released her fingers at once, instead cradling her hand in his own. "Have you called the doctor yet?"

"No."

"Do it now. One of us is going to be stuck here all night, and it might as well be me—I can't do any work at home, anyway; on top of everything else, the Internet chose today to go down, too. Once the police leave I'll set up shop in the office here and try to figure out what's attacking my system."

"What about Elizabeth?"

"If she shows up, I'll tell her you want to talk to her when she's done with the police. I would have said her reaction to the missing money would be telling, but this murder kind of makes anything else seem like no big deal."

Janet stared at him for a moment before she nodded and stood. She bent over to kiss him on top of his head and said, "I'll see you at home, then."

He hooked her arm and stood as she turned away. "Are you okay?"

Nearly nose to nose, they stared at each other. Janet finally shrugged. "I don't know. It's been a . . . well . . ."

"I know," he said, and pulled her close. They stood together for a moment before he smoothed a hand over her cheek. She leaned into him and felt butterflies form in her stomach at his tender smile.

He tilted his face down and gently touched her lips with his own. Heat zinged through her core before he pulled away. "See you later." He squeezed her uninjured hand and she knew his words were a delicious promise.

Finch cut across the space to meet her at the door. "Don't go far—we might have more questions for you, no matter who your dad is." He looked as if he wanted to stop her from going, but his partner called him over, and Finch sent one last wary look over his shoulder. O'Dell winked at Janet, and she felt a puzzled smile form as she walked out the door to the parking lot.

The humidity outside was so thick that she felt like she was cutting through it with every step, and a blast of heat hit her in the face when she opened her car door. She turned the key in the ignition, got all four windows down, cranked up the AC to full blast, and got back out of the car while it cooled down. She had to wipe her sweaty hands on her jeans to tap a number into her phone screen.

After a few rings and a quick word with the receptionist, she was forwarded to the scheduler at her doctor's office, only to find out her doctor was on vacation for the next two weeks.

"That must be nice," she muttered.

"The other two doctors in the office are taking her patients while she's gone," the scheduler said in a bored voice, listing the names with such apathy that Janet forgot them as soon as they were mentioned. "Do you want whoever's first available? We just opened up clinic hours this weekend."

Janet assessed her finger. "First available is fine." She made the appointment for Sunday morning and climbed back into her car. The air blowing out of the vents wasn't cool, but it wasn't hot, either, so she closed the windows and steered her car toward home. In just a few minutes, she pulled up to the duplex she and Jason had bought a year ago.

Newer beige wood siding cut perfect lines along the front of the house. She loved the color—so clean, so fresh—but Jason said it lacked energy. Earlier in the spring, small red and white flowers had filled the planter boxes just under the windows on their half of the house, but they were long wilted and dead from the summer heat, and Janet was glad, despite what Jason said, that she'd planted plastic flowers in the second-floor window boxes.

A moving van stretched across the front of the home; their new tenants waved her over from the other side of the building, but she pretended not to notice. It had been a long day already, and she didn't feel like making small talk with strangers. The two separate entrances were tucked discreetly away from each other, and she walked into her home without a backward glance.

The first thing she saw was a pair of crumpled checks from their new tenants sitting on the hall table: the security deposit and first month's rent.

She took out her cell phone and called Jason.

"I thought you were going to deposit the checks from Kat and Mel two weeks ago—you know, right when they handed them over?"

"I know, and I'm sorry. I thought I did, but then I found them in the middle of a stack of papers in my office. I was going to deposit them today, but then . . ."

She rolled the tension out of her neck and purposefully relaxed her shoulders. "It's fine. I'll do it tomorrow. Is everybody still there?"

"Yep, and regulars are starting to arrive. I wish you could see Nell talk to that idiot cop. It's classic."

"Is she running the conversation?" Janet asked, grinning despite the gruesome topic.

"He can't get a word in edgewise, and last I heard, she was telling him all about her dog's digestive issues."

"You're sending them home, though, right?"

"Yes. I told them that when you open back up tomorrow night, the first drink's on the house. Beer guy finally came—I had him load up the cooler, so you should be set for tomorrow."

"Elizabeth?"

"Nope." She blew out a sigh, and Jason said, "I'm making some progress on the Internet thing, so hopefully I'll be home later," before disconnecting the call.

Janet's finger throbbed painfully, and her head was starting to throb, too. She wandered to the main room and sat on the couch, tilting her head back to stare at the ceiling. As she tried to remember where in town the closest walk-in health clinic was located, her cell phone rang. She didn't recognize the number, and after she answered, she wished she'd let the call go to voicemail.

"Listen, Detective O'Neil—sorry, O'Dell—there's nothing else I can tell you about Ike Freeman, our staff, or our security system. Nothing." O'Dell was the nicer of the two detectives from earlier, but she was too tired to be very polite.

"I wanted to talk a little bit more about Ike. Can you come in early tomorrow? First thing?"

Janet made a face. She didn't like the sound of the invitation.

"I know your dad—well, I know of your dad. When he was appointed federal judge, we helped out with the background check on his family—"

"Yes," Janet interrupted. "I remember it." She and her father hadn't been on speaking terms back then, and she'd successfully evaded the FBI and local police for weeks, not caring to have any part in anything her father wanted or needed. Eventually her father had come to town to track her down, and Janet was more surprised than anyone that it had led to the beginning of a father-daughter relationship, the first she'd ever had.

"I'm not going to pull any surprises on you, Janet, just a few questions I didn't want to ask in front of an audience," O'Dell said. "I'm sure you'll want to do your part to help with this case."

She grimaced, but she heard herself agreeing to go in before she could think better of it. "Fine. I'll see you first thing tomorrow morning."

# CHAPTER SIX

"First thing in the morning" was subjective. Janet set her alarm for eleven fifteen, just to be on the safe side, but didn't roll out of bed until shortly after noon.

Her pajamas were rumpled and her hair lay tangled on one side, but as she brushed her teeth, she noticed that her skin was clear. She'd quit smoking about a year earlier and continued to find unexpected benefits.

After taking a quick shower, she spent a few minutes drying her hair and then threw on jeans and a tank top.

She was heading toward the kitchen when Jason called out, "Shoes!" He leaned back to look at her through the open doorway.

She slid her feet into the flip-flops she'd left by the door the night before and walked into the work zone that was their kitchen.

Jason had started renovating it shortly after they'd moved in by tearing the old, dilapidated kitchen down to the studs. A major project had then come in for his security business; another followed, and another after that. They'd been eating out and using the microwave extensively ever since. Now, with the malware attack, Janet wasn't sure when he might get back to working on the kitchen. Just then, he had three laptops spread out on a sheet of plywood over two sawhorses where the island would someday live.

"Did you sleep at all?" she asked, pressing her body against his back and kissing him between his shoulder blades. He turned and draped an arm around her shoulders. His eyes were bloodshot and his hair was rumpled.

"Hi, Janet!" called another voice, this one deep and gravelly. She looked quickly around the room and then at the computers when the voice said, "Down here."

"Wex?" In the lower corner of the left computer monitor, Jason's college roommate waved, live via webcam. His dimples deepened when she asked, "Did you cause this, Wex, or are you fixing it?"

He chuckled and ran a hand through his floppy brown hair. "I'm trying to get Jason to fix it, so I don't have to charge him, and then he'll be able to do it himself next time."

"Oh, please, spare me the learning-experience bullshit and just tell me what to do!" Jason said, only half joking.

Janet smiled at Wex, and then headed through the kitchen into the hallway where the fridge and coffeepot had been relocated half a year earlier. She fixed a cup of coffee and drank it as she made her way back through the kitchen to the front of the house.

"Can I have some?" Wex called as she walked by.

"Stop ogling my woman!" Jason said, and then unplugged the webcam, making Wex's laugh the last thing they heard from him. He followed Janet. "Sorry I'm distracted." She set her drink on the plywood and he pulled her close. "Good morning." She leaned into the hug and felt her body relax into him. He chuckled when she let out a low moan.

"It's okay, you're busy. How are things coming?" she asked his chest.

He stepped back and leaned down, softly touching her lips with his, then it was his turn to moan. "Mmm. I missed you last night. I thought I could lick this thing on my own, but I had to call Wex early this morning. Damn virus." He shook his head. "It's wormed its way into my operating system. Wex thinks he can isolate it before it does more damage, but it's locked up my whole system."

"Are you suspicious of the timing?" Janet asked, suddenly wondering if Ike's killer was a computer whiz, too.

"No," he said, frowning. "Wex thinks it's been lurking on my hard drive for weeks, and something I did, some combination of keystrokes, triggered it into action."

"Wow. Sounds very sophisticated."

"It is," he agreed, running his hands up and down Janet's arms. He cocked his head to the side. "I'm due a lunch break soon."

"How soon?" She ran her fingertips lightly over his chest. Heat flooded her stomach and she pressed her hips closer, nipping hungrily at his lower lip.

His breathing grew louder and it took him a moment of exploring her mouth to answer. "I've got Wex for another hour."

"Ugh!" she moaned. "I'll be at work by then."

Jason's cell phone rang. "Wex," he said, looking at the screen. He tapped a button that silenced the phone, then leaned closer to Janet and planted a scorching kiss on her lips. His phone rang again, and he rubbed a hand through his hair and blew out a loud sigh. "Gotta go. I'll see you tonight!" he said, then jogged back to the kitchen.

Her lopsided, dopey smile remained until she opened the door and a blast of heat melted it off her face.

"Morning!" a cheery voice called from the street.

Janet squinted past the glare of the sunlight and saw a woman carrying a pillow up the drive. Behind her a moving truck was still half-full.

"It's me, Katherine—but you can call me Kat," she said.

Kat had long, wavy brown hair that swung back and forth like a pendulum with each step, and she tossed the pillow up in the air as she approached.

Behind her, her partner, Mel, labored up the driveway with three boxes stacked high in her arms. Mel had short, sandy-blond hair, and wore hiking boots, gray cargo shorts, and a T-shirt. She gave off an air of cool efficiency.

They'd all met three weeks earlier when the two women had toured the open half of the duplex and signed the rental papers.

Janet pivoted and reached back inside the house, her fingers closing around the checks on the hall table.

"I'll head to the bank," she called to Jason, whose only response was a grunt. She turned back to Kat, who was still smiling widely. "I'm, ah . . . I'm running late. You're unpacking, huh?"

Kat hugged the pillow before answering. "Yup, almost done. We want to get the truck back by three, so we can get our deposit back, and I think we'll make it."

"Well . . . great," Janet said. "Welcome!" She barely avoided a hug as she edged past Kat.

In the car, her pulsing finger reminded her that her doctor's appointment was still days away. Blood had continued to seep from the wound all night, and now something else was oozing out as well, something creamy and whitish that definitely didn't belong in a finger.

After a quick trip through the bank drive-through, she headed to the nearest walk-in medical clinic.

The waiting room was packed, and when she signed in, the administrator guarding the clipboard said, "Mornin', sweetie. Looks like the wait is right around two and a half hours to see a doctor."

"Two and a . . ." Janet looked around the room slowly. Despair, pain, and suffering wafted through the air. She didn't have hours to waste *here*.

She crossed her name off the list and headed back to her car. She had bandages and antibiotic cream at home. She'd be fine. She touched the edge of the bandage to wipe away a smear of blood and had to bite her lip at the pain.

It was just a cut, for God's sake!

Janet determinedly headed downtown, ignoring the regular

pulsing through the pad of her finger, and turned the music up to drown out the pain.

"You said first thing in the morning," O'Dell said when he came out to the lobby. His eyebrows were knitted together, but he didn't look truly upset. "Oh, and call me Patrick."

Janet squinted up at him, wishing she'd had the foresight to stop for a cup of coffee on the way. "We don't all work nine to five, Det—Patrick."

His eyebrows shot up and he nodded with a half smile. "Well, come on back." He opened the door to the right of the bulletproof glass that enclosed the receptionist. "My office is through here."

Janet kept a few steps behind him as he wound his way through a maze of cubicles. O'Dell shared one of the very few offices with a door at the far end of the space. Two desks faced each other in the cramped room. He motioned for her to sit in one of the two visitor chairs by the door. The wall facing her was covered in mug shots—a grim row of men and women snarling unhappily at the camera.

O'Dell finally cleared his throat. "Thanks for coming in."

"Sure. I'm not sure what I can do to help, though."

They stared at each other for several long minutes before O'Dell cleared his throat again. "I feel like we got off on the wrong foot yesterday."

"Not you—your partner," Janet said with a frown.

O'Dell nodded. "Mark's very well regarded and is as thorough an officer as you'll find here." When she didn't answer, he added, "He's very . . . enthusiastic."

"Me too," Janet said flatly, and a smile threatened to break out on O'Dell's lips.

"Well, like I said last night, I know your father—well, of your father—and I figured you'd want to do right by him, to do right by this case."

She squinted up at him and leaned forward in her seat. "What does that mean?"

"It just means I know he's good people—you're good people. I hope you'll keep your ears open and let us know if you hear anything about the case, that's all. We rely on the fact that most people are . . . well, good."

She snorted. "Is that all? Did I drive all the way down here for you to tell me that most people are good?"

Surprisingly, he blushed.

"Patrick, I'm not sure about your training or background, but next time you have something similarly urgent, feel free to call or text, okay? You already have my number."

"Sit down." Janet hadn't even noticed she'd stood. "That's not why I asked you to come in." He waited for her to sit, then *he* stood and paced the tiny office. "I wanted to tell you what we know about the victim."

"About Ike?" she asked. "I already know all I need to know about Ike. He came in almost every night, ordered five drinks—three of them during happy hour to keep his costs down—and usually drove himself home, unless he'd had a few drinks before coming in, in which case we'd call him a ride."

"Do you know about his family, though—his history?"

"Well . . . no. I guess not."

"His story is a sad one, but not uncommon. His family is mostly gone, and he turned to drink at some point. We spoke to his only daughter last night to break the news, and she said they'd been estranged since her mother died a number of years ago. She was at home last night meditating. He was all alone."

Janet kept her face impassive. Everyone had a sad story to tell. Ike's didn't sound more tragic than any of her other regulars'. "Is that all?" she asked, standing again.

His green eyes bored into hers. He seemed disappointed by her disinterest. "For now. I'm counting on you to keep in touch if anything else comes up—especially that surveillance video from your boyfriend. That sure would be nice to have."

O'Dell escorted her through the office to the lobby. "We'll probably come back to the Spot tonight—we need to talk to your customers about Ike and see if anyone remembers anything from Wednesday night."

Janet made a face but nodded. She'd figured the cops would be back. "You and Finch?"

"*Detective* Finch, and it'll probably be just him. Now, now," he said when she groaned, "he's one of our best and has been on the force a long time. Ike deserves that, don't you think?"

Janet didn't answer as she wondered what her now-dead customer deserved.

"Busy day?" O'Dell asked as they stood in the doorway together, looking out onto the hot sidewalk.

"Headed to work. Did you see the news covered the crime last night? With all those live shots from our parking lot, business will be crazy tonight."

"That's grim," O'Dell said.

"It's a grim world."

"Doesn't have to be," O'Dell said.

"You're right," Janet agreed, "but it is, and I want my staff to be ready. Speaking of staff," she said, watching O'Dell's face, "what can you tell me about my bouncer, Frank Ellis?"

"Frank?" he repeated, a little too innocently.

"He said on his résumé that he was a cop here. When I asked him about it after he applied at the Spot, he told me the job wasn't what he expected and he quit, but I think I should have checked that out, you know, made sure it was an accurate reflection of why he left."

"Hmm," he said, and crossed his arms, leaning up against the door frame. "I'll give you the number for HR, they can answer any questions you have about Frank, or any of our employees." She pursed her lips, but he wasn't done. "Oh, we'll also want to talk to that other bartender who was working Wednesday night. Elizabeth? Detective Finch went to her house, but no one was home."

"Mmm-hmm," she said, crossing her arms and smiling at O'Dell. "I'll make sure to connect you with our HR department."

He cocked an eyebrow and the corners of his lips lifted in

amusement. "Fine. You want to know about Ellis?" He dropped his arms and moved closer to Janet. "The official release papers say he was honorably discharged after serving eight months on the force to care for a sick relative."

"And?" She tried not to breathe in his aftershave, but it was such a welcome combination of sandalwood and citrus that she leaned toward him while he answered to get another noseful.

"And that's bullshit," he said, his voice dropping. "He was too rough with citizens. He racked up a dozen use-of-force complaints in his first six months. Chief put him on probation, and he didn't slow down. Boss finally told the union he had to resign on his own terms or he'd be fired. He resigned." He looked behind him at the reception desk, then turned back to Janet. "Your turn. Elizabeth?"

"She's scheduled to work tonight," Janet said, distracted enough with O'Dell's new information about her bouncer that she forgot about his cologne.

"What time?"

She shook herself, focusing on the detective. "Seven. She's scheduled to work seven to close."

O'Dell patted her on the shoulder and she pushed through the door, wading through the hot, humid air to get to her car.

So Frank was a liar, and nobody had seen Elizabeth since the night Ike was killed. It was a lot to process so early in the day. Her finger throbbed as she grabbed the steering wheel—and she thought absently that she'd have Cindy Lou cut the lemons from now on.

She put the car into drive and pulled away from the curb. If O'Dell thought she'd help him with his murder case because her father would want her to, he was mistaken. In fact, it only made her want to step as far away from the crime as possible. She wouldn't lift a single finger—throbbing or not—to help.

# CHAPTER SEVEN

"Speak of the devil," Janet said, looking at the screen of her phone when it rang. She tapped a button and said, "What do you want?"

There was a beat of silence as her father processed her tone. "I miss you, too, and I love you."

She laughed grudgingly, almost hating the fact that a man she hadn't known for most of her life was somehow able to read her moods as well as Jason.

"What's going on, Dad?" she asked, navigating the streets of Knoxville as she made her way toward the bar.

"We haven't talked in a while, and I wanted to check in to see how you're doing."

"Oh, really?" Janet asked.

"Is it so difficult to believe a father would want to check in on his daughter?"

"This call has nothing to do with the body found behind my bar last night?"

There was a long pause, and Janet cringed when she realized her father might have been telling the truth. Finally, he said, "Well, now I am curious, Janet. Please, do fill me in."

"Uhh . . . It's not a good time. I just pulled up to work." It wasn't exactly true, but she was only a few blocks away and there wasn't nearly enough time to explain a murder.

"Let's talk tomorrow—first thing in the morning," her father said with annoying authority.

"Sure, sure, first thing," she said with a smile, knowing he'd be in the middle of meetings and court hearings by the time she rolled out of bed.

She disconnected the call and, a few minutes later, pulled into the parking lot at the Spot. She pursed her lips when she saw the police caution tape was still blocking off the Dumpster area. "Where are we supposed to put the trash?" she asked the car.

She walked up to the deserted building, unlocked the door, and headed through the dark bar to the light panel near the office to flip on the daytime lights.

Back in the office, she fired up the computer, determined to go over the books one more time. Before she could log in, though, there was a knock at the back door. She looked at her watch; she wasn't expecting any deliveries that day.

She pushed the miniblinds apart and saw the beer truck parked behind the bar, and the deliveryman smiling sheepishly at her through the glass.

She wrestled open the steel door. "Hey, Bud. What's going on?" she asked the burly man leaning against the door frame. Janet grinned. She loved that the man who delivered their Bud was named Bud.

"I shorted Jason a couple cases of the lager yesterday. I only realized it when I was going through inventory this morning and I wanted to make it right."

"I hadn't even noticed it yet," she said, holding up her clipboard. "I was just about to go over the books; things have been . . . busy lately."

"Where do you want them?"

"Straight in the cooler, if you don't mind."

He nodded and headed back outside. Janet turned back to her computer, but she was distracted by the rolling thunderclap of sound as Bud opened the back of the delivery truck. She scrunched up her face and tried to focus on the accounting figures in front of her while Bud moved through the office with his cart. Cases of beer went in the door and the empty cart came back out. She finally closed her accounting program and waited.

"I broke down these boxes," Bud said, holding the flattened cardboard in both arms. "Do you want me to throw them out back for you?"

Janet grimaced. "If we can," she said, thinking about the police caution tape. She led Bud through the empty bar and out the side door to the alley, and stood there, her hip propping open the door and her arms crossed over her chest.

"Whoa." Bud surveyed the caution tape around the Dumpster. "This is where it happened?"

"Yup," she said. "Did the police talk to you?"

"Nah. The old guy just asked if I knew somebody named Ike. I don't, so he watched me unload and I got right outta here," Bud said.

He tossed the boxes over the yellow tape into the recycling bin, then he adjusted his waistband, and his eyes lingered on the exit sign.

Janet stared for a moment. Did Bud know about the security camera hidden inside? His eyes flitted from the sign to Janet and he grinned, but she didn't know him well enough to say whether the smile was nervous or just a smile.

"Thanks again, Bud."

"No problem." He took a pack of cigarettes out of his chest pocket and tapped one forward. "Hey, sorry again about the mix-up. It won't happen again on my watch." With a final glance at the exit sign, he waved and then disappeared around the back of the building.

Bud had always been friendly, and he'd delivered beer to the bar since she and Jason bought it, but she didn't know anything about him. Why was he interested in the exit sign? She chewed her lower lip as she headed back inside.

"Hey, boss!" Cindy Lou applied an extra coat of bright red lipstick. As usual, she was scantily clad. Today's outfit was a micro-mini jean skirt and a red tank top with a plunging neckline.

Jason was right: she was going to have to say something before they got a health code violation. She opened her mouth but then felt her eyes glaze over. Who was she to tell someone else how to dress? She didn't want to be *that* boss. After all, Cindy Lou was a grown woman.

"Do you know who's out there?" Cindy Lou asked.

"Oh, it was just Bud, but he's done now."

Cindy Lou cocked her head to the side, and one corner of her mouth pulled up. "No, I saw Bud, darlin'. I'm talking about the lady? She tried to follow me in, but I told her we didn't open for another hour or so. I figured she'd get back in her car and drive away, but she didn't."

Janet walked over and they both looked through the glass door into the front parking lot. Sure enough, a woman was taking a large black trash bag from the passenger seat of an old, beat-up yellow car. She hefted it over her shoulder and headed toward the alley-way. Janet walked through the bar, keeping an eye on the woman through the windows running along the wall.

The woman froze when she caught sight of the police tape wrapping the Dumpster and stood there for several minutes. Janet was just deciding whether to get back to work when the woman finally put her bag down and sank out of sight.

Janet hopped onto the bench seat of the nearest booth and looked down through the window. The woman squatted on the pavement, staring at the Dumpster as she rummaged through her trash bag.

"What the . . ." The woman took out a dozen tea candles, a wooden cross, and wireless speakers. A lighter followed, and within minutes, a mini memorial covered two parking spaces. It wasn't until Janet pushed open the side door that she heard the Christian music blaring from the speakers next to the woman.

"What in the heck is goin' on out there?" Cindy Lou asked

from behind her. Janet turned around to see her tying an apron around her waist. The short apron's pockets were only deep enough for a credit card, yet it was still longer than her bartender's skirt. Janet raised her eyes to the ceiling and tried to focus.

Frank came in the front door and joined them at the window.

"Need me to take care of it, Janet? She's on private property, she can't just set up shop here."

"No—thanks, Frank. I'll go talk to her." Janet squared her shoulders and pushed the door open. Her finger gave a sudden throb, and she turned back to Cindy Lou. "Why don't you start prepping the fruit while I deal with this?"

On the pavement outside, the woman now sat cross-legged by the curb, her face and hands raised to the sky as she swayed to the music. Janet cleared her throat loudly and the woman lowered her gaze; the sadness in her blue eyes was so profound that for a moment, Janet couldn't speak. Already, beads of sweat pooled at the woman's hairline; her face was pale and her hands trembled. She looked like she was in her early twenties.

"Peace and greetings," she said in a misty voice. "My name is Larsa Freeman."

Janet's eyes opened wide at the last name. "Are you related to Ike?"

"He was my father." Larsa closed her eyes. "I'm embarking on a spiritual journey of justice and have vowed to sit here in prayer and meditation until my father's killer is caught."

Janet spun around and marched back into the bar, slamming the door behind her. She stalked past Cindy Lou and headed for the swear jar, taking a bill out of her wallet as she walked.

"A twenty? What in the world is that for?" Cindy Lou asked.

Janet shoved the bill into the jar. "Fuck."

# CHAPTER EIGHT

Janet knew two things with certainty: Larsa Freeman should have been at home or with family, and Larsa Freeman wasn't going anywhere. She rubbed a hand across her face, trying to find the inner strength to keep from cursing again, when a commotion to her left caught her attention.

"Gosh dang it, Frank! Janet said to stop calling the police every five minutes!" Cindy Lou yelled.

Frank, his voice patronizingly calm, said, "I'm doing my job. That woman is on private property, and if Janet doesn't have the balls to get rid of her, I'll do it."

While her employees fought, Janet snuck another look out the window at Ike's daughter. In the withering heat, her arms were raised again, her lips moved, maybe in prayer. She sat just feet away from where Janet had found Ike. Didn't the woman have anywhere else to go to mourn? Any other family? What if she didn't? The thought pulled Janet up short.

When the argument behind her escalated, she finally turned. "Guys!" She opened her mouth to continue but both of her employees rushed to have the last word.

"Janet," Cindy Lou said, "I told him—"

"It's not your bar, Cindy Lou—" Frank interrupted.

"Enough!" Janet yelled over the pair. "I've had enough. Frank, I told you yesterday to stop calling the damn cops every time someone looks at you crossways. I do not want police here unless someone's dead, and that's final." All three cringed at her word choice, but she plowed ahead. "You need to start listening to Cindy Lou, because, from now on, she's the . . . the assistant manager of this bar. Her word is *the* word if I'm not here."

Cindy Lou's mouth dropped open and Janet noted with satisfaction that Frank's did, as well. But before he could give voice to his sour expression, red and blue lights from a police cruiser flashed across their faces.

"Damn it, Frank!" She certainly wasn't going to let the cops haul away a woman who'd just lost her father!

Stalking past her bouncer to the side door, Janet called out, "Larsa! Larsa, I have a table all set up for you in here, hon. I don't want you getting heatstroke while you wait for justice." She waved to the cop, who was just getting out of his squad car. "I think there's been a misunderstanding. False alarm—no problem here!" She ushered a surprised Larsa in and shut the door without a backward glance.

"Frank, tell the police officer you were mistaken and then get table twenty-one ready for Ms. Freeman while I fix her a drink."

Before Frank could react, Cindy Lou said, "Frank, honey, after her table's ready, I'll need your help changin' out a keg. Thank you." She tried to hide her grin but failed.

Frank huffed out something rude that Janet couldn't quite hear before he stalked past her to wipe down the table and set out some coasters.

"What do you want? Bloody Mary's on special tonight." Janet steered Larsa through the bar.

"Oh, I don't drink," Larsa said in that same dreamy voice. "Alcohol's the devil's work, clear as day. I've been sober for eight and a half years and counting."

"Devil's work. Ah, right," Janet said, fixing Frank with a death stare when she caught him smirking. "Can I . . . can I get you anything? Water? Tea?"

"Well, I guess I'd love a glass of sweet tea."

"Cindy Lou, one sweet tea for Ms. Freeman. First one's on the house."

She left the whole lot of them behind and walked into the office, flung herself into a chair, and threw an arm over her eyes. A teetotaling, antialcohol prayer warrior was going to be taking up prime real estate inside the bar—or causing a scene outside of it—until Ike's killer was caught. As much as she hated to admit it, she was stuck. She would either have to help Detective O'Dell with this case or slowly lose customers until she was out of business. People didn't go to a bar to be reminded of murder, death, and sadness, but to escape all of that. She had to hope the police would find the killer—and soon.

———

By eight o'clock that night, the Spot was standing room only. Customers were four deep around the bar and people hovered aggressively by the tables, ready to jump in as soon as a seat opened up. They were officially over capacity for the first time ever, and Frank had a crowd waiting outside the door.

"Two out, one in," he called to Janet as she passed by with a tray full of beer.

She nodded but didn't slow down, and a moment later, she set the drinks down with a flourish. "Anything else, guys?" They were new customers—their first time there, Janet guessed. They'd asked for some kind of fancy microbrew she'd never even heard of and had then gleefully asked for the menu after she told them their five choices.

"Menu?" she'd said. "There isn't a menu. We have five beers on tap; I don't need to write them down, for God's sake!"

They'd chortled at that and then ordered five light beers. Now they were drinking them with a kind of curiosity she reserved for the zoo.

"How is it?" she asked, already wishing she hadn't.

"It . . . it just doesn't really taste like anything, does it?" said a man with a pencil-thin beard that rimmed his jawline. "It's not hoppy, it's not malty. What is it?"

"It's light," Janet snapped. On her way back to the bar, she stopped by Larsa's table. The soft flickering glow of her tea candles made the woman look fuzzy. "Can I get you anything?"

"Maybe some more hot water with lemon?"

Janet bustled back up to the bar and grabbed a mug from the shelf.

"Is she drinkin' more free hot water?" Cindy Lou asked grumpily as she pulled two pints of beer at once.

Janet didn't have time to answer—the bar was busier than she'd ever seen it, and they were down a bartender, since Elizabeth hadn't shown for her shift again.

The stack of dirty glasses took up half the lower counter space, and Janet's eye twitched when a nearby customer missed his table and a full glass of beer splashed onto the ground.

"Need some help?"

Janet turned to find Mel, her new tenant, standing opposite. "What can I get you?"

"I'm serious—I used to be a bartender. I can bar-back for you or deliver drinks. It looks like you could use more hands."

"Oh . . . well I, uh . . ."

The cacophony of requests being shouted at her made her agree before she could really consider the offer; soon, Mel was behind the bar, cleaning glasses and pulling pints next to Cindy Lou.

It took three more hours for the crowd to finally thin.

"What's the matter, boss? You look grumpier than a one-handed acrobat!" Cindy Lou grinned. "You'll be able to pay all your bills for the month from this one night!"

Janet frowned. She didn't want to complain, but she didn't like all the chaos. She'd had to stop those hipster fools from drinking and dashing; the ringleader of the group had nearly come to blows with Frank in the parking lot until she'd stepped in and Pencil Beard's girlfriend finally pulled out a fifty-dollar bill. They'd drained two different kegs before the rowdiest of the crowd had left, and the ice machine couldn't keep up with demand, forcing Janet to institute a three-cube cap around ten o'clock. "We just weren't ready for it, that's all. We need to grow slowly enough that we can handle it. I don't want people trying us out and never coming back because they got bad service," she finally answered.

Cindy Lou turned to look at Janet for a long moment and finally asked, "You all right, sweetheart?"

"Stress," Mel said. "Her eye's twitching from stress." Janet slapped a hand over her eye and Mel said, "I'm taking off. I told Kat I was heading out for one beer," she added with a smile.

"How are you both settling in?"

"Good. We weren't sure it was going to work out, moving in and all, and I wanted to thank you for that, and talk to you about—"

"Frank!" Janet shouted over Mel when she saw her bouncer sipping from a can of beer. "You're not allowed to drink until your shift is over!"

He grumbled but put the beer down on the table next to him. Distracted, she said, "Thanks, Mel. We'll work out what to pay you tomorrow."

Mel didn't move for a moment, but she finally nodded and walked away.

"You haven't heard from our sweet Elizabeth yet?" Cindy Lou asked when Janet took her post behind the bar.

"Nope. You?" Janet frowned when Cindy Lou shook her head. "I understand taking a sick day, but at least have the courtesy to call in with an excuse!"

"Ain't you worried, boss?"

*Worried she's got my money*, Janet thought darkly, finally dropping her hand from her no-longer-pulsing eye. "No," she said aloud, "I'm not worried. I think she's just taking some time off."

"It ain't really like her, though, is it?" Cindy Lou asked as she topped off the bowls of trail mix from a bag under the counter. "And the timin'? I mean, she's one of the last people to have seen Ike alive. Now he's dead and she's missin'?"

"She's not missing!" Janet said. "She's an inconsiderate employee who couldn't be bothered to tell anyone she was taking some days off." She slammed the cooler lid up and rearranged the bottles inside for something to do. "And it's not the first time, either. Remember a couple of years ago?"

Cindy Lou chewed on her lip but didn't say anything.

"It was the same thing! She took a week off with no word to anyone, then came right back in like nothing happened. No explanation or anything!"

Cindy Lou's worried expression didn't waver, and after a moment, she turned away from Janet, in either resignation or disappointment.

Janet stared moodily at the tap and then shifted her focus to Larsa. "What are we going to do about that?" she asked Cindy Lou.

The other woman shrugged. "Beats me why you even invited her in here."

Janet frowned at the grieving daughter, but when Larsa looked up and they locked eyes, she forced a neutral expression back onto her face. She scooped some trail mix into a clean plastic bowl and headed toward her guest, determined to have a tough conversation about Larsa's future at the Spot.

"Need a snack?" she asked, sitting down across from Ike's daughter.

Larsa blew out a breath before plunging her hand into the bowl and plucking out two cashews. "I know I can't stay here—your bouncer has made that perfectly clear."

Janet's left eye pulsed in warning. "Did he say something to you?" His arrogance was starting to do more than just annoy her.

Her face heated up. This was her bar—she could invite whomever she wanted, and Frank had no business interfering.

"Let's just say I know not to come back."

Janet's temper flared, and before she could stop herself, she was saying the exact opposite of what she'd planned to when she walked over. "Larsa, you are my guest. You will be here as long as you want, and I'll make sure Frank knows that, along with the rest of the staff." Her glare landed on Frank, who was sipping surreptitiously from his beer can again.

"Well, that's so . . . that's just so . . ." As Larsa teared up at the offer, Janet inched away, preparing to stand. "Wait." Larsa hiccupped and took a gulp of water from the mug. "Wait, I'm sorry. It's just, you're being so nice. It means a lot, you know?" Janet stuck one leg out from under the table and shifted her weight, but Larsa laid a hand on her arm. "I know my father was in here a lot. I hope he wasn't too much trouble?"

"Oh, well . . . I mean, he was one of our regulars, that's for sure." Janet tried to stay vague, she didn't want to be the one to tell Larsa they'd had to send Ike home—and suffer his anger and yelling when they did—almost as often as not.

"He wasn't always so hateful, you know. He used to be . . . well, better, I guess."

"Weren't we all?" Larsa's lower lip quivered as she attempted a smile. Janet settled into her seat; she knew a thing or two about dads who didn't live up to expectations. "What went wrong?" she asked, realizing not only that Larsa needed to talk this one out, but also that she might not have had anyone else to turn to.

"Listen, I'm not saying he ever would've won Dad of the Year or anything. He always drank too much, and he was never around as much as he should've been, but he was never the same after the accident."

"What accident?" Janet settled back into the seat and focused on the other woman.

"I guess it was just about ten years ago. He was driving home, probably drunk, and hit someone."

"God, how terrible. What happened?"

"The first cop on the scene drove Dad home. They didn't come talk to him about the, uh, the accident until that night. By then, he'd slept off whatever alcohol was in his system."

"Wow," Janet said. "What happened to the other driver?"

Larsa blanched. "It wasn't—it wasn't another car. It was a guy on a bike." Janet gasped and Larsa said, "He was killed. My dad hit and killed a college kid who was riding his bike to class."

Janet's mouth twisted in shock, but when she saw Larsa's face fall, she racked her brain, trying to find something redeemable about the situation. "Well, I mean . . . maybe the kid wasn't riding with a headlight. Cyclists can be hard to see, sometimes. Maybe it wasn't your dad's fault."

"It was nine thirty in the morning." Larsa's wide blue eyes brimmed with unshed tears. "The boy was heading to an early-morning biology class and my dad was already drunk—or still drunk from the night before. At any rate, he shouldn't have been driving, and he shouldn't have gotten off without charges."

That information startled Janet into silence. Finally, she said, "He didn't get charged at all? He hit and killed a person and didn't face any charges?"

"Not as far as the law went, no, but believe me, there were consequences. He was never the same. He drank more and talked less. He and my mom had a huge fight one night and he walked out. I hadn't really talked to him since."

"When was that?"

"Ten years ago."

"You didn't talk to your dad for ten years—and now he's dead? You must feel . . ." Janet let the sentence trail off, unable to put her thoughts into words.

"Unsettled, like there's no closure. It's just . . ."

"Awful," they said together.

"Thanks for letting me sit here. I don't know why, but it makes me feel better to think I'm doing something that might help." She dropped her gaze to the mug of hot water between her hands and fell quiet.

Janet didn't ask the other woman exactly how sitting in her bar was going to help. Instead she stood, taking two empty water glasses with her.

On her way back to the bar, she nearly ran headlong into Detective Finch. The frown she had been trying to hold off finally came through. Finch waved off Frank's handshake attempt, nodded briskly at Janet, and then walked toward the bar without a word.

Janet smacked the beer out of Frank's hand as she passed and felt a satisfied grin cross her face when he curled his lips and crossed his arms but remained silent. She dumped the trash into the can behind the bar, set the glasses into the sink, and stifled another smile when she overheard Nell, clearly answering one of Finch's questions.

"I don't know, Officer, I guess I'd say Ike was an insufferable fool who had no friends, no manners, and no idea of how to be a good human—but I'm sure somebody out there is sorry he's dead."

Nell's glasses took up half of her face. The large black frames would have made anyone else resemble a fly, but with her silvery-white hair pulled back into a low bun and dark red lipstick, Nell oozed sophistication, even as she sat on the bar stool drinking well vodka on the rocks.

Janet tried to listen in as she dipped two dirty glasses into the spinning brushes on the left side of the sink and then dunked them into the basin of cold, mostly clean water on the right.

Finch, his voice low, said, "We're trying to find out where Ike's car might be. Do you remember seeing it Wednesday night?"

Janet froze. Of course! Where was Ike's car? In the chaos of finding his body, it hadn't occurred to her that it was missing. Just as she wondered whether the police were thinking it might have been a carjacking or theft gone wrong that left Ike dead, Nell answered.

"No, but I do remember Elizabeth taking his keys. He was fit to be tied when she snatched them off the bar."

"Elizabeth, the other bartender? She had Ike's car keys?" He whipped out his notebook and scribbled down a few words.

"Mmm-hmm." Nell swirled the ice cubes in her glass with a straw. "If I recall, Ike told her to eff off, but he actually said the word, if you know what I mean."

Finch nodded seriously. "Was he often angry like that?"

The brushes on the automatic glass washer spun, cleaning lipstick and sediment from the two new glasses in Janet's hand while she focused on the conversation.

"Every time he got kicked out, he swore it would be his last time here." Nell worried at a bracelet. "He always came back, though—had nowhere else to go, I'd guess."

"His behavior must have made people angry. How did Elizabeth react?"

"She was calm. I mean, it wasn't the first time." Nell took a sip of her drink and winced. Cheap vodka never went down smoothly, but Nell wouldn't spring for top shelf. Instead, she squeezed the wedge of lime that had balanced on the rim of her glass and motioned to Cindy Lou for another.

Finch was quiet until Cindy Lou moved down the bar again. The drying rack was full, but there were still a dozen dirty glasses, so Janet kept at it, glad for the mindless task while Finch was asking questions.

"Was everyone always so calm? What about Janet?" the detective asked Nell.

"Well, Janet doesn't suffer fools. If Ike yelled at her, she yelled back. That's just how she is, though—she doesn't mean anything by it. She'd probably give you the shirt off her back if you needed it," Nell added.

"Did her boyfriend let that pass?"

"Did Jason let *what* pass? He's not going to pick a fight with every jerk here, I mean, that'd be a full-time job." Nell's glass clunked against the bar as she set it down. "Is that all? You're cramping my style tonight. I've got my eye set on that tall drink of water at the corner table—he's new. I think I've got a shot. What do you think?"

Finch's eyebrows arched comically, and his mouth opened but no words came out.

"What, you don't think an old woman's got game? You'd be surprised." She straightened her massive glasses. "You just gotta be direct and tell the man what you're interested in. They almost always bite."

"Oh . . . uh . . ." Finch stumbled back a step in his hurry to get away. "Well, thanks for your, uh . . . candor, Nell."

He hastily walked to the back corner of the bar and looked down at his notebook—maybe gathering his thoughts after the visual Nell had put there.

Janet moved down the bar with a grin. "You had to go there, Nell?"

The older woman set her glass down primly. "What do you mean? If someone's going to ask me so many questions, I'd like them to remember me at the end of the day. Oh, and by the way, you might want to tell your new guest over there to pipe down. She was just regaling some new customers about her sobriety. 'One thousand eight hundred twenty-seven days sober and counting' just seems like a lot of information for a casual customer, you know?

Janet blew out a sigh at Larsa's tendency to over-share, patted Nell's hand, and moved down the bar until she faced the side door. The condiment container was running low on cherries and limes, so she set to work refilling it from the bin of prepped fruit in the cooler.

As she worked, she pondered the new information from Detective Finch. Ike's car was missing and Elizabeth had taken Ike's keys before he left the building. Now he was dead, his keys and car were missing, and no one had heard from Elizabeth since.

She tried to swallow but her mouth was completely dry.

Where was Elizabeth? Had she killed Ike and left with his car? If she was having money trouble—and Janet suspected something was going on with her if she was stealing from the till—was it too much of a leap to think she might have been desperate enough to kill?

"Would that be okay, Janet?" Nell stood across the bar, her eyebrows raised.

"Oh, sorry, I didn't hear you. What?"

"I was just saying I wonder if you could pour me a sweet tea. The vodka's tearin' me up tonight, for some reason."

"Sure, Nell. No problem."

Before she could deliver the drink, however, Finch approached with more questions.

"Did your boyfriend have any luck with that surveillance video?"

Janet slid the tea to Nell. "No. That's why he's not here helping out tonight: he's been working around the clock, trying to get his whole system back up."

"I'll bet," Finch said, his expression conveying the opposite sentiment.

"What's that supposed to mean?"

"It means it's pretty convenient for your employees that the video's not there. Elizabeth was the last person who talked to Ike and the last person to have his keys, and the one thing that would help solve all the mysteries is mysteriously down. It doesn't look good. Do you see what I'm saying?"

Janet bristled at the insinuation. "All I see is a crime that's not solving itself. I hope you'll put the time in to get justice for Larsa, if not for Ike, instead of expecting someone else to do your job."

Finch leaned across the bar and sneered, his glare burning through her. "Doing my job depends on asking people like you to give a shit about someone besides themselves. Forgive me if I seem hopeless. And tell your boyfriend I've got a subpoena coming soon. Just waiting on the judge to sign off. Tell him we'll have to cast a wide net if he can't get us what we need." He pivoted and stalked out of the bar, pushing past Frank as he left.

Jason would not be happy about cops rifling through his things. He dealt with many high- and low-profile clients, and none of them would like the thought of law enforcement snooping around his computer and files.

Why was Finch hell-bent on blaming someone at her bar? Her eye gave a final, mind-bending pulse, then settled down. She had to find Elizabeth before the police did. If she could only find her bartender, she could solve more than one mystery.

# CHAPTER NINE

When Janet got home at close to four in the morning, she found Jason passed out over his desk in the basement. He frowned in his sleep, and the low blue light from his computer monitors cast shadows over his face. She kissed him gently on his shoulder, scribbled Finch's warning onto a sticky note, and slapped it on the largest monitor, then crept back upstairs. She settled on the couch with a blanket, then sloshed some wine into a glass and felt some of the tension leach out of her shoulders for the first time in hours with that first sip. It didn't last long.

After her phone, which had died earlier that night, charged enough to turn on, an alert sounded with a message from Detective O'Dell.

"The coroner's report came in. I thought you might be interested to know Ike was killed with a knife—the same one your boyfriend and Larsa identified as Ike's."

Janet paused the message and pressed the phone against her temple. It sounded terrible when O'Dell said it like that, but they all knew that Ike carried a Swiss Army knife. He would sometimes use the bottle-opening feature at the bar when he felt service was too slow. She frowned and then started the message back up.

"It was a single stab wound to his gut," O'Dell continued, "and the coroner says it would have been a slow, brutal death—it might've taken him twenty minutes to bleed out. She's ruled his death a homicide. Someone was angry, that's for sure. My investigators are going to want to talk with your staff again—especially this Elizabeth person—and your boyfriend. I'm counting on you to keep your ears open, Janet."

She stared at her phone after the message ended. Someone was angry at Ike, but who?

The longer she sat there, the more she thought about Ike's history and how what he'd done in his past seemed a more likely reason for anger than simply his being an obnoxious customer at the bar.

Could Ike's murder have anything to do with the cyclist he'd hit and killed a decade ago? Had someone's anger flared after ten years passed without a single repercussion for the uninvestigated and uncharged crime?

She was sure police knew about the event, but—and this made Janet grimace—what if they didn't? She groaned into the empty room and then pulled the blanket over her head and screwed her eyes shut. She didn't want to get involved, but it was becoming hard not to. With the dead man's daughter now invited to practically live at the bar and police calling with daily updates, as much as she hated it, she was going to have to do something.

Where was Elizabeth? She'd been with the bar for the whole year Janet had owned it, as well as the year before that, when Janet had only been an employee herself. Elizabeth wasn't the most reliable person, but the behavior was still concerning.

Janet decided with another groan that she would call O'Dell in the morning—right after driving to Elizabeth's house.

———

*Crrrrrunch.* Janet swore at the sound, then backed her car away from the parking block that had just scraped the underside of her car. The front end of the vehicle made an identically awful sound as it scraped back over the block in reverse, and she swore again.

The sun shone down relentlessly as Janet got out of her car. The black asphalt oozed sluggishly under her feet, the tar that covered its cracks mushy already from the morning heat. The slam of her car door was the only sound in the apartment complex, and Janet stood assessing the space for a moment.

Chunks of gray stucco had fallen off parts of the building, but someone had attempted to paint over the holes, even coming close to matching the original color of the outside walls. The freshly mulched flower beds were void of any plants except for some knee-high weeds in one shady patch by the rental office. It wasn't one of the nicest parts of town, but it wasn't bad.

Janet looked down at the paper in her hand to check Elizabeth's address again and then made her way toward number 215.

At the door, she saw some business cards tucked into the frame; they were from both O'Dell and Finch—and that meant the door hadn't been opened since Ike's body was found. Janet frowned, not liking the deserted vibe that emanated from the space.

She knocked, but no one answered. After a quick glance around the property, Janet unzipped a small leather case, then assessed the lock in front of her. As she was deciding which pick to use, the door next to Elizabeth's opened.

"This girl's had more visitors in the last two days than the last two years combined," said an old man with graying brown hair and a frown. "Who are you?"

"Who're you?" Janet shot back, casually tucking her lock-picking set under one of her arms when she crossed them.

"I'm the grumpy old man who don't like all the noise from a half-dozen visitors!" He wore a red plaid robe tied at the waist, light blue pajama pants, and house slippers. Steam curled up from the mug of coffee he held in front of his chest.

"All the noise of six visitors over the last two years?" Janet challenged. "I'd say you're lucky. That's—what? One person knocking every four months?"

"What's that?" He cupped a hand around his ear and leaned toward Janet. She repeated her sarcastic remark a little louder. "No need to shout." He scrunched up his face in distaste. "It's the last two days I'm fed up with. What's everyone want with Elizabeth? Is she in trouble? The other two wouldn't tell me anything—just kept asking questions, and I don't have nothing to say about nobody, you know? I keep to myself and mind my business."

Despite what he said, it seemed like he was dying for a chat. "So, what'd you tell the cops?" she asked, sliding the leather case into her shoulder bag.

"What?" Again, she raised her volume, only to be shushed dramatically before he answered. "Nothing. Just like I said, I got nothing to say about the girl next door." He savored a sip of coffee, then added, "She's a pretty good neighbor, even though she's up until all hours of the night doing God-knows-what with God-knows-who. I bet her mama's rolling over in her grave knowing she dropped out of college to work in a dive bar, but she probably does her best to do her best, you know what I mean?"

Before Janet could unpack everything the gossipy neighbor had just shared, he started up again.

"It's nothing to me if a woman wants to make a living and support herself, but she was planning on going to medical school— or was it dental?—but then she didn't. And I don't see why her plans had to change just because her plans changed, okay?" A small, yappy brown dog barreled around his legs. "Hey, dog, get back in here." He scooped up the small pet and deposited it in the coat closet. The yapping continued, but it was muted behind the door.

Janet cocked her head to the side; she wouldn't have pegged this guy as a dog person. She shook herself. "So, you've lived next to Elizabeth for a long time, huh?"

"Long?" He scratched his head, still frowning. "Long enough to know her mom wouldn't be happy with her choices."

Parent guilt via neighbor. Nice. "You said her mom is dead? When did that happen?"

"What was that?" She put forth a Herculean effort not to roll her eyes and repeated her question. He winced at her new volume and said, "A couple of years ago. Ah! Vet, that's it! She was going to become a vet, not a dentist! I knew it was something like that." He shook his head sagely and took another sip from his mug. "She dropped out of school and since then, nothing. Just a big lump of nothing."

Janet assessed the nosy neighbor, who seemed determined to judge Elizabeth. "Did Elizabeth drop out of college right after her mother died?"

His brow furrowed and, after a moment, he nodded. "I guess that's right."

"Does she have any family left?"

"Don't know."

"I don't suppose the two events were related, do you?" He lowered his mug slowly, his face taking on the confused look of someone who'd just lost their train of thought. "Like, maybe she didn't have the money to continue her education, or maybe she just lost her spirit or passion or will to learn after her mom died. I don't suppose you checked in on her, made her a cup of coffee, or offered to help in any way?"

The man pulled the belt of his robe tighter around him, but he still didn't speak.

Janet's nostrils flared and she was breathing hard. "Yes, she's an adult, but she's young! I'd say Elizabeth is doing her best to get by after life pulled the rug out from under her by taking her mother before she was ready to be on her own. The girl probably needs more help and less judgment from both her friends and neighbors. Did you ever think about that?" To her surprise, she found that she'd moved closer to the stranger and was touching his chest with her finger. She blew out a breath and took a step back, dropping her hand to her side.

He finally cleared his throat and took another sip of his coffee. "Sounds like you're speaking from experience."

Janet felt blood rush to her cheeks. "You're always too young to lose your mother, no matter your age," she finally said.

"Paul Massie," he said, sticking out his hand. "You want some coffee?"

Janet blinked and then shook his hand. "Janet Black. Elizabeth works for me, at my bar." He held the door open, but she shook her head. "No, thanks. I was just . . ." She looked at Elizabeth's door. "I just came here to check on Elizabeth. So, you haven't seen her?"

"Not lately. She's a good kid. She'll get it together—especially if she's got you on her side." Paul nodded, dismissing her, but continued to lean up against his door frame, watching her, until she turned to leave. She looked back to see if Paul had closed his door, thinking she could try to pick Elizabeth's lock after he was back inside, but he stared at her until she climbed into her car, only closing his door with a final nod after she'd cranked the engine.

Janet wrinkled her nose. Was she on Elizabeth's side? Just days ago, she'd been ready to fire her, certain the bartender was stealing from the Spot. Now the petty theft seemed like no big deal—at least, compared with murder. She didn't like the emotions that were blooming inside her.

Elizabeth was all alone in this world, except for a nosy neighbor and apparently the people she worked with at the bar. Was Janet so heartless and cruel that she couldn't be bothered to care enough to help find her?

With a groan she headed home, knowing what she had to do, but already irritated with her plan.

# CHAPTER TEN

She poured herself a cup of coffee and stared at the phone. She needed to make the call. She was going to . . . gulp . . . get *involved* and be *helpful.*

*Ugh.* She shuddered and dropped down onto the couch, then dialed the numbers; when O'Dell answered, she filled him in on what Larsa had told her the day before.

"A cyclist, huh?" he said.

"I'm sure you know about it already, but Larsa mentioned it, so I just thought . . . I wanted to make sure . . ." She frowned into her coffee. She had to step up for Elizabeth's sake. "It just seems a better motive for murder than anything else I've heard."

"I'm actually just heading out to talk to the victim's family, to let them know what happened," O'Dell said. After a pause, he added, "Why don't you come along?"

"What?" Janet spluttered. Coffee slopped out of her mug onto the table as she hastily set it down. "Why would I do that?"

"I got to talking to your dad yesterday—"

"He was certainly a busy beaver . . ."

"—and he said you have a knack for reading people. He said

you're uncommonly good at it, in fact. I just thought, since you're being so helpful, you'd want to ride along."

"Oh, I've got so much to—"

"I'm meeting the family at one thirty. I'll pick you up on the way." He hung up before she could come up with an excuse that would get her out of it.

She was still staring at her phone in disbelief when it rang in her hand. This time, it was the bank.

"Miss Black, we wanted to let you know the checks you deposited yesterday came back insufficient funds."

"What?"

"We wanted to let you know the—"

"I heard you, I just . . . are you sure?" The checks were for her new tenants' first month's rent and security deposit.

"Yes. I wanted to make sure you noted it in your register, so your balance was correct."

Janet disconnected and pressed her hands into her temples. Insufficient funds? She walked to the minibar across the room. Her hand moved past the vodka to the bottle of Kahlúa. She eyed her coffee; maybe just a splash. She sloshed some in and then stalked back across the room to the front door, where she looked out the window at the unit next door and took a long, slow sip of her fortified morning drink.

She thought they'd done a good job of vetting the new renters —she and Jason had even had them fill out a credit report form, and Mel and Kat had both checked out. The money should have been deposited before they moved in, but it wasn't, and now they were stuck with a couple of freeloaders.

There was no movement from the other apartment, but as she stared crossly at the front door, she realized Mel might have been trying to tell her something about their finances the night before at the bar. She felt a light touch on her shoulder and turned to find Jason holding out a plate of scrambled eggs.

"I thought you'd need lunch but would want breakfast," he said with a smile.

"Our renters are broke," she said. She took the plate with a grateful smile and told him what the banker had just told her. She sat down on the couch and shoved a forkful of eggs into her mouth.

Jason stared out the front window, rubbing his chin. "I don't know, Janet. I get a good vibe from them."

"Is it a broke vibe?" She stabbed a piece of bacon with her fork. It cracked into three pieces, none of them on the tines.

"No, a good vibe. Let's talk to Mel about it and see what she's got to say. We'll take it from there."

"We aren't running a charity, Jason. It's a business! The goal isn't to find people who need a handout." Her feelings of responsibility for Elizabeth had sucked the generosity for anyone else in her life right out of her. She frowned at her boyfriend; he smiled back.

"I know, but let's hear what they have to say. Maybe it's just a misunderstanding." Jason sat opposite her and leaned forward, his elbows resting on his knees.

"You know what the problem is? You're too nice," she said. He snuck a piece of bacon out from under her hovering fork. "Hey!"

"Not *too* nice. *Just right* nice," he clarified. "So nice, in fact, I'm going to help you in the shower today."

"Is that right?" she asked, a grin slowly turning up the corners of her lips.

"Mmm-hmm." He took the plate out of her hands and set it on the table between them.

Her stomach flooded with heat. "I don't have much time," she said, looking at the clock over his head.

"Trust me. You have time for this." He pulled her up and led her to the bedroom.

———

She stayed in the shower after Jason left, and so did the lovey-dovey smile on her face. Over the last year, she had gotten used to feeling like she was in control of her life for the first time in a long time. She had a steady relationship with a great man and a solid job at the bar she owned. Even though she could feel chaos creeping back into her well-ordered world with Ike's murder and her apparently broke tenants, she needed to remember the good things she had, and protect them.

By the time she toweled off and got dressed, Detective O'Dell was knocking at the front door.

"Are you ready?" he asked when she opened the door. She looked behind her, but the house was empty. Jason must have gone down to his office in the basement.

"Nope," she answered while running a comb through the tangles in her hair.

He laughed as if she'd made a joke and then turned and headed toward his car.

"No cruiser?" She tossed the comb on the hall table and pulled the door closed behind her.

"No, no, my cruiser days are long gone. I drive this baby." He patted the top of his unmarked Ford Crown Victoria with affection and laughed at Janet's horrified face. "It's not so bad once you're in it."

The Crown Vic wasn't brown or tan, but a murky color in between. As Janet pulled open the passenger door, she saw the black leather seats, which would be hotter than an iron against skin in this weather. Luckily, she wore jeans, but she still let out a low groan when she sat as the heat seeped through the denim.

"We get most of our cars at auction. Nobody else would take this beauty, so it's been mine for the last two years."

"Lucky you."

They drove in silence until Janet's curiosity got the best of her. "How's the investigation going?"

"Still lots of questions and not many answers."

"Have you spoken to Elizabeth?"

"Nope—no answer on her cell or at her apartment door. You heard from her?"

"No. Nothing." She tapped her fingers lightly against her thigh. O'Dell's curious stare was more pronounced this time, and she felt her cheeks heat up under his scrutiny. "These people we're going to see," she said, "do they know why we're coming?"

"Not exactly." He turned his attention back to the road. "But I hear that Margaret and Dan Daniels are sharp people; I'm sure they suspect my visit has something to do with their son."

Janet nodded slowly but kept her eyes trained on the scenery outside. For all her bravado, she wasn't looking forward to getting close to this family's emotional turmoil.

As they pulled up to an average-looking brick colonial in a neighborhood full of average-looking brick colonials, O'Dell turned toward her. "You're just here to watch and listen. You're not a detective, you know?"

"You invited me!" She crossed her arms.

"I know, but leave all the talking to me, okay?"

Janet nodded again and followed him up the front walk. Lush greenery surrounded them on all sides, including a stunning flowering plant bigger than she was. Even the buzzing of the bees seemed louder here. The sound of Detective O'Dell's fist against the door was practically absorbed by the house.

After just a moment, a woman answered. "I'm Margaret. You must be the gentleman from the Knoxville Police Department?"

As O'Dell introduced himself, Janet assessed the woman. She didn't know what she'd been expecting—perhaps some sort of grief-ridden, devastated mother. Instead, a sprightly, energetic, strong, and muscular woman stood before her. Yes, her hair was gray, but she was taller than Janet and far from stooped over; she had the lithe, long, taut arms of someone who practiced yoga for three hours a day. When O'Dell introduced Janet as his associate, Margaret kindly invited them inside.

"Dan!" she called as she motioned for Janet and O'Dell to follow her down the hall. They found a man sitting in a blue wingback chair in the living room. He couldn't have missed them when they'd walked up to his home—his chair faced a huge picture window that looked out over the street—but he looked up, surprised.

His eyes were sad and weary as he stood to welcome them. He shook hands with O'Dell first, then Janet, and when he reached out for her hand, she saw scratch marks on his arm.

"Rosebushes won," he said, then shrugged his cuff down and circled around to his wife's side.

Where she was strong and tall, he was beaten and stooped. Life had chewed him up and spit him out, and it was clear that Ollie's father was only barely hanging on. He had a pasty complexion, and his hair, which according to a family photo on the wall used to be jet-black, was now a shocking silvery white, as if grief had leached all the color from his person.

O'Dell cleared his throat and Janet jumped. "What?"

"I was just telling Margaret and Dan that you and I are both newer to Knoxville. They've lived here their whole lives."

"Yes, that's right. I've been here about two years." When everyone continued to stare at her expectantly, she added, "It's hot."

O'Dell gave her a funny look before clearing his throat again. "Thanks for seeing us on such short notice. I wanted to let you know, in case you hadn't heard yet, that Ike Freeman is dead."

Margaret sucked in a sharp breath and instinctively flung an arm around her husband just in time to guide him back to his chair. He collapsed into it, his shoulders shaking as he sucked in great gusts of air. She looked up and motioned O'Dell and Janet and toward a door before murmuring something into her husband's ear and following them into the kitchen.

"I'm so sorry. We talked last night about how your visit might have something to do with our son's death." Her expression turned dark. "It's always a blow to hear that man's name in this house. My husband has never gotten over it, of course, nor have I."

O'Dell patted Margaret on the shoulder. "I wanted to be the one to break the news to you, so it wouldn't hit you unexpectedly while you were out and about."

"I do appreciate it, Detective. What happened?"

O'Dell told her about the murder investigation while Margaret bustled around the kitchen making tea. He left out many details of the crime but let her know they hadn't yet arrested anybody.

Margaret nodded, not exactly in satisfaction, but as if she was accepting the inevitable. "I can't say I'm sorry he's dead. He changed our lives forever." She dropped a tea bag into a mug and set it on the counter, then took a pint of milk from the refrigerator. She finally turned to face Janet and O'Dell. "When Ollie was killed, it—it was just awful, you think it's the lowest moment in your life. But then when that man got off without a single charge . . . well, it was like losing Ollie all over again."

"What happened?" Janet asked.

The kettle whistled, and Margaret poured boiling water over the tea bag before answering. "Ollie and one of his roommates were riding to class that morning. This was before everyone started wearing helmets, but I'm not convinced a helmet would've helped," she added, her cheeks flushing red. "Plastic and foam are no match for tons of metal and pints of alcohol." She dunked the tea bag in and out of the water and stared blindly through the window above the sink. "Ollie was in front and had just enough time to yell out a warning to his roommate. Ike missed the other boy by inches—Ollie saved him.

"The rest isn't part of the official record, but it's what we've been able to piece together. A friend of Ike's in the police department was the first on the scene, and he sent Ike home without a Breathalyzer. Ike got an extra eight hours before he was called downtown for questioning. By then, he was sober and Ollie was dead."

She took the tea bag out of the mug, set it in the sink, and poured in some milk and sugar. "I'm going to bring this to Dan. Thanks for stopping by with the news, Detective. Good day."

When they were back in his car, O'Dell asked, "What do you think?"

"I think Ollie's family is still angry."

"With Ike?"

"Well, yes, but also with your department."

"Grief can do interesting things to people," O'Dell said.

"Do you believe them? That a cop kept Ike from getting in trouble that day?"

"I don't know," O'Dell said, starting up the engine. "It's hard to imagine it happening. I'd never help out a friend that way. Would you?"

Janet looked out the window, considering his words. Instead of answering she asked another question. "Have you seen the original police report from the accident?"

"No. But I'll check it out, see who was on the call." Janet nodded and he changed the subject. "Forensics found two sets of fingerprints on the knife that killed Ike: Ike's and someone else's, which are not in the system."

"Do you suspect one of Ollie's parents of killing Ike?" Janet asked, suddenly wondering why they'd really come. "Dan Daniels probably couldn't deliver a deathblow, but Margaret looks tough."

He shook his head. "It's just interesting to know that whoever else handled Ike's knife isn't a hardened criminal. Your boyfriend's never been arrested, either, has he?"

She pinched the bridge of her nose and released it before turning to face O'Dell. "What exactly are you trying to say?"

He eased the car to a stop in front of her house. "Just that it's oddly convenient that a secret, hidden camera that hardly anyone knew about was tampered with before a man was murdered outside your bar. Pretty lucky for the killer, huh?" Janet stared at him, stunned by how baldly and arrogantly he'd stated the accusation. "It's your duty to help us with any information you have about this crime, Janet. Don't forget."

The nerve of this cop. Had today's excursion all been a sham to get her reaction to his baseless claim against her boyfriend?

Her face felt tight. She climbed silently out of the car, then slammed the door with extra force. She was done being helpful—especially if the cops were going to start making wild accusations.

The sound of O'Dell's engine faded away as he drove down the street. She straightened her shoulders and walked slowly up the path to her house, still simmering.

She only had one job—no, make that two—and she was failing at both lately. She ran a bar and she was a landlord. The bar didn't open for hours, but she was going to landlord the shit out of her tenants before she went to the Spot.

# CHAPTER ELEVEN

She stalked into the house, aware that she needed to calm down before she spoke to the renters. As much as she hated to admit it, Jason was right: she could easily fly off the handle if she wasn't careful. She headed right for the minibar in the main room and filled a glass with ice before drumming her fingers against the countertop and looking over her choices. She finally pulled a bottle of gin off the shelf, took the tonic from the small refrigerator under the counter, and lined up a lime and a knife on the cutting board. Her finger gave a throb, though, and she hurled the lime into the trash.

"Are you going to get that checked out?" Jason asked. "Oh, and darlin'? It's two thirty in the afternoon. Are you sure you're ready for that?" Janet tilted the glass to one side and assessed her finger. "Is this about the renters?" he asked, nodding at her drink. "Sometimes people just need a second chance, Janet."

She huffed a frustrated breath out her nose. Detectives were zeroing in on this kind man as a murder suspect. It was insane. She didn't want to tell him about the accusation, though, so she latched onto his assumption. "It's not a charity, Jason, it's a business. You're too soft."

"Soft?" he asked, taking several slow, deliberate steps toward her until they were standing toe to toe. "There's nothing soft about me."

Janet gulped as he clasped his hand over hers and slowly lowered the drink to the counter. When she let go, he gently set the highball glass on the table behind them.

*Again?* her eyes asked, and he smirked. Even though they'd been together for eighteen months, her heartbeat quickened at his expression: it was scalding hot.

With a flick of his wrist, he sent the remaining items on the counter flying into the sink; the sound of the cutting board and knife clattering into the stainless steel basin barely registered, though, as he slowly pressed his body closer to hers.

He walked her back until she was snug between him and the countertop, then he slowly lifted her onto the bar, their bodies rubbing together deliciously, before he settled between her legs. Jason nipped her earlobe as his hands worked to untuck her tank top, and he finally splayed his fingers across the skin of her stomach. The streaks of desire shot all the way down to her toes and fingers.

"I love this bar," he said, undoing the clasp of her bra and sliding one strap down her arm. "It's so convenient."

Convenient. That's just what Detective O'Dell had said about the killer. Janet huffed out a breath and reluctantly stopped Jason's hands from exploring. "We need to talk."

His eyes still smoldered, but he leaned back a fraction. Before she could explain, the doorbell chimed.

"Hold that thought, darlin'," he said as he walked to the door, "because I'm holding mine."

Janet took a shaky breath before sliding off the countertop and reclasping her bra. By the time Jason opened the door, she was leaning against the leather club chair, looking, she hoped, reasonably presentable.

It was Mel and Kat.

"Sorry to intrude," Mel said, looking uncomfortably between Jason and Janet. "We wanted to introduce you to Hazel."

She stepped aside, and Janet gasped as a baby became visible in Kat's arms.

"You have a baby?" she asked, flabbergasted. "Why didn't you tell us?"

"We just got her," Mel said with a slight smile. "Kat is on the foster list for the county, and Hazel was found yesterday. A case-worker came by last night, approved our new place, and another delivered the baby this morning."

"Found?" Jason asked, crossing his arms. "What does that mean?"

Mel frowned and Kat put a hand on her arm. "It's a sad story," she said. "Her mother was arrested. Apparently, she'd left Hazel home alone to run some errands—"

"Errands? She was out buying drugs!" Mel interjected angrily.

"—and got arrested," Kat finished, as if Mel hadn't interrupted. "She didn't want to get in even more trouble for leaving Hazel home alone, so she just didn't tell anyone she had a baby. It took the neighbors two days to call the police about the crying."

"God," Janet breathed, looking at the peacefully sleeping baby with a mix of horror and awe. "She's okay?"

"She is now. She was in the hospital overnight until doctors could regulate her temperature and get plenty of fluids in her little body," Kat crooned. "Now she'll be okay—we'll keep her safe."

"We wanted to let you know some friends are going to drop off a crib," Mel said. "They might block the driveway while they unload —we just didn't want you to think we were being inconsiderate."

"Speaking of inconsiderate . . ." Janet looked meaningfully at Jason, but he just grinned.

"Welcome home, little Hazel," he said before turning and walking into the kitchen.

"Mel, can I have a word?"

"Get Hazel back inside—I'm worried the sun is too bright out here," Mel said before watching Kat walk to their half of the duplex. Only when the door closed did she turn back to Janet. "I know—you don't have to say anything. I'm working on it."

"Working on what?"

"On getting a job. I came into the bar yesterday to tell you the check might bounce, but I'm working on it. We knew Hazel was coming, and I intend to do right by her, but I just need a couple of weeks to make it work."

She held Mel's gaze for a moment before nodding once. "Two weeks. This isn't a free hotel."

"I know—and thank you."

Janet watched Mel walk into her house and then shivered when she felt hot breath on her neck.

"I knew you wouldn't do it. You talk a tough game, Black, but you're a big ol' softie on the inside." Jason was grinning when she turned toward him. She unsnapped his jeans and lowered the zipper. His smile widened.

"Shut up."

Neither spoke, then, as they picked up where they'd left off on the bar.

———

Hours later, Janet pulled up to the other bar in her life, the Spot. She groaned when she saw Larsa sitting on the parking block by the Dumpster, her candles already flickering and the tinny sound of spiritual music audible over Janet's engine.

She slammed her car into park and cursed under her breath. There it was again, that feeling that things were spiraling out of control. Her chest felt tight; the tension Jason had so kindly worked out of her body at home was coiling back around her. She rolled her shoulders, trying to recapture some of the glow she'd enjoyed just moments ago.

"I hope you're having a blessed day," Larsa said as Janet climbed out of her car. Listening to her dreamy voice was like eating cotton candy, and it was starting to give her a toothache.

"It's been an interesting one, that's for sure," she said as she walked to the front door. Larsa turned off her speakers, so the only sound was the jingle of Janet's key ring hitting the metal frame as she unlocked the door. She crossed the threshold and paused, took a deep breath and blew it noisily out, then finally called over her shoulder, "Well? Are you coming?"

Larsa quickly blew out the candles but left them on the curb. She shoved the speakers into her oversized bag and scuttled into the bar behind Janet.

"Interesting is good," she said. She was pale and sweating again, and Janet held out a glass of ice water for her when she passed.

"How many days now?" Janet asked, thinking the woman looked closer to five days sober than eight and a half years, or whatever she'd told Nell the number of days was earlier.

"Huh?" Larsa stared back before blinking in understanding. "Oh, today is day two thousand four hundred fifty-eight. I'm so blessed." She took a long pull of the ice water on her way back to "her" table.

Janet's nose scrunched. She was certain Nell had told her that Larsa's sobriety number was in the one thousands.

She took out her cell phone and her free hand clenched when she saw that the Wi-Fi wasn't working again. She checked the computer in the office, and sure enough, the Internet was completely down. She texted Jason, then opened the calculator app on her phone as she walked back out into the bar.

Larsa had originally told her that she'd been sober for eight and a half years.

$365 \times 8.5 = 3,102.5$.

But just now she'd said 2,458 days, and now that Janet really thought about it, Nell had quoted Larsa as saying 1,827 the other night. Which was it? In her experience, alcoholics were very precise about that number, sometimes down to the hour of their last drink.

She headed over to ask Larsa, but the other woman spoke first. "What made it so interesting?"

After a moment's hesitation, Janet said, "I went with the police to talk to Ollie Daniels's family." Distracted by her numbers query, Janet suddenly worried that reopening old wounds might jeopardize Larsa's sobriety—however long it had been. Then again, Larsa *was* sitting in her bar, hoping to find her father's killer . . .

Larsa, who had been in the middle of settling into her seat, froze with her arm outstretched, her fingers just hovering over her purse on the table in front of her. She took a deep breath before asking, "And how are they?"

Janet was struck by the real depth of feeling in Larsa's voice. "They are . . . devastated. That's the only word I can think of to describe them. They're still devastated over their son's death all these years later. Your father's death seemed to bring it all back to the surface—especially for Ollie's dad."

"Of course they are devastated. Their family was ruined after the death." Larsa bent her head and Janet got the impression she was saying a prayer.

"It sounds like it ruined your father, as well." Janet kept her eyes trained on Larsa for her reaction.

For a moment, there wasn't one, but finally the other woman nodded slowly. "The fact that he wasn't charged seemed so lucky at first. Of course, it soon became his cross to bear. The death ruined my family, as well."

There wasn't much to say to that, and after a moment, Janet got to work behind the bar, combining bottles of liquor, mopping the floor, and wiping down the ice machine. Larsa finally spoke again as Janet eyed a bin of lemons and limes with distrust.

"I tried to talk to them, the family—Ollie's family—and even with the other boy on the bike, but they just couldn't separate me from my dad.

"My mom killed herself, you know, about a year after the . . . the accident. She couldn't take the notoriety of being associated with it all. Knoxville's growing, but it's still a small town, and everyone knew."

Larsa picked up the sweating glass of ice water and took a long draw, then set it back down and stared at it curiously.

"You know, I don't think she ever tasted alcohol. At least, if she had, she stopped completely when my dad started going down the road he went down. It's hard to live with the knowledge that your husband killed somebody else's kid. She just couldn't do it."

"Larsa, I'm so—"

"I'm not telling you this so you'll feel sorry for me." She took two tea candles out of her bag and lit them carefully. "I guess I just want you to know what he was up against. Of course, he blamed himself for my mother's death, and in my anger at the time, I did, too. In fact, I hadn't talked to him since the night my mother's body was found—until a couple weeks ago, anyway."

Janet looked up from the fruit bin. She thought Larsa had said that she and her father hadn't spoken in years. Janet pushed the bin away and really focused on Ike's daughter.

Larsa's eyes flicked up to meet Janet's before she refocused on her ice water. "A friend let me know he'd been in another accident while driving drunk. My father only had minor injuries, but the car was damaged. I got in touch—I just wanted to tell him to stay off the roads. I really had the best of intentions, you have to know that." She tucked her lighter back into her purse and stared at the candle flames dancing in front of her. "Before I knew it, though, he was shouting at me and I was shouting back. I hung up after saying something awful—just awful," she repeated before falling silent.

Janet said quietly, "What did you say?"

She shuddered. "I said, 'You cannot imagine the guilt I feel for being so relieved that you won't be able to hurt anyone else.'"

Janet's eyebrows drew together. "Because he was going to be charged, finally?" she asked softly. It suddenly made sense—what was driving Larsa's behavior. More than just the sadness of a grieving daughter, the guilt of her angry last words to her father must have been eating away at her. No wonder she hadn't wanted to admit that they'd spoken recently.

Larsa didn't answer, though, as she was folded over in prayer, her lips moving without sound.

Janet decided not to ask about the conflicting number of days Larsa had been sober. The woman obviously had a lot on her mind. What was it to Janet if she couldn't keep her sobriety straight?

She bent over the cutting board, moving a knife through the fruit with caution, but halfway through the first lemon, she stopped, distracted. With all that Larsa had just told her, her mind kept boomeranging back to one thing—person, really: the roommate on the other bike who had watched Ollie die.

Had the ten-year anniversary of Ollie's death reignited the outrage of those who'd been closest to him? She wondered what the other boy on the bike thought about Ike's death. More importantly, she wondered where he'd been the night Ike was killed.

# CHAPTER TWELVE

Janet couldn't wait to get out of the bar, and as soon as Cindy Lou walked in, she headed for her car, unsure of where she wanted to go but certain she had to get some distance from Larsa.

How anyone could survive such devastation in their life, Janet didn't know, but even more unsettling was how the other woman's story made Janet think about her own past.

She'd been raised by her mother, a loving woman who more than made up for the fact that her father had walked out on them before she was even born.

Janet's world had been rocked, however, after her mother died several years ago. Her father had tracked her down and shared a completely different story about why he'd been absent for her whole life. He'd had the audacity to blame her mother for not wanting *him* and not even telling him he had a daughter.

It had been a confusing new reality for Janet to come to terms with, and Larsa's story brought it all to the surface. A man Janet had learned to hate in her youth had turned out to be a steady, calm influence in her life—at least, when she let him.

By the time she was able to focus on the road, she was already pulling up to the downtown library. Stuck at a light for a few minutes, she clucked a celebratory cheer when a car pulled out of a metered spot just ahead. "Do I have any quarters, though?" she muttered to herself as she wedged her car into the spot.

She checked the change tray and found just enough to get her a half hour inside.

"Can I help you, ma'am?" an elderly librarian called as she walked through the front door, but Janet waved her off and headed to the computer section. She signed up for a machine and settled in between two elderly people.

It was much easier to navigate on a real computer than on the small screen of her phone, and soon she was reading Ollie Daniels's obituary from the *Knoxville Times*.

Ollie had been nineteen when he was killed. The article also listed the names of his two roommates, Abe and Benji, one of whom had been at the accident. She searched for both online and in just a few clicks she had their information, amazed to find that they both still lived in town. She looked at the clock: it was already after four. Business would start picking up soon back at the bar. This hunt for information would have to wait until the next day.

———

Janet heard crying as soon as she stepped out of her car. She felt her blood pressure increase and wondered what she was going to do with Larsa. It was one thing to sit unobtrusively in a corner booth, but it was completely another to wail and disrupt her paying customers. She pushed open the door to the Spot, prepared to have a come-to-Jesus conversation with the most spiritual person she'd ever met, but she pulled up short when she was met by the tear-stained face of Cindy Lou.

"I—I—I'm so sorry, Janet," she sobbed. "You know Chip is leaving for college in just a few weeks? We just got his first tuition bill in the mail, and I thought I was so excited to get rid of him—I mean, not rid of him, but to get some extra time back—but now I —I—I just don't know how I'll get along without him!"

Janet's eyes widened and she glanced from Cindy Lou to Larsa, who looked guiltily away. She tried to focus on the problem at hand; she couldn't have tears behind the bar, even if Cindy Lou was going to miss her only son when he went away to school.

"Isn't he going to UT Knoxville?" Janet asked. The university was right in town.

"Yes, but he'll be living in the dorms. I might only see him once a week!"

She doubled over in tears and Janet winced; her outfit was so tight and short that drastic movements like sobbing and bending over quickly made the R-rated ensemble teeter toward NC-17.

"I have just the job for you today, Cindy Lou," Janet said, thinking fast. She'd been meaning to organize the cooler for weeks but hadn't thought of it until Bud deposited dozens of cases of bottles and cans. "Did Bud come by while I was gone? You can head into the back and cool off while you organize—"

Instead of calming down, however, Cindy Lou wailed even louder and threw her head back in angst. "No!"

"Okay." Janet instinctively stepped back. "Oh—oh, I've got it! Our renters are fostering a new baby, and I know they must be overwhelmed. Why don't you head over and see if you can help out —give them a break for a few minutes—and come back to work once you've calmed down?"

"A baby?" Cindy Lou sniffled, looking up at Janet with watery eyes.

"Yes, a beautiful baby girl."

Cindy Lou grabbed her keys and turned to Larsa before heading out the door. "Th-thanks for your in-insight, Larsa." She took a loud, shaky breath. "You're right. T-t-time does move too fast!" With another sniff, she was gone.

Janet turned her back on Larsa, exasperated that the woman had not only put *her* in a funk that day, but had also apparently sent Cindy Lou spiraling out of control.

She ran a hand through her hair, then rolled out the tension in her shoulders. It was time to get to work. The condiment container was full, the ice chest was replenished, and everything behind the bar was clean and sparkling. But they were short two rows of their most popular beer—and Cindy Lou said Bud hadn't been in yet. She depended on him, and he was usually so prompt and consistent, but it had been a solid week of mistakes and missed deliveries. She hoped she wouldn't have to change distributors.

She checked the walk-in cooler to see whether they could make it through the night when the very deliveryman in question knocked on the back door.

Janet opened it, prepared to give Bud a piece of her mind, but for the second time in less than ten minutes, she stopped before she spoke. Bud, usually so open and friendly, looked nervous as he glanced everywhere but at Janet's face.

"Sorry . . . traffic . . . ," he mumbled as he held out a clipboard for Janet to sign, still not making eye contact.

"No problem, Bud. You know where it goes."

He worked faster than she'd ever seen; the usually chatty deliveryman loaded up the walk-in cooler with cases of beer and left the bar without saying goodbye.

She watched him climb into the truck and drive away, wondering what was going on there. Something wasn't right. He'd been acting funny since . . . well, since Ike's murder.

She closed the door and turned the dead bolt, then groaned as pain sliced her finger. Despite her liberal use of hydrogen peroxide and a triple-action ointment, her finger hadn't gotten better. The long-awaited doctor's appointment wasn't until the following day, and the cut had turned a funny shade of green that surely wasn't healthy. The throbbing was like a nonstop low tone in the background, always with her and getting louder by the hour.

By seven o'clock, business was going strong. It was another busy night, and Janet looked around her bar with satisfaction. Her regulars sat in their unofficial assigned seats and were happy to be there after the crowds following Ike's murder.

"It's like church on a regular Sunday compared to Christmas or

Easter, ain't it?" Cindy Lou asked. She was back from visiting with the baby and more chipper than before.

Janet grinned. Nell caught her eye and motioned for another round. Janet poured vodka over ice in a shaker, mixed it, filled a clean rocks glass with ice, dropped two limes onto the rim, and poured in the chilled liquid.

The older woman's silvery-gray hair shone under the low lights at the bar, and Janet wondered if she'd ever know *her* sad story. Nell had been a regular for as long as Janet had worked there, but she didn't know much more about her than she'd learned after the first week.

There were other regulars, too: the one-night-out-a-week section, the barflies desperate for contact, and the lonely old people pining for better days. Some might have seen the motley crew as pathetic, but Janet was glad to know they all had a place at the Spot. Sometimes, all you needed was somewhere to call home —to be comfortable and to be yourself—to make the difference between a good day and a bad one.

As the crowd thinned and people filed out of the bar for the night, Janet bused a table by the door and overheard Frank talking to Larsa.

"I'm just saying, if you want one, it's on me."

"I'm pretty sure it wouldn't help," she responded, her dreamy voice flatter than usual.

"I'll bring one over. If you change your mind, it'll be right there."

Janet watched suspiciously as Frank left Larsa's table and headed behind the bar, reemerging moments later with a bottle of beer. She cut him off halfway to the woman's booth.

"What do you think you're doing?" She snatched the beer from Frank's hand. "She doesn't drink. Why are you bringing her this?"

"Like I told her, it might help her tonight. She seems low."

"So you decided to pressure a recovering alcoholic into having a beer? Her father is dead and she's in the throes of sadness and depression, for God's sake!"

Frank looked unabashedly back at Janet. "Uh-huh."

"Stop talking to the customers and do your job, Frank." She was livid, but softened her tone when she turned to Ike's daughter. "Go home, Larsa. You kept watch tonight; we'll see you tomorrow."

"I just wish I'd taken him seriously," Larsa said gloomily into her water.

"Frank? Nobody takes him seriously—"

"No, not Frank. On the—on the phone? It was just before my father and I argued that last time. All he could talk about was a ghost from his past, and I could only focus on the present. If I had just stopped talking long enough to really listen, I bet he'd still be alive." She pushed up from the table and slung her bag over her shoulder before heading out the door.

Janet watched her walk away, worried for Ike's daughter's mental health. The poor woman was blaming herself for her father's mistakes. What a heavy burden to bear.

She loaded the white ceramic mug onto her tray, along with two empty glasses of water, then handed the beer to a customer at the next booth over. As she wiped down the table, she wondered which ghost had haunted Ike just before he died. It seemed like there were plenty to choose from.

# CHAPTER THIRTEEN

"Where have you been?" Janet asked as she watched Jason walk across the bedroom through one slitted eye. "It's the crack of"— she turned her head and pried her eye all the way open to look at the clock on the bedside table—"nine! It's the crack of nine! What are you doing?"

"Janet, a massive virus has disabled my entire computer system. Wex has been here since midnight, and it's going to cost me an arm and a leg, but I can't have my system compromised. I should have had him come here two days ago, but I really thought he could walk me through it."

"Wexford Restin is here?" Janet asked as Jason changed into a clean shirt. She sighed when all his skin was covered up. "If your old hacking buddy is going to do the job for you, doesn't that mean you can come back to bed?" She patted the spot he'd just vacated.

He took an involuntary step closer to Janet before stopping himself with a grin. "No, God only knows what Wex will hack into if he's left alone." He walked to the door and then stopped and turned back. "We'll be in my office for the rest of the morning. Are you headed to the doctor today?"

"Och," Janet groaned, knowing it might be days before she saw her boyfriend again. "Yes, finally."

"Good," he said before disappearing down the hall.

She stayed in bed for another minute and then climbed out to get ready for her own busy day, which would start with tracking down a stranger.

———

The knock echoed in the hallway of the fancy apartment building in downtown Knoxville. Janet had managed to slide in the main door behind a resident, and she bounced on her feet, hoping Benji Watts would answer his door.

With the sudden rattle of the lock and twisting of the door-knob, Janet found herself face-to-face with a bald man who looked like he was caught between two different worlds. A few tattoos crept up from the neck of his dress shirt, and he wore an expen-sive-looking suit and tie. He pulled the strap of his messenger bag over one shoulder and held a bike helmet in his other hand.

He stopped just short of walking into her, and fumbled with his keys. "Can I help you?"

"Benji?" He nodded. "I hope so." She took a step back to let him out. He locked the door behind him and motioned for her to walk with him to the elevator. "I . . . I guess I'm looking into Ike Freeman's death." She kept her eyes trained on Benji's face to see if the name drew any kind of reaction. It did.

He stopped walking and looked at her again. "Who are you?"

"I own the bar outside of which he was found murdered."

"You're here why?"

"It turns out the police don't have a lot to go on, and I thought it made sense to investigate Ike's past. It sounds like you are a big part of it."

Benji snorted. "You could say that. He definitely changed my life."

"It was a terrible loss," Janet said.

"It *was* terrible—terrible that it happened and terrible that Ike wasn't charged with murder. He's a criminal, but he walked free. It was unbelievable. Still is."

He started walking again, and Janet followed him down the hall.

"I wasn't there, you know, when it happened. I was still at home; my first class wasn't until noon that day. Abe saw the whole thing, though. Right in front of his eyes, his best friend was snatched away. The first cop on the scene drove the man who did it home, like a taxi service." He jabbed at the down button for the elevator and shook his head.

"It sounds like you haven't forgiven Ike."

"He never asked for forgiveness!" Benji said, and his voice echoed in the empty concrete hall. He shook his head and lowered his voice. "You're right: I haven't forgiven him." He blew out a breath and jiggled his keys in his hand. "But the crazy thing is, even if the cops who showed up had given him a Breathalyzer, chances are the same thing would've happened. It's astounding how cyclist rights are trampled on a near-daily basis across this country."

"Cyclist rights?"

"People think cars own the roadways, but it's simply not true. The law gives cyclists just as much of a right to be on the road as motorists, yet time and again cyclists are treated like second-class citizens and literally run down by drivers who think they shouldn't have to share the road. It's ridiculous. I mean, we're people, okay? Some drivers are more careful when they see a dog on the side of the road than when they see a cyclist."

Janet narrowed her eyes and tried to make sense of the man in front of her. "What do you do, exactly?"

"I'm a lawyer at Dystel & Schmatt," he said, naming one of the largest law firms downtown, "but I also work pro bono to repre-sent cyclists who've been injured." They were on the elevator now, heading down to the ground floor. "You wouldn't believe how many *police officers* don't even know the law. Cars have to wait either until it's safe to pass a cyclist or until they have enough room to go wide around them if there's not a bicycle lane. Lots of cyclists get charged with blocking traffic if they take up any space at all on the road, though, like they're supposed to ride through the potholes or something!" He tsked in outrage before the ding of the elevator doors interrupted him; they stepped off together into the wide, open lobby.

"Did you know I was premed in college? I was planning to become a doctor, but then Ollie was killed and rage changed my passion from health to litigation. The fact is that Ike was drunk. He should have been charged with drunk driving and vehicular manslaughter. Instead, he got a taxi ride home, paid for by the city. My goal is to make sure that doesn't happen again to anyone." He slipped a hand inside his briefcase and flicked his card to Janet. "I'm late for work, but if you have any more questions . . ."

She followed him out of the building and watched him unlock his bicycle from a covered rack in the parking garage.

"Hey, Benji! When's the last time you saw Ike?"

He put his bicycle helmet on and clicked the latch together under his chin before answering. "I've actually never seen him in person—only in the papers." He threw one leg over the bike and, with a last wave, pedaled down the street, his unbuttoned suit jacket flapping in the wind.

She felt like scratching her head. Benji certainly didn't seem upset to learn Ike was dead, but she couldn't really blame him. As he disappeared into traffic, she realized she hadn't even asked him where he'd been the night Ike was murdered. God, she'd make a terrible investigator. He had said one thing that stuck with her, though: he hadn't been riding with Ollie the day he was killed. Their other roommate, Abe, had been. She dug around in her purse, finally finding the old receipt on which she'd scribbled their addresses. She wondered if the person who'd watched Ollie die still felt any anger toward the man who killed him.

# CHAPTER FOURTEEN

Abe also lived in a nicer section of Knoxville, but his neighborhood was less urban and Janet felt even more out of place. Everything from her car to her clothes to her hair screamed that she didn't belong in this suburban utopia, littered with expensive jogging strollers, luxury cars and SUVs in every driveway, and stucco as far as the eye could see.

It could have been her imagination, but as she knocked, she felt like a couple walking by slowed to watch her. It made her want to turn around and let them know she wasn't going to steal anything.

A beautiful brunette woman wearing tight-fitting yoga pants and a matching tank top and jacket that likely cost more than Janet averaged in tips each night opened the door. "I'm sorry, sweetheart, but we're not interested." The woman's twang was strong; she was clearly a native of Knoxville, or somewhere else down south.

Briefly curious as to what this woman thought Janet was selling, she said, "I'm looking for someone named Abe."

The woman's eyes narrowed. "Who may I say is asking for him?"

"Janet Black." She held out her business card and the woman snatched it out of her hand then pushed the door closed. Janet heard her yell up the stairs for Abe.

Footsteps pounded down the stairs. The woman pulled open the door again, still assessing Janet through narrowed, now suspicious, eyes.

A man came to stand next to her. "Vanessa?" She shrugged and stared at Janet, so he looked over, too. "Hi, I'm Abe."

He was tall, slim, and muscular, with sandy-blond hair, wire-framed glasses, and long, Nordic features.

Janet zipped up her hoodie, which was at least a size too big with frayed seams at the hemline, and flicked a look at Vanessa before saying, "Is there somewhere private we can talk?"

Abe squeezed the woman's hand, then motioned that he would follow Janet down the walk. Vanessa's eyes disappeared into slits as Janet turned to head toward the street.

"Sorry," Janet said, glancing back, as they reached the sidewalk. "I think she's—"

"Don't worry—my wife is used to it. Patients sometimes show up here. How they find me, I'll never know. Are you a patient?" He stopped walking to look her over, his eyes resting on the white bandage on her finger.

"No! I'm . . . well, I guess I'm looking into the death of Ike Freeman."

"Ah," Abe said, his face scrunched together in not quite sadness, but something near sorrow.

"You heard?" Janet asked.

"I saw it on the news the other night. I was sorry to hear it. Yes, I really was," he said in answer to Janet's surprised expression. "His life wasn't an easy one. It took me years to forgive him for killing Ollie, but I did, and I was sorry to see he wasn't ever able to . . . to get his life on track." He flicked Janet's card back and forth against his hand as he spoke. "I actually became a doctor because of him."

"Really?"

"Ollie and I were both physical therapy majors, but being there when he was hit and not knowing what to do while I waited for the ambulance . . . well, it changed me. It put me on the path I was supposed to be on."

"What did you think when Ike wasn't charged in Ollie's death?"

"I thought it was a total miscarriage of justice, just like everyone else. You'd think five eyewitnesses would have been enough to challenge the official version of what happened, but it wasn't. I can't make sense of it, but I'm glad it forced me and Benji to rethink what we were going to do with our lives. That's the only good to come from the terrible accident."

"You're with KPD?" Abe asked, finally glancing down at Janet's card.

"Oh, no. I'm, uh, I'm not." She knew Detective O'Dell well enough to know she couldn't pull off impersonating an officer without getting into trouble.

Abe looked down at her business card and frowned. "You own the Spot? What are you, like, a private investigator?"

"Oh, no." She chuckled at the thought.

"What do you have to do with—"

"I'm really just checking facts in a nonofficial capacity," she said with authority.

He squinted down at her. "What does that mean?"

Janet sighed. "It means Ike was found dead outside my bar, and his daughter is having this . . . prayer vigil on my property until his killer is found. So, I guess I'd like to speed that process along."

Abe blinked several times, and then shrugged. "Well, it's been hard on Ollie's family, but I'm sure they're finally feeling a sense of closure. Knowing Ike was out there, living his life, while their son wasn't was difficult for them—for Mr. Daniels, especially."

Janet asked a few more questions but didn't glean any new information, except that Abe's wife seemed the jealous type.

Vanessa glared down the walk through a small crack in the curtains. Janet's bar-fight radar was running hot, so she held out her hand to Abe to say goodbye.

"It's a felon," he said matter-of-factly.

"Excuse me?" Janet said, affronted. "A few misdemeanor run-ins with the cops when I was a teenager certainly doesn't make me—"

"No—no," Abe said with an uncomfortable laugh, "your finger. The kind of infection you've got is called a felon."

"Oh . . . uh, good to know. I have an appointment scheduled with my doctor for later today, hopefully she can fix me up." She waved before heading down the front walk, feeling like she'd just wasted her morning. Benji and Abe both seemed about as vaguely unaffected as could be expected when someone who had altered the course of their lives ten years earlier finally met what they must have seen as a fitting end.

An idea occurred to her, and she stopped walking and turned back toward the house. "Oh, hey, one last question: when did you last see Ike?" She was thinking about Larsa's ghost-from-the-past comment, wondering if Ike had actually seen a familiar face recently that had sent him over the edge. Abe didn't answer, he was scrutinizing her card again.

"Do the police know you're out here, talking to people about a murder case?"

"As if I'd take on all of this on my own?" Janet asked, arching her eyebrows incredulously. Abe cocked his head to the side and narrowed his eyes, and she decided to leave before he could delve more deeply into how she was connected to the case.

As she drove away, though, she realized he hadn't answered her last question and wondered if that was by design.

# CHAPTER FIFTEEN

Janet had just over thirty minutes until her appointment, so she grabbed lunch at a drive-through on the way to the office. But after two bites of hamburger, her stomach clenched.

What was she doing, investigating a murder? It was crazy, and though she hadn't been impersonating a police officer, she hadn't been far off. She'd never felt so out of control! She laughed without humor in the silence of her car, because that was really saying something. Her life had not been the smoothest over the last few years.

Something oozed from under the bandage around her finger; she dabbed it with a napkin and tossed her trash into the takeout bag before putting the car in drive and heading toward her doctor's office. There, she sat impatiently in the lobby, reading an old, torn-up magazine for twenty-seven minutes before her name was called.

She stood, and her finger gave a last, painful pulse, as if it knew treatment was near. But her brow furrowed when she saw that the woman waving her over wasn't wearing cat-and-dog scrubs like the other nurses in the office. Instead, she wore a crisp, black business suit.

"I'm so sorry, hon—I forgot to have you fill out the financial responsibility form, and we'll need to get payment for your services first." She handed a clipboard to Janet over the counter.

"You don't know what they're going to do yet, though. How can I pay for it?" Janet asked, feeling her face heat up. "I know I don't have insurance, but I'm here for a cut finger, not chemo!"

The woman adjusted her glasses. "Yes, well, it's just office policy, hon—nothing to get offended about."

She looked at the clipboard distastefully before pulling out her wallet. "How much?"

"Well, as you so succinctly said, we don't know yet. We'll just go ahead and put a five-hundred-dollar hold on your credit card and then charge you the exact amount when our billing department determines what that is."

"What? That's just . . . that's so . . . it's just a cut!" Janet said.

The woman merely raised her eyebrows and looked pointedly at the forms.

"I don't have five hundred dollars!" she snapped. "I've got renters who don't pay and employees who steal, but I *don't* have five hundred dollars!"

"Well, I'm sorry to say that's exactly why we've got the policy in place," the woman said with a smugly superior expression.

"This is unbelievable!" Janet stared at the receptionist and waited for her to come up with another plan. After all, the customer was always right. But the woman only stared back, and finally Janet, her finger now pulsing in time with her heart, shoved her wallet back into her bag and marched out of the office. She was officially pissed off.

She threw herself into her car and slammed the gearshift into drive, her foot heavy on the gas as she navigated the streets of Knoxville. She'd called Cindy Lou in early to sign for deliveries that morning, so she could get her finger looked at. Instead, she'd chased false leads all over town and nearly gotten fleeced by a doctor's office!

She parked on the street in front of the duplex and snorted in disbelief when she saw her renters—no, her squatters—sitting outside, sunning themselves, as if they didn't have a care in the world.

She climbed out of the car and called to the woman not holding a baby. "Mel! We need to talk!"

Mel headed toward her slowly, clearly sensing a shift in Janet's demeanor.

"You guys can't stay if you can't pay—it's that simple. This isn't a free boardinghouse; it's not a stop on your European vacation where you can run out before having breakfast without paying.

"This rental home is a business for us, and if you want to stay, you need to pay money to live here. If not, you'll need to be out by the end of the week." She resolutely did not look at the baby, suddenly angry that these women were unable to organize their lives.

Mel nodded solemnly, and her lack of reaction somehow stifled Janet's anger.

"Well. Okay then. I'm glad we've got that straightened out." Instead of going into the house, she got back in the car and headed to the drugstore. They were out of bandages at home, and it was clear that she needed a new treatment plan to fix whatever was happening in her finger. The skin was red, tight, and angry looking, with some pearly-white liquid oozing out one end of the cut.

She marched to the back of the store and picked out the biggest box of bandages on the shelf, then grabbed a bottle of hydrogen peroxide and a bottle of rubbing alcohol. She was going to kill whatever was growing in there, no matter how much it hurt —and it was only going to cost her nine dollars.

She pivoted for the cash register and nearly ran into another customer.

"Janet!" Detective O'Dell also had his arms full. He was balancing an eight-pack of toilet paper, a giant red sports drink, a bag of candy, and a value-size container of Tylenol. "I just came in for the Tylenol. I should know by now to always get a cart," he said with a self-deprecating grin.

Janet crossed her arms over her chest and leaned toward the detective. "I have a question about the case."

O'Dell squinted back at her, losing his friendly smile. "So do I."

"Oh?"

"Where is Elizabeth? We're starting to wonder if she really exists." He hitched the package of toilet paper under his arm and looked at her with unabashed curiosity.

She tensed up. "Of course she exists! She's one of my original bartenders at the Spot."

"You mean she was."

"No, she is. I just don't know where she is right now."

"Is that common? Has she missed work like this before?"

"Yes." Janet shifted her load to free up her injured hand. "You don't often become a bartender because you've got your shit together, you know?"

"Why do you become a bartender?"

Janet looked up sharply, but for once, O'Dell wasn't smirking. He seemed genuinely curious.

"It's what you do when you've got great people skills," she deadpanned. O'Dell didn't laugh, and Janet added, more seriously, "It's happened before—with Elizabeth—but it's unusual. It isn't like her, and I'm—I'm worried about her."

"We're worried, too, Janet. It doesn't look good. She's either involved in something or got in the way of something, you know?"

"Well, she's not involved in anything!" she said with conviction she didn't feel.

"That's worrisome, too, isn't it?" O'Dell replied. "Finch checked her apartment—had the manager let him in yesterday afternoon—and said nothing was out of place, but there was no sign of her." They stared at each other for a moment before he said, almost reluctantly, "You had a question for me?"

She took a breath and her shoulders dropped. She no longer felt combative—just tired. "Larsa was at the bar yesterday, again. She said her dad had been in an accident recently. Do you know anything about that?"

O'Dell's eyes widened in surprise. "Well . . . it was a single-car accident maybe a month ago."

Janet's fingers twitched. "What happened?" It was a pain in the ass not to have access to the case file.

"An anonymous passerby called 911 about a car off the road and a man bleeding. Dispatchers sent an ambulance, and EMTs treated Ike for a concussion at the scene. When our officer arrived, he was so drunk that he didn't really remember the details of the crash— his blood alcohol level was over twice the legal limit to drive. He should have been served papers to appear in court a few weeks ago, but there was a filing error, so it just crossed my desk."

"Any idea who this Good Samaritan was who called 911?"

"We're working on it." O'Dell frowned and subconsciously made a humming sound as he blew out a breath. He finally shook his head. "One more for you: I just got a call from Dispatch. They fielded inquiries from both of Ollie's old roommates. Care to explain what you're doing?"

Janet crossed her arms but didn't answer.

"I'm uh . . . I'm late for work, but watch out, Janet. You're not a cop, so don't act like one." He gave her a final stern look before heading for the checkout stand.

She waited until he was out of the store before she moved. As she stared at the shelf of bandages, she honed in on a recurring theme for Ike. How did he get home from his most recent accident? Why had Ike been able to continually skirt the law when he was alive? Was his friend still on the force?

# CHAPTER SIXTEEN

"Late for work?" Janet stared at O'Dell twenty minutes later. They stood toe-to-toe in her kitchen and she was furious.

"Yeah," he answered, not taking his eyes off his notebook. "My guys got here fifteen minutes ago."

"What exactly is going on?" She watched a trio of men, wearing navy blue KPD polo shirts, carrying things up to the kitchen from the basement, through the TV room, and out the front door.

He plucked a piece of paper from the plywood island and cursed. "Splinter!" He handed her the paper and then put his finger to his mouth, still wincing in pain.

This was where being helpful got her: with her house being legally ransacked by cops. Unbelievable.

"Look, Janet, I'm investigating a murder, and if that means I have to collect your boyfriend's computer equipment to make sure he's being truthful when he says the crime wasn't recorded on his surveillance cameras, then unfortunately, that's what we're going to do."

"'Collect'? I wouldn't exactly use that term," Jason said as he came up from the basement, his cell phone pressed against one ear. "More like illegally confiscate." Another cop walked past with a large hard drive and Jason said, "Be careful with that!" He turned back to O'Dell. "I have over fifty thousand dollars of hardware down there, and if any of it comes back dented, scratched, or otherwise damaged, you'll be paying—" He broke off midsentence and moved his phone in front of his mouth. "Yes, I'm still on hold for Phil Walderman. It's urgent." He looked over at Janet. "This is going to cost us a fortune." He then stormed back down the steps that led to his office.

"A lawyer?" O'Dell said, recognizing the name of the local attorney. "Save yourself the money. We got a subpoena signed by a judge to take everything. A lawyer won't be able to do anything about it."

"Are you sure? Did the judge know Jason has information on other clients in his system? You can't look through someone's entire office to find information on one case."

"Actually," O'Dell said with an attempt at a conciliatory tone, "we can."

Janet tried to read the piece of paper he'd handed her, but in her anger, she couldn't focus. "Why would we lie? What could we possibly gain by not handing over evidence that would solve a murder? Do you think it's good for business—"

"You said it was yourself! You said business would be crazy the night after Ike's body turned up, and Finch said you were right. Standing room only! I'd say it's been great for business."

"That's—that's just . . . I mean, that's totally off base! Yes, the initial thrust was, but it's not a long-term strategy for growth. How can you—" She was so angry she was spluttering, unable to finish a single thought. Instead, she picked up her cell phone.

"Oh, are you gonna call your daddy now and see if he can get you out of this mess?" O'Dell asked.

She looked up from her phone in time to see his smirk.

"No!" she said, even though that was exactly what she'd been intending to do. "I'm going to text Jason and tell him we'll take out a second mortgage and sell the bar if that's what it costs to get a lawyer down here to make sure you don't trample all over our rights. You can't come in here and destroy a man's business—especially when you have no proof that he's done anything wrong!"

"Good luck."

"What do you mean?"

"I mean good luck finding a lawyer on a—" He stopped, took a deep breath, and then released it slowly. "What is it about you that drives me so nuts?" He shook his head like he was shaking off a swarm of gnats. "This is a murder investigation, Ms. Black, that's it. It's not a personal vendetta against you or your boyfriend."

She stared at him, thinking about what he'd been about to say. A spark of knowledge hit, and she stepped closer, her finger jammed against his chest. "You did this on purpose. It's Sunday, and you must have gotten this subpoena filed when?" She looked down at the paper still grasped in her other hand. "Yes, on Friday, but you didn't act on it until today, Sunday. You knew we wouldn't be able to find a judge to counteract this filing on a weekend!" She looked up from the paper in shock. "You're just as bad as a criminal!"

O'Dell scoffed. "I'm the exact opposite of a criminal. The fact that you can't see that just confirms what we're doing today is the right thing."

Janet stalked past him and yelled down the stairs, "Any luck on Walderman?"

"Still on hold. They'll probably bill me four hundred dollars for this call alone!"

A woman with dark hair slicked back into a bun stepped around Janet, carrying another hard drive. A man behind her gripped two monitors by the stands. Janet watched both walk out the back door and deposit Jason's items into a waiting van.

"Now you're just being punitive," she said, turning to O'Dell. "What are you going to do with the monitors? That's just—that's just plain mean." While keeping an eye on him, she shouted, "Jason, do whatever we need to do here, okay? This isn't right. Let's make it right."

"Careful," O'Dell said, tucking his notebook under his arm and fixing her with his most irritatingly superior stare.

"Is that a threat?"

"No, just a friendly warning. If you bet on the wrong horse, here, and Jason isn't as innocent as you think, he might just drain your accounts defending himself, and then you'll lose him, this house, *and* your bar."

Janet sucked in a gasp at his audacity, then spun away from him, not wanting to look at his smug face for a second longer. Jason came back up the stairs and she looked up at him, a question on her lips.

"W—" But before she could get Wex's name out, he shook his head almost imperceptibly. Her eyes flicked to O'Dell. "Who else can you call?" she asked, trying to cover up her earlier question.

Jason frowned at O'Dell. "Whoever we need to, to make this right."

She frowned, too. Why was O'Dell so certain Jason was involved in a murder? What did he know? What was she missing?

# CHAPTER SEVENTEEN

It was dead.

Janet was halfway through her shift Sunday afternoon and the bar was practically empty. Janet studiously avoided making eye contact with Larsa at her corner booth, and Nell, the only true customer there, sat out of sight on the other side of the Beerador, nursing a drink.

She'd left the house in utter chaos with Jason near the breaking point, prowling up and down the stairs like a caged cheetah.

Now she was the one ready to pounce. She paced behind the bar, wondering what was going to happen to his business—to their business—and their home. Sunlight streamed into the dark room when the door opened, and Janet squinted toward the light. "Jason? What are you doing here?"

He grinned. "Figured I might as well hang out here, rather than watch them tear apart our house." He had a bounce in his step that she hadn't expected.

"For someone who was yelling at a lawyer on the phone an hour ago, you sure seem . . . chipper."

His grin widened. "It was a pretty good act, if I do say so myself."

"Act? What are you talking about?"

He straddled a stool across from her and swept a hand through his dark hair. "After you passed on Finch's message about the subpoena, I told Wex what needed to happen. Can you believe he got the problem licked in two hours? That bastard hacked me right past the malware and then sent a line of code back that'll disable the jerks who wrote it for months." He nodded in satisfaction.

"What do you mean? You and Wex were working through the night and all morning. If you weren't trying to fix the virus, what were you doing?"

"Copying everything over to new external hard drives and then wiping my machines clean. If KPD can get past my passwords and into my system, which is doubtful, they won't find a thing."

A shocked laugh escaped before Janet clamped her lips and smacked him on the arm. "Jason, that's going to make you look so guilty!"

"They can't make me guilty just because they want me to be, and lack of evidence in itself isn't evidence. Plus," he shifted in his seat, "I couldn't risk them getting ahold of my files. If word got out that the security guy's computer wasn't secure—" He stopped abruptly with a shake of his head that said he might as well sell pizza for a living.

"Jason," she moaned, "it's all about perception with these guys. If you look guilty, they're going to dig in!"

"Let them," he said dismissively, reaching out to grab her hand. "I'm sorry that I had to worry you, but there wasn't time to explain."

"I get it. I know how important your job is, and I'd never get in the way of that."

"I know. That's one of the reasons I love you."

She grinned at him for a moment before shaking herself. God, she hated feeling so sappy.

Jason laughed, sensing her internal struggle. "I have something for you," he said with a sly smile.

"What?" she asked, suspicious of the change in his mood.

Before he could answer, though, Bud, the beer deliveryman, walked in the front door.

"I knocked around back, but no one answered."

"A Sunday delivery, Bud?"

"Well, Mondays get so busy, I thought I'd get a jump start." His hand tapped out a beat against his leg, and the loose coins in his pocket jangled like a tambourine.

Jason waved her off, slipped off his stool, and walked around the bar to pour himself a glass of water while Janet dealt with the delivery.

"I know Cindy Lou will miss seeing you," she said as she led Bud through the office to the back door. She propped it open and watched him fill his cart with cases of beer.

She counted the bottles as Bud wheeled them into the cooler and then signed the paper on his clipboard. When the truck pulled out of the lot, she went in search of Jason.

She didn't have to go far; he was waiting for her by the alley exit.

"So, mystery man, you ready to spill the beans?" Janet asked.

"Out here." He pushed the door open, then pointed at the eaves of the roof. "See anything different?"

Janet scanned the roofline but didn't see anything out of place. If she really squinted, she could make out the tape still covering the security camera hidden in the exit sign. "You didn't fix the camera?"

"In fact, I have." He crossed his arms over his chest and grinned.

She leaned against the door frame. "Well, then, riddle me this: why does it look exactly the same?" she asked.

"Because I am the top security expert in town and even the cops can't contain me." He wagged his eyebrows.

She rolled her eyes at her boyfriend. "Obviously. But what does that have to do with *that*?" She pointed at the tape covering the camera. She'd been on an emotional roller coaster for the last few hours and was suddenly tired of Jason's game.

His grin wavered. "I punched a tiny hole in the tape and then replaced it over the lens. Now it looks like the camera's still covered, but it's not—there is a crystal-clear shot of this alleyway." He turned and pointed vaguely to a different part of the roof. "I also installed a second hidden camera a couple of days ago that nobody knows about." He crossed his arms and frowned. "I'm still having some trouble with the wiring for the cameras inside. I'll need a few more days to untangle *that* problem." He paused for a moment, then turned to look slyly back at Janet. "With both cameras up and running, we'll be set for anything that happens out here in the future."

Janet threw her hands in the air. "But what about the past? That's what I'm interested in!" Didn't Jason understand? The police suspected him of *murder* and that meant they needed to find out who'd covered the camera, so the detectives could move on to their next wild guess at who killed Ike!

"I've got some information on that, too," he said, giving her a strange look. Jason held open the door and motioned for her to walk in first. She dropped her head back and groaned but walked into the bar, waved to Cindy Lou as she arrived for her shift, and followed Jason back to the office.

He sat down in the chair and logged on to the computer, then double-clicked on a thumbnail image; the shot showed the empty alleyway behind the Spot, from the surveillance camera they had just seen in person.

"It's from yesterday." Jason tapped another button and the video zoomed forward. Soon, Cindy Lou walked into the frame, and Jason slowed the video to real-time playback. As usual, she had more skin showing than clothes, and just as Janet was trying to decide if her top would be classified as low-cut or high-rise, another person walked into the frame—slunk, really.

"Is that Bud?" Janet asked incredulously.

"The one and only," Jason said with a sly smile.

She looked back at the screen when his grin widened. In the few seconds she'd been looking away, Cindy Lou had lost most of her clothes. With a frantic energy she had a hard time connecting with Cindy Lou, her assistant manager and beer delivery guy were getting it on big-time.

"How does her back bend like that?" Janet asked, but Jason only shrugged.

While Cindy Lou appeared to be completely engrossed in the task at hand, Bud's eyes continued to flick to the hidden security camera often enough that it wasn't coincidence—he obviously knew the camera was there.

"Do you think he's the one who tampered with the camera?"

"Keep watching," Jason said.

"I don't think I can." She scrunched up her face. With her eyes squeezed nearly shut, the images on-screen blurred out enough that she couldn't see actual flopping body parts but was aware when the deed was done. She opened her eyes only after both parties were fully dressed again. "I sure hope she washed her hands before she got back to work."

"Are you watching?" he asked.

"Yes," Janet grumbled, squinting at the screen again. Bud tucked his shirt in and took a step toward the door after Cindy Lou. But before he walked in, he reached right up to the camera and moved his thumb over what he thought was the tape covering the lens. He then nodded in satisfaction and disappeared into the bar.

"I think we found our guy." Jason clicked something that reversed the video. Another tap on the keyboard froze the frame on a close-up of Bud's face.

"But how did he know the camera was there in the first place?"

Jason blew out a short breath. "He came out into the alley with some boxes the day I was installing it. I'd have never guessed he knew what I was doing, but it must have made him suspicious enough that he took a closer look."

"Oh my God!" Janet covered her mouth with her hand. "Do you think Bud killed Ike?"

"Nah." Jason leaned back in his seat and swiveled around to

face Janet. "I saw Bud collect a spider in a cup from the walk-in cooler and then set it free outside. He's not the violent type. I think it was just Ike's bad luck that he was killed near Bud and Cindy Lou's meeting place."

The sudden sound of knocking came from both sides of the office, at the back door to the parking lot and the door to the bar. She opened the outside door first and came face-to-face with Bud.

"Is my clipboard here?" he asked sheepishly, peering around Janet into the office space.

She followed his gaze and was immediately distracted by the sight of Cindy Lou standing on the other side of Jason. Her silvery bandeau top was like a sandbar of coverage in the expansive ocean of skin between her eyes and hips, where a micromini jean skirt clung hopefully.

*Uniforms. We need uniforms at the Spot*, Janet thought dispassionately.

"What's that, boss?" Cindy Lou asked, staring at the computer screen. She looked at Jason and then shifted her gaze to Janet. Before either could answer, her eyes moved again and she adjusted her top with a bright smile. "Oh, hey, Bud! I wasn't expectin' to see you today." She ran a hand through her hair.

Janet swallowed hard and realized this was their chance to get some answers. "We actually wanted to talk to both of you. It seems there's been something going on, and we need to get to the bottom of it."

Bud took a jerky step backward, while Cindy Lou laughed a little too loudly and stepped into the office. She pulled the door closed behind her.

"I guess y'all found us out. I can't believe we kept it a secret for this long, Bud!" Her gaze shifted back to the computer screen and she said, "Seriously, Jason, what the heck is that?"

No one answered, and she looked back to the doorway. "Bud?"

Janet tore her eyes away from Cindy Lou to see her lover's reaction, but the doorway was empty. Seconds later, the beer truck's engine started with a roar.

# CHAPTER EIGHTEEN

"Wait!" Jason yelled. He ran out of the office and banged on the driver's-side door of the truck just as Bud slid the engine into gear. The truck lurched and Bud banged on the steering wheel but made no move to get back out until Jason knocked on the door again.

Then he and Jason walked back into the office. Cindy Lou's face, cheerful just moments earlier, had frozen when Bud left. Now tears threatened and her lower lip trembled. Janet said a quick prayer that her assistant manager could keep it together.

Jason closed the door so all four stood in the small office space together. It was silent for what felt like a long time.

"So," Janet said, looking between the pair. "Secret lovers?"

Bud's face flushed scarlet, and Cindy Lou took a tremulous breath before answering.

"Well, I guess it ain't so secret anymore," she said with a brave attempt at a smile. "But, you know what? I'm glad it's out in the open. Now we don't have to sneak around. They don't care, right, Janet? Jason?"

Janet didn't say anything; instead, she inspected Bud, who absently stroked his hand. His left ring finger, to be more specific.

After another few awkward moments of silence, he spoke. "Listen, I don't want any trouble. I mean, this was just for fun, right?"

"Just for . . . just for fun?" Cindy Lou's voice was barely louder than a whisper. Her pale skin flushed scarlet from her cheeks all the way down her shoulders, like beer foam spilling over the edge of a glass.

Bud shifted his weight and said, "I mean . . . I, uh . . . I've got a wife and two kids at home."

Cindy Lou sucked in a noisy breath and her piercing wail flooded the room. "A wife? Kids? What are you talkin' about? I mentioned Chip a dozen times, and how he's leaving for college soon, and I'll be all alone—and you never thought to mention your dang wife? Your k-k-kids?"

Janet's face felt pinched, and she was furious that Cindy Lou had let herself be played so fantastically. What was it with everyone in her life being unwilling to see the truth of things? Jason was so intent on not helping the police that he couldn't see he also wasn't helping himself. Her renters were a mess and had no money and no jobs, yet thought they could sign a lease and foster a baby.

Now Cindy Lou was shocked that secret alley sex wasn't the launching point for a long-term relationship?

"Wake up, Cindy Lou," Janet snapped, glaring at Bud. "You're Dumpster diving with this guy, and you think he doesn't have a secret? Use your head!" She looked down her nose at Bud, who flinched under her cold stare. "That's a man with something to hide."

Her eyes shot over to Cindy Lou in time to see her employee's face crumple completely. The bartender ran, sobbing, from the room. Bud slunk out to the parking lot, and drove away.

Janet bit her lip. The silence coming from the other side of the office was louder than Bud's truck. In her peripheral vision, she saw Jason cross his arms. She could feel him staring at her but couldn't quite bring herself to meet his eye.

"What's wrong with you, Janet? Do you think Cindy Lou

needed to hear that from you just now? Where's your compassion?"

"Compassion?" She rubbed her hands over her face and sank heavily down onto the threadbare couch. "Compassion leaves you with broke renters, crappy employees who disregard what you say, and police trying to dig up dirt on you that doesn't exist. I don't think we can afford to be compassionate anymore, Jason!"

Disappointment wafted from her boyfriend like freshly applied aftershave. He grabbed his coat and wallet from the desk, his face taut, his lips tight. "I'm going home," he said. "I have work to do."

He walked out of the office without a backward glance.

"Oh . . . okay," Janet said to his retreating figure. "I'll, ah . . . I'll see you . . ." But she was alone. He was gone.

The phone rang and she answered wearily.

"I can't come in tonight for my shift. I'm sick," a very healthy-sounding Frank said.

"Sick?"

"Yeah, sorry."

"What kind of sick?" Janet asked. Here, finally, was someone at whom she could justify being angry, but she was too tired to expend the effort.

"The kind of sick where I don't feel like working, okay?"

"Well . . . I don't have anyone else I can call to come in—"

"Now that I think of it, I'd better just cancel my shift tomorrow, too. Might still be contagious."

In the background, she heard laughing. Maybe some music, too.

An inner calm took over, and her clenched shoulders relaxed. She took a deep, cleansing breath. "Frank, don't come back. You're fired."

"But—but, Janet—"

She gently placed the phone down onto the receiver before resting her head on her folded arms.

The door opened and Cindy Lou murmured, "I'm sorry, Janet.

I'm sorry I'm such a dang disappointment," then slunk back into the bar like a beaten dog.

She scrubbed a hand over her face. Why couldn't she have handled that better? She'd never set out to be the kind of boss who'd make an employee cry. Now Cindy Lou was apologizing to her. Cindy Lou! Apologizing to her! Her most loyal employee, who never called in sick and always had a smile for everyone, had just been emotionally torpedoed by a lover—and Janet had piled on the way Frank would have.

She groaned at her own behavior. Her life had begun to feel like a runaway train, and she was flying off the rails along with it.

In the bar, Cindy Lou slumped over the ice chest, staring dejectedly out at the front door.

Janet leaned up against the cooler too, so they were shoulder to shoulder. "I'm sorry I'm such a bitch." She took her wallet out of her back pocket, then peeled a dollar out of the fold and tucked it into the swear jar. "I've been a hell of a jerk"—another dollar—"but I'm going to own it. I was mad at Bud and took it out on you. That wasn't fair."

Cindy Lou nodded, but her eyes didn't leave the door.

Janet blew out a sigh. "I should tell you that I fired Frank, that asshole." Two dollars that time. "And I will try to stop being such an award-winning cu—"

"Janet, no!" Cindy Lou gasped.

"Okay—bitch"—Janet stifled a grin as she put a fiver into the jar—"for at least the rest of the night so that this shitty day"—another dollar—"can end with enough money in the swear jar for one hell of an extra tip for my employees. I mean, ffff—" Cindy Lou slapped a hand over her mouth to cover a smile. "Ffffuck, it's been a long day." She ended with the final bill in her wallet, a twenty. "Do you forgive me?"

Cindy Lou nodded. "I was a fool, Janet. I know that."

"And I should have been there to support you. Not knock you down even more."

Cindy Lou threw an arm over Janet's shoulders. "You fired

Frank?"

"Uh-huh."

"Well. There's one good thing about today."

———

Four hours later, business had picked up and they had a sizable crowd—especially for a Sunday night.

"Watch Jimmy," Janet said to Cindy Lou. "He might need a taxi." The new customer appeared to be on a mission to drink as many happy-hour specials as possible.

Nell had sidled up to him and they were discussing cataracts, with Jimmy boisterously advocating skipping surgery and just going blind. Nell's extra-large glasses turned opaque under the lights as she pondered that idea. Janet grinned, then turned when the door opened and a crowd poured in.

They really could have used Frank that night, so despite their argument, Janet texted Jason, asking him to come in. The bar was nearing capacity, and she didn't have anyone to check IDs at the door, so drink orders were backing up while she and Cindy Lou checked IDs before each order.

A small commotion at the front door caught her eye as she pulled a pint. "What's going on?"

"Huh?" Cindy Lou opened two bottles at once and slid them across the bar to waiting customers.

"Nothing, nothing." Janet opened a tab for someone but scanned the front of the bar until she spotted it. Well, her. Two people moved to reveal a woman slumped against the door, preventing anyone else from coming in. The door rattled, and the woman flipped her head up. Her long blond hair parted, revealing Larsa.

"Larsa, hon, what are you doing?" Janet called. She was so distracted, beer spilled over the side of a pint glass and down her hand. "Damn it!" She wiped off the glass and handed it across the bar. "Cindy Lou, I'll be right back."

"Seriously?" Cindy Lou looked over and swiped the back of her hand across her forehead. When she saw the situation at the front door she nodded. "Get on back here ay-sap, boss!"

Janet hustled around the side of the bar and made her way through the crowd to the front door.

Larsa chuckled when the door behind her pulsed again as someone tried to push it open from the outside.

"Larsa? Are you okay?"

The other woman's eyes opened wide. "Janet. I've had a day, you know?"

"I was wondering where you were!"

"You were?" Larsa drew the hair away from her face and held it back on top of her head, her eyes welling up with tears.

"Well, yeah, sure. Come on up to the bar, away from the door," she added, reaching out to guide Larsa away from the entrance.

Larsa finally leaned forward, just as the door pushed open. The unexpected bump sent Ike's daughter sprawling into a group of people nearby.

A beer from that group flew through the air, spraying a stream of liquid across Larsa's face as the bottle plunged back down to the ground.

Janet and Larsa locked eyes seconds before Larsa's tongue snaked out and tasted the beer dripping down her cheek. Janet's jaw dropped at the move, and Larsa's eyes widened when she realized what she'd done.

"Oh!" she gasped.

"It doesn't count!" Janet said with conviction. "That doesn't . . ."

Larsa mopped her sleeve across her face and tried to stand, but her legs were unsteady. While Janet swooped down to rescue the beer bottle before someone stepped on it, Larsa wailed, "Oh my God!"

"Larsa! Larsa, it's going to be all right!"

But the other woman fell against the wall, shook her head, and pushed back off before stumbling through the crowd of people.

By the time Janet made her way out into the parking lot, Larsa was gone.

She rubbed a hand across her forehead and blew out a noisy breath through her nose. "What in the hell just happened?" She was worried about Larsa, but there wasn't anything she could do about the other woman now. She headed back inside and took her place behind the bar, handing out drinks as fast as people could pay for them.

"Don, Chris, are you ready for another, or are you headed home?" she asked two men seated at bar stools in front of her.

She scanned the room as she waited for their answer, and did a double take when her renters walked into the bar with their baby.

"We have good news," Mel said with a guarded smile. "We found some money to put toward rent. It won't cover everything we owe, but it's a good start."

Janet's eyes narrowed. "Oh yeah?" She dried her hands on a rag tucked into her apron string. "How much?"

"It's enough for this month's rent and half the security deposit. Not perfect, I know, but it's a start, don't you think?" Kat looked hopeful as she held out an envelope; Janet took it and peered inside at a stack of cash.

"Do you think you can pay next month's rent and the other half of the deposit in thirty days?"

Mel stole a glance at her partner before nodding. "Yes."

Kat started yammering on about all of the baby's accomplishments that day, which included things like smiling and touching her toes.

Janet wasn't impressed, but she also wasn't really paying attention. She looked inside the envelope again, then interrupted Kat. "Where did you get this money?"

"Well, the timing just couldn't have been better," Kat answered when Mel didn't. "It's from the state for child support for the baby. We had so much help from friends offering to donate items that we don't need it."

Janet stared wordlessly at her tenants for a moment while she gathered her thoughts.

Hours ago, she might have told them to save the money for the baby, not use it to pay their rent. She might have told them that from what she'd heard, babies grew quickly, needed new clothes every other week, and ran through formula like the people in her bar ran through beer, and they'd likely need the money *for the baby*, as the state intended.

But.

She was a new woman. A more responsible user of words. So, instead, she said, "What about the other half? You think the state's going to cover that for you, too?" But before they could respond, Janet's attention was drawn to a commotion on the other end of the bar.

Jimmy, the customer Janet had recently identified as being on the edge, had officially fallen over it. He leaned over the bar and yelled at Cindy Lou, his finger shaking just inches from her face. Nell scurried off her bar stool and hustled away.

"Cut off? Who are you to cut me off? You don't make the—the —argh!" He'd leaned too far forward on the stool and misjudged where the bar was. His elbow missed the counter completely, and he pitched forward and fell off the side of his stool to the floor, narrowly missing the corner of the bar with his chin as he went down.

He braced himself against the floor and Cindy Lou took the break to call the cab company. She turned to Janet and held up two fingers, indicating his ride was only a couple of minutes away.

In the meantime, Jimmy was gearing up for another outburst. His fingers reached up for the edge of the countertop. Janet could see the wheels turning—albeit slowly—and his face growing redder by the moment.

Her mouth twisted in distaste. With Frank fired, it was up to her to physically remove this unruly customer. "Boy, did you pick the wrong day to mess with me," she muttered as she rounded the corner of the bar. But before she got to Jimmy, another set of hands latched onto the scruff of his neck. He was cut off mid-snarl as Mel literally lifted him off the floor and set him down on his feet hard before propelling him forward.

Cindy Lou, the receiver still pressed to her ear, called out, "His ride is thirty seconds away!"

Mel slammed the idiot down into a seat by the door and pressed her hands against his shoulders in a death grip, keeping him in place until Cindy Lou said, "Now!" and pointed to the door.

Mel hefted him back to his feet and escorted him out into the parking lot. The taxi pulled up in front of the glass door and Mel deposited Jimmy carefully into the backseat. She slammed the door, then tapped the roof and watched the car drive away, her arms hanging loosely at her sides.

The bar had fallen quiet during the scuffle, but when Mel walked back inside the establishment, the other customers erupted in cheers. Mel's grim expression didn't change, but Kat squealed, clapped, and hugged her when she arrived back at the bar.

"So, anyway, what were you saying about money?" Mel asked, as if they hadn't been interrupted.

Janet's mouth hung open again. She had no idea what kind of background Mel had, but that hadn't been learned in a simple self-defense class. Before she could second-guess herself, Janet said, "I was saying you need some—some money, that is—and you can earn it by working for me. I need a bouncer. Are you interested?"

"What kind of hours are we talking about?" Janet glanced at Cindy Lou in disbelief before Mel, her face impassive, said, "I'm just messing with you. Of course I want the job! Obviously, I need it—we need it."

Janet smiled faintly. She wanted to know more about Mel's work history—hell, her life history—but before she could ask where she had learned to kick ass, a man walked into the bar. He rubbed his sweaty hands on his pants, leaving dark streaks behind, then scanned the crowd.

"Abe?" Janet called out. "What are you doing here?"

# CHAPTER NINETEEN

The tall, sandy-haired man scanned the perimeter of the space, before his eyes landed on Janet. He nodded solemnly, then walked forward.

"Is . . ." He looked around the room again, zipping and unzipping his light jacket in time with his foot tapping against the floor. He finally brought his eyes back to Janet and tried again. "Is Larsa here?"

"No. No, she's not."

"Oh, I thought . . . I thought you said she was going to be here until the police caught Ike's killer."

"Yes, she was in a bit of a state tonight. I don't know why, she rushed out before I could ask."

"Oh!" His hand stilled when his zipper was halfway down the coat. "Did the police make an arrest?"

She blew out a sigh. "No . . . I don't think so, anyway." She looked at the door, wondering how she could check on Larsa. Until that night she'd thought she might never get the woman out of her bar; now she was worried she wouldn't be able to find her. "Hey, can I get you a beer? On the house." She wanted to know why he was here, and if Larsa couldn't ask, she was going to.

He held Janet's gaze for a long moment before finally nodding. She went behind the bar, pulled two draft beers, and carried them to an empty table in the corner. Larsa's table, she thought with a grimace.

"I see you haven't had your finger taken care of," Abe said as he sat down and shrugged out of his coat.

She plonked the beers down. "I'm going to a walk-in clinic first thing tomorrow," she said with conviction. Her finger had seemed to get worse after she'd treated it at home, instead of better.

Abe took a zip-top bag out of his pocket and set it on the table. "I grabbed a few things from home that might help, just in case you still needed it—and I see you certainly do." He opened the bag and unfolded a large gauze rectangle, a scalpel, a needle, and two small bottles of liquid. He pointed to the smaller bottle. "The iodine will clean out the wound after we drain it." Then he picked up the larger bottle and the syringe.

"Whoa, wait just a minute. You're going to dr—drain it?" She gulped and her heart rate zipped into overdrive. She looked down at her finger, certain that the throbbing she felt would be visible from the outside. It wasn't.

"Don't worry, I'll numb it first." Abe took the very worrisome-looking syringe and drew some liquid from the larger bottle. "Lidocaine," he said while snapping on blue gloves before he held out his hand. She reluctantly rested her hand on his and he got to work. "The first poke is the only one you'll feel." The needle hovered over her hand; she peeled her eyes away from the shiny tip, and as soon as she looked up, Abe struck the needle down into her finger.

"Shh-YOW!" She tried to jerk away, but Abe was surprisingly strong. After a moment, though, the burning sensation faded, and for the first time in days, she didn't feel the constant throb of pain pulsing in her finger.

"See? I told you," he said with a smile. He put the syringe down and picked up the scalpel. "I could tell this was pretty painful when you were at my house." He chatted as if they were at a ball game, discussing how the season was going. She watched him work, fascinated that, even as he drew the blade along the lateral line of her fingertip, she felt nothing.

"Yup, look at that," he said as a yellowish-green liquid dripped from her fingertip onto the gauzy pad below. "That was festering inside you. Time was not your friend—this finger was only getting worse every hour you left it untreated." He poked and prodded around all sides of the cut skin. Whatever he saw made him nod, and then he poured liquid from the small vial directly onto the wound. "The iodine will disinfect anything bad that's still in there. Incidentally, where did you get injured?"

"Back there, cutting lemons."

"Well, next time, I'd just pour some eighty-to-one-hundred-proof alcohol right over the cut. That would do a pretty good job clearing it right up."

She sighed. Surrounded by alcohol, and it had taken her four days just to buy rubbing alcohol at the drugstore. By then, it had been too late.

Abe bandaged her finger with a simple wrap and then set about cleaning up his operating station. Within minutes, he was taking off his gloves and nodding at her hand in satisfaction.

"It should feel a lot better by tomorrow," he said, stuffing the trash back in the bag.

"Thanks." Janet inspected her finger with a wide smile. Abe held his glass out and they clinked before both taking a sip. After a moment of silence, Janet said, "Why were you looking for Larsa?"

Abe blinked. He took another sip of beer before he answered. "I feel . . . I don't know, a strange connection with her." Janet raised her eyebrows and he continued. "Her father irrevocably changed my life ten years ago—and hers, too. Now that he's dead, I feel the weight of the situation. I can talk about it with you and I can talk about it with my wife, but I really feel like I need to talk about it with someone else who feels that same weight."

"Wow." Janet leaned back against the leather of the booth. She had felt many things in her life, but she'd usually wanted to feel them alone. She opened her mouth to say as much when a screech from the doorway of the bar brought the regular din of the crowd to silence. Abe's head whipped around and panic swooped across his face like a sudden storm.

"Who is—" Before she could finish her question, though, Abe stood, an uncertain, tremulous smile on his face.

"Vanessa, what are you doing here?"

"What am *I* doing here?" Vanessa stalked toward Abe and Janet like a mountain lion, her long, dark hair loose and wild around her face. "What am *I* do—" She broke off and huffed out three rapid breaths, blinking in rhythm with her gasps. Finally she snarled, "What are *you* doing here?"

"Vanessa, you remember Janet, the owner of this establishment. Janet, I'm sure you remember my wife." Abe scratched his head as he looked at Vanessa's furious expression.

"I knew it," Vanessa whispered. By now, the crowd had returned to its normal volume, although they were still getting some furtive glances and outright stares from the tables nearby. "I just knew it, Abe Nyack. I knew you were having an affair, but I never thought you'd stoop so low as to mess around with someone like *her*." She jabbed a finger toward Janet and glowered in her direction before turning a venomous eye back to her husband.

"Hey!" Janet said, affronted by the accusation and rankled by the revulsion.

"Vanessa, what are you talking about? I came here to find—"

"Oh, I know exactly what you're looking for, mister, and you know where you're not going to find it anymore? At home. You better pack your bags if you're shacking up with her! You're sure as hell not welcome in my bed!"

Abe opened his mouth, but Vanessa cut him off again, fury turning her face purplish red.

"You know what? You almost had me convinced that you were at work last week when you were out all night, but then your secretary called and said she didn't know how to enter the receipt from the coffee shop into the accounting system. 'Was it business or pleasure?' she asked, and I said, 'The coffee shop at the hospital?'

She said, 'No, the one downtown—the twenty-four-hour café.' Now, are you going to try and tell me you worked on a patient at four in the morning *in a café?*" Her eyes cut accusingly toward Janet and then back to her husband. "I guess I don't have to ask what kind of 'work' you were doing!" She hit the air quotes around the word "work" like it was a knockout punch.

"What are you talking about?" Abe asked.

"Are you going to make me say it?" Vanessa asked, her voice rising again to a shriek. "Were you with her Thursday night, Abe? How long has this been going on?"

"No, no—" Janet tried to interrupt to set her straight, but it was like stepping in front of a rabid dog.

Vanessa turned to growl at Janet. "I know exactly what you two were doing, but I am a lady, so I won't say it out loud, you man-stealing *whore.*"

Janet looked to Abe for support, but he stared at his wife, slack-jawed. He looked like a man who'd been caught, but not like a man who'd been caught cheating.

Vanessa was gearing up to launch into falsetto when Janet yelled, "Wait just a minute! I wasn't with your husband that night, Vanessa. My boyfriend and I were home together—at our house."

"Oh, sure. That's a pretty convenient excuse!" Vanessa snapped. "What were you doing?"

"Just about everything," a deep voice rumbled past Janet's ear. "And I'll be honest: we tried a few new things that night that I won't soon forget." Jason's hands smoothed over her shoulders and ran down her arms possessively. "A lady probably couldn't handle the details, though," he added. "A woman could." He squeezed Janet's shoulders and then wrapped his arms around her chest.

Janet leaned into her amazing boyfriend and noted with satisfaction that Vanessa's breathing didn't slow, only now, her chest heaved with anticipation. Abe didn't even look at Jason, just rubbed the back of his neck with one hand and stared blankly at his wife.

The color drained from Vanessa's face until she was as pale as their lightest beer. "I . . . I don't . . . ," Vanessa stuttered, her mind seemingly unable to make the transition from woman scorned to woman stunned. Abe took the momentary silence to press his hand into her back and usher her out the door. Janet heard him mumbling apologies to the crowd as they left.

"Thanks, Jason, I—"

"You're not off the hook—not by a long shot. I just couldn't stand to see that woman try to drag you down. I came in to help out because it's busy, but we've got things to discuss, Janet." He took the beer out of her hand and drained half of it before turning away and crossing to the bar. Cindy Lou gave him a wide berth as he rounded the corner.

Janet didn't want to think about what she'd done wrong, so she thought about Abe instead. If he hadn't been at home with his wife and he also hadn't been at work, where exactly was Abe on the night Ike was killed?

# CHAPTER TWENTY

Business stayed strong long after Vanessa and Abe left, and although Jason wasn't talking to her, Janet was glad to have him there. With Mel manning the door and Jason, Janet, and Cindy Lou pouring drinks and clearing tables, they fell into a rhythm that barely kept them from drowning in drink orders and dirty tables.

But as the bar emptied, Janet felt her boyfriend staring at her, disappointed, and a faint throb of guilt bubbled up the walls of her stomach. Watching Abe's wife accuse him in such a broken way had made her appreciate all the people in her life just a little bit more—especially Jason.

Finally, as she bused a table in the corner and he pushed the mop broodingly past, she said, "Okay, all right? I get it. I'm sorry I was a jerk. I—I already apologized to Cindy Lou. Is that what you've been waiting to hear?"

Jason didn't say anything. The only sign that he'd heard her was that he stopped pushing the mop forward and instead worked on a stubborn splotch on the floor.

"I was frustrated." Janet pushed her hair away from her face and stood from the table she'd been wiping down. Although she was feeling contrition, she couldn't help but put her hands on her hips as she said, louder than she'd intended, "I know that's no excuse for how I treated Cindy Lou today, and I'm sorry."

Jason looked up. "It's not just Cindy Lou. What about Elizabeth and the renters? You've been too hard on everyone lately!" She threw her hands up with a groan and opened her mouth to explain, but he cut her off. "See, you're not even really sorry. You're just going through the motions," he scoffed. "Things aren't good, Janet."

"What do you mean?" Janet asked. Her hands dropped from her hips and dangled by her sides.

"They're not good," he repeated, "and I—I need some space."

Her heart stuttered once, twice, then stopped beating all together. "What do you—space?"

"I'm sorry, I just—I have to be honest. I'm really disappointed in you."

Her mouth went dry, and she scooped up a glass of water from the table. It was halfway to her lips when she remembered it wasn't hers—just a dirty glass from a random customer.

She set the glass down hard. "Disappointed? I'll tell you what's disappointing. You've had your security system back up and running since *Friday*, but you haven't told the police? You haven't checked the other outside cameras to see whether we might know who the killer is?"

"Janet, I'm not going to help the police when they're so determined to trap me—"

"You're so busy not helping the police, you've become a target of their investigation, and now I'm getting wrapped up in it, too! So guess what? *I'm* disappointed in *you!*"

Jason's step faltered, and for a moment he looked at Janet with a kind of sad, injured stare that seemed to sink straight into her soul. Before she could take it back, apologize, beg for his forgiveness, though, he backed away.

"I need a break." She nodded mutely, a sudden rush of emotion bringing moisture to her eyes that she had to blink away forcefully.

"I can't help with—with *this* anymore, do you understand what I'm saying?"

She looked up sharply at his wording in time to see him wince. "What does that mean?"

"It means I'm going."

"Jason, what are you—"

"Good night, Janet."

She hadn't moved yet when his headlights swept across the room as he backed out of his parking space.

"What the . . ." What had just happened?

She finished clearing the last table and turned to find Mel and Cindy Lou staring uncomfortably at each other.

"Go home," she said, a sudden exhaustion taking over that was so complete, she could hardly stand. "I'll see you both tomorrow. Cindy Lou—"

"I know, boss. You don't have to say anything."

Cindy Lou stepped forward and flung her arm around Janet's shoulders. "You know I love you, boss. So does Jason." She squeezed her shoulders. "See you tomorrow."

Cindy Lou and Mel walked out together and Janet finished closing up the bar, flicking away a tear when she locked the front door. She opened all the miniblinds and turned off the neon signs. Then she pressed down on the light panel, plunging the bar into darkness.

She took a gulp of air, then another, trying to keep it together. But her knees felt weak, and alone in her bar, she sank down against the wall and finally allowed the breakdown to come.

Sobs racked her body. Her frustration, her anger, and even her sorrow and embarrassment came in hot waves. She was a failure. She was a disappointment to her boyfriend. She was a bad boss. The list seemed endless, and she wallowed in it deeply, giving voice to all her insecurities.

She sure as hell wasn't going to do this again, so she might as well get it all out now, alone, when no one could see.

When the tears slowed to a trickle, she took a shaky breath, and then another.

"Damn it, Jason," she said to the empty room, frowning through her tears. She hated when things didn't make sense, and her boyfriend had her twisted in knots. The more she thought about it, the more it didn't make sense. Why hadn't Jason checked the other outside cameras? Why was he leaving her exposed to cops who were determined to see the worst in her—in them?

She wiped her eyes and sat up straighter. Was it possible that *Jason* was the one hiding something? Had she misjudged him from the beginning? She snorted into the quiet room. Maybe her dad was wrong; maybe she wasn't the great judge of character he thought she was.

Under normal circumstances, she'd have driven straight home and confronted Jason, but he'd said he wanted—no, needed—space. And she was going to honor that.

She made up the couch in the office, fumbling with the blanket, her mind racing and frozen in turns.

She'd been alone before, and if she had to, she could handle it, of course she could. But that didn't stop fresh tears from leaking out of her eyes.

Curled uncomfortably on the threadbare couch, she tried to distract herself by focusing on Ike's murder. Alone in the office, staring at the ceiling and listening to the low, steady buzz of the halogen light at the desk, she didn't believe for a minute that Jason hadn't found the video from the night Ike was killed; it would have been the first thing he looked for after Wex hacked him back into his own operating system. Even with the tape covering the back alley camera, other exterior cameras would have captured something about Ike's death. So what was Jason hiding?

# CHAPTER TWENTY-ONE

The next morning, Janet awoke to pounding at the office door. She had slept fitfully, tossing and turning on the uncomfortable couch. The pounding continued, and she stood unsteadily, wincing as her bare foot touched the cold concrete floor.

"What?" she yelled—or at least tried to. The word came out like she'd run it through the dishwasher, muddled and wet. She cracked the miniblinds open and winced again as the bright sunlight hit her red, swollen eyes. Detective Finch stood on the other side of the door, flipping his key ring around like a lifeguard with a whistle. "What do you want?" she asked, refusing to open the door.

She'd thoroughly read the subpoena the day before; they had no right to search her office, but she wasn't going to take any chances.

"Janet Black, you look like hell."

"Seriously?" she called back. "You're seriously going to open with that line?"

He barked out a laugh and banged on the door again.

She wrenched it open, and the blast of heat hit her in the face like a nine-iron.

Finch assessed her from top to bottom, with the blanket wrapped around her, one foot bare. "Have you been crying?" he asked with a deepening frown.

"No," Janet answered mulishly. "Goddamn air conditioner is stuck on, and the wool blanket I found in the closet is irritating my skin, but if I took it off my face, I was freezing."

"Is that right?" He stared past her to a pile of tissues by the couch.

She pulled the door closer. "What do you want?"

"I just wanted to ask, one last time, if there's anything you're not telling us about Ike, about Elizabeth—about anything at all."

"Are you for real? Your department just ransacked my house, accused my boyfriend of a felony, and basically told me I'll lose everything no matter what. You're not welcome here."

"A man is dead!" He stared at her, a sudden heat in his voice. "I don't get the impression that you even care."

"Of course I care," Janet said, wrapping the blanket tighter, despite the hot day, "but I care more that you seem hell-bent on pinning a murder on an innocent person, instead of actually solving the crime, which means whoever's guilty is getting a free pass!" She glared at the cop and stepped back to close the door.

"I don't want any surprises, Black. Do you understand?" The sunlight cast shadows on the wrinkles on his face, making him look older and more haggard than usual.

"Yeah, well, me neither. No more Sunday subpoenas. Our lawyer's going to . . ." Her mind, still fuzzy from sleep, couldn't come up with any kind of credible threat, and Finch snorted when she fell silent.

"Despite what you might think from watching TV, this case is getting colder by the minute. Chances are it will fade away, just like too many others."

She watched him walk across the lot to his car and felt an odd prickle of confusion. Even as O'Dell doubled down on pinning the crime on Jason, Finch seemed to suggest they were out of leads.

Which was it?

Before she could deep-dive into Finch's motivations, her phone jangled in her pocket.

Her heart leapt. Was Jason calling to talk?

She fumbled to answer the call before it went to voicemail.

"Oh," she said, unable to hide her disappointment. "Hey, Dad."

"Jason said you need some background checks on the people involved in this murder. Give me their names and I'll fast-track it for you. I should have the info to you later today—maybe tomorrow if I can't get ahold of the right person."

"What?" Janet stared at her phone as if it were a bug.

"Jason said there's a lot you guys don't know about Ike Freeman's death—and there are a few things Jason can't tell you. So, I'm going to bridge the gap for you. How about that? Your old man coming to the rescue. I like the sound of that, don't you?"

"No," she replied. She actually hated the sound of that. Her voice took on a wheedling tone. "What does he know about this crime that he can't tell me?"

"It's complicated."

"Yeah." She laughed humorlessly. "I guess."

Because she couldn't think of a reason not to, she listed off all the names of the people she'd come into contact with since Ike's murder, including Ollie's family and roommates.

When she finished, her dad said, "I'll get back to you with anything that sticks out. You okay?"

"Sure. I—well, I will be."

"Love you, Janet."

"I, ah . . . I love you, too, Dad."

"I know." He disconnected without another word.

She folded the itchy blanket over the back of the couch, then pulled on her clothes and shoes and stood, staring out the window.

So Jason had secrets. But she didn't think he was the only one. The more she thought about Finch's visit, the less she liked it. Jason had managed to circumvent O'Dell's computer grab in large part because Finch had warned them about the pending subpoena on Friday. Was that a lapse in judgment on Finch's part, or something else?

Now Finch was telling Janet the case was cold, and whoever was guilty likely wouldn't be caught, even though O'Dell had just made a major move against Jason.

What was Finch's game?

Sunlight flared off the back windshield of a black truck up the block as it pulled away from the curb and into traffic, and she scrunched her eyes shut against the glare, but the image burned into the back of her eyelids.

Suddenly, her eyes flew open, and, squinting, she stared at the space where the truck had been.

Surely not, it couldn't be—

"Shit!" She grabbed her keys and took off at a run through the small parking lot, then skidded to a stop at the empty spot a block away. She was at a drab, isolated stretch of street, usually littered with trash and bordered by nothing but the parking lot for the Spot; a run-down, abandoned house; and a city bus bench. She couldn't believe her eyes. Parked less than two hundred feet from the back door of the bar, Elizabeth's car was wedged behind a crappy camper trailer. It had been invisible from the office window until the huge black pickup truck that had obscured it from behind pulled away.

The old, gray Chrysler Sebring was unremarkable, save for the aggressively pink rabbit's foot hanging from the rearview mirror. It was Elizabeth's car.

She tried all the doors, but they were locked. She leaned in close to the trunk and gingerly sniffed, then sank against the car when she didn't pick up any dead-body smells.

She rifled through the handful of parking tickets on the dash. The oldest one was dated the day that Janet found Ike's body. Elizabeth's car hadn't moved since her last shift at the Spot. But where was Elizabeth? The question now seemed more important than ever.

She hit the roof of the car in frustration. According to O'Dell,

Finch had checked out Elizabeth's place—and nothing had been amiss. Was that true?

She shivered despite the heat. What if it wasn't? Elizabeth's car had been abandoned and no one had heard from her—including that nosy neighbor—since Ike was killed. She was the last person known to have the keys to Ike's car, which was also missing.

Janet hit the roof again, this time with more force. She'd let Elizabeth down so far, but it was time to correct that. She was going back to Elizabeth's apartment, and she wouldn't stop digging until she found her.

She gulped. Hopefully there wouldn't be any actual digging involved.

———

The apartment manager, a slight, tanned, skinny man with shockingly white teeth named Dale, frowned. "It's an unusual request," he said, scratching his chin, "and I'm afraid it's not allowed."

"I'm just really concerned about her, you understand. She hasn't been to work in days."

"Well, it's against the rules laid out in section one twenty-four of the lessee's handbook." Dale flipped through a three-ring binder he'd just pulled off the shelf behind his desk, then held out the book to Janet.

"I know, and I know you just let the police in, but we still haven't heard from her—"

"Police? The police haven't been on the property since Arty McMaster had a kegger that got out of control about five weeks ago—"

"It's not a secret," she interrupted. "I know they didn't find anything—but I'm still worried." She shot Dale her most ingratiating smile. "I kind of thought, with your help, I could just poke around and see if anything looks out of place."

"I don't know what you're talking about. You're the first person asking about Elizabeth," he said, scratching his head.

"Detective Finch from KPD wasn't here?"

"Nope, and I'd know—I'm the only one authorized to open doors without the lessee's consent. It's right here in the binder," he said, pointing at the book again.

She closed her eyes, glad she'd come, and then opened them wide, her friendliest smile imploring Dale to help. "I need to get into Elizabeth's apartment to make sure she's okay. You can be a hero today or a zero, Dale. It's up to you."

Five minutes later, she skulked in the alcove by Elizabeth's door. Who knew Dale would choose to be a zero? She'd have to work on that smile.

Janet slipped her lock-picking set out of her pocket. With the tension wrench at the bottom of the keyhole, she raked her favorite pick across the top edge until she felt the final pin budge. She cranked the lock over and pushed the door open.

The whole thing took less than thirty seconds, and she dropped her tools back in her pocket before walking into Elizabeth's home.

A burst of color hit her when she stepped over the threshold, and the furniture was unexpectedly floral. She guessed the couch and armchair had been her mother's, because they were well-made pieces that didn't match the other, self-assembled, Scandinavian items in the room. It was like midcentury modern had met a flowery explosion from 1996.

Clothes and shoes littered the main room, as if Elizabeth left things right where she took them off without regard for a laundry basket or shoe rack. Well-traversed paths darkened the cream-colored carpeting between rooms. On the edge of one such path, a huge stain flowered out from under the dining room table.

She hadn't heard a sound since the slow creak of the door when she'd pushed it open. "Elizabeth?" she called out.

There was no response.

She walked through the main room into the dining room and tried again. "Elizabeth? Are you here? It's Janet . . . from the Spot?"

No one answered, and she crouched down to touch the edge of

the large stain on the floor, only to snatch her fingers back. It was soaking wet. The wet spot spanned half the room. On the table above lay a broken bowl, a cutting board, and a hammer. It looked like some liquid had spilled out of the broken bowl and poured off the table. An oval-shaped section of the wood finish had bubbled up, ruined.

"What is going on?" She breathed in a smoky smell and, with a mounting sense of unease, moved away from the wet spot and walked through the dining room into the kitchen. "Shit," she muttered slowly. The microwave lay, broken, on the floor; black scorch marks feathered up the cabinet to the counter above. A smoky burnt-plastic smell filled her nostrils.

It looked like one holy hell of a battle had gone down in Elizabeth's home, but who'd been fighting?

Perhaps more important, who had won?

Janet backed out of the kitchen and stared, once again, at the wet spot under the table. Terrible thoughts raced through her mind. The hammer glinted menacingly in the sunlight from a nearby window. Had it been used as a weapon? What had happened to Elizabeth? Was she caught up in a murder? Was the wet area where someone had tried to clean blood? Each scenario she came up with was worse than the last.

She sucked in a breath at a sudden noise from the hallway outside. She had to get out before someone found her here. At the door, she saw both Finch's and O'Dell's business cards lying on the ground—they must have fallen when she'd walked in. She pressed her ear against the metal and started counting. When she got to thirty without hearing anything else, she carefully stepped back outside, then cringed when the door swung shut. The crack of noise echoed in the concrete walkway.

Elizabeth's old, crotchety neighbor's dog barked and yipped up a storm at the sound. She turned and headed toward the parking lot but froze when she heard another door open. The dog's yipping was now louder, a tiny, all-out roar.

"You again?" Paul said when he spotted her. "What are you

doing here?" The dog lunged toward her at the end of his lead, barking his heart out.

She turned, her friendliest smile plastered back on. "I thought I'd try Elizabeth one more time, but she didn't answer. You haven't heard from her, have you?"

"No, but I thought I heard a door." He crossed his arms and raised one eyebrow.

"Must have been a car in the lot," Janet said.

He frowned, and the dog lunged toward Janet again.

She wiped what felt like a sheepish smile off her face and said, "Well. Let her know I'm looking for her, okay?"

"You and the rest of the city," Paul said.

"Did you see a Detective Finch Saturday?" Janet asked.

"Nope. Saturday was quiet. Just how I like it." He stared pointedly from Janet to the parking lot with a sour expression.

Instead of saying goodbye, she frowned back at Paul, then sidestepped the noisy pup and headed for her car, and home.

She tapped her fingers against the steering wheel at a stoplight; the sound was like a hammer, pounding nails of worry into her brain. Something bad had happened at Elizabeth's apartment—or something illegal—and Finch had clearly lied about checking on her well-being.

Finding Elizabeth's place in such disarray changed everything. Janet was the only "family" Elizabeth had, and now it was up to her to be there for the young woman. If it was already too late—if Janet's worst fears about what had happened at Elizabeth's apartment proved true—then it was up to her to find out who had done what to Elizabeth and why.

# CHAPTER TWENTY-TWO

"Hey!" Mel walked over to Janet's car as soon as she pulled up to the curb in front of the house. "Is everything okay?"

"Sure," Janet answered. Mel raised her eyebrows and she blew out a sigh. "Well, no, everything's not okay. My bartender's missing, now presumed injured or dead; Jason 'needs a break,' whatever the hell that means; and I have no idea what I'm supposed to do —" She'd been about to say "without him," but her throat constricted and she choked out a stuttered breath before saying, "No idea what to do about this whole situation."

When she looked up Mel was staring contemplatively at her own front door.

"I'm sorry—you already have your hands full with a new baby to take care of. How is . . . Mabel. No, no . . . ah, Mazel?"

"*Hazel* is great," Mel said, with a smile that appeared and disappeared so fast Janet wasn't sure she'd seen it.

"Great?"

"Well . . ." Mel ran a hand through her hair. "It's just . . . exhausting, okay, it's freaking exhausting. Kat's got this maternal thing down, but I feel a little lost. And tired, did I say that already?"

"Come on. We need drinks," Janet said over her shoulder as she unlocked her door. "You tell me your problems, I'll tell you mine." She led Mel to the minibar. "What can I get you? I'm having a Bloody Mary."

"Make it two," Mel answered, taking the knife away from Janet and hacking two wedges from the lime sitting on the counter.

"Jesus, what did that lime do to you?"

Mel shrugged and said, "Kat's the cook, sorry."

Janet gathered the Tabasco and Worcestershire sauces, tomato juice, vodka, celery salt, and ice, and soon the women were sitting on the couch with drinks in hand.

"So babies are hard work, huh?" Janet took a long, slow sip. "I guess that's not a surprise, though, really?"

Mel took a sip of her drink and blew out a breath. "Perfect. Just what I needed." She leaned back against the cushion. "No, not a surprise, but knowing that it's going to be difficult doesn't make it any easier when you're living it."

"Amen," Janet said, and the women clinked glasses. "Any idea how long you'll have her?"

"The mother is making her way through the court system. The grandmother's got her hands full with Hazel's brothers and sister, she can't take on a baby, too." Janet clucked and Mel said, "Now all four, including Hazel, are effectively in the system. No telling how long it will be. Could be five more days, could be five more months."

"And then you'll—you'll just give her back? To this woman who seems incapable of making any good choices?"

"Yeah," Mel said, and a heavy silence fell over the room. When both of their glasses were empty, Janet stood. "Another?" she asked, already walking to the minibar. She froze at the halfway point, though, when she glanced into the kitchen.

All of Jason's computers had been seized the day before, yet there, on the "island" plank of wood, sat two monitors, a keyboard, and a hard drive. The monitors glowed in the dark room, and after a moment of shocked silence, she recognized the image on both screens as the back alley at the Spot.

"What is this?" She set the glasses down and walked into the kitchen. "Did you see Jason today, Mel?" She pulled a bar stool close to the computer.

Mel followed her into the construction zone. "Sure. The lights were on over here all night, and then he left . . . let's see, I guess I was giving Hazel a bottle around eight this morning and he waved as he walked to his car. I think he said, 'See you soon,' and then drove away. You haven't talked to him since last night?"

"No . . ." Janet filled her in on what she'd found at Elizabeth's apartment and her concern that something bad had happened to the bartender. "And now I get home and Jason's not here, but his computer is."

"Where is this video taken from?" Mel asked, gesturing to the monitor.

Janet squinted at the screen, wondering the same thing. It was the Spot, all right, but the camera was pointed at her bar from across two parking lots. "It must be . . . Wait . . ." She leaned in for a closer look. "This is taken from—"

"Old Ben's property?" Mel interrupted.

Janet studied Mel for a moment. "How do you know Ben Corker? He sold the restaurant next door long before you came to town."

"It's written down right here," Mel answered, pushing a small pad of paper toward her. "It says, 'Old Ben's place, Wednesday to Thursday.'"

Janet inspected Jason's handwriting, then turned back to the screen. "Jason used to have a security contract with Old Ben," she said slowly. "But when Ben was ready to retire, he couldn't find a buyer for the building, so he shut it down and stopped paying taxes on the property. When the foreclosure notices started to appear, he moved to Florida without leaving a forwarding address."

"Was he still paying Jason?"

"I don't know. It looks like it, doesn't it?"

"And look at that angle." Mel nodded appreciatively. "It shows the whole side lot of the Spot."

"It's lucky, actually. There used to be two big oak trees between our parking lots, but one fell down in a massive hailstorm in the spring, and we had the other one taken out just last month. What a waste of money that was," she grumbled, still incensed at the hefty price tag of that particular maintenance project.

"Janet."

"What?"

"Press play."

Janet snorted when she realized that Mel was right—she was stalling, feeling nervous about what they might see. Suddenly she was glad she wasn't alone. She struck the space bar and the still shot came to life.

Mel's finger snaked out and pressed the space bar again, and the video of leaves blowing across the parking lot froze. "Wait. Should we be watching this, or should we tell the police that we have it first?"

Janet scowled at the mention of cops and turned back to the monitor without answering. She tapped the space bar. According to the time stamp in the corner of the screen, it was just after midnight, early Thursday morning. In less than twelve hours, Janet would find Ike's body. Neither spoke—the gravity of what they were about to watch weighed heavily on them both.

Old Ben's property was up a slight hill from the Spot, so the angle from his security camera gave them a nice overview of her parking lot.

She remembered Cindy Lou saying that it had been a quiet night, and she was right; the parking lot was unusually empty.

A figure came stumbling out the door of the bar. "That must be Ike." She frowned at the screen, "but where's Frank?" The protocol was clear: a drunk customer was supposed to be deposited directly into the taxi by a staff member. On that night, Frank should have been outside with Ike, but he wasn't.

"Didn't Frank tell you he walked Ike to the taxi?"

"Yes," Janet said, incensed that it had taken her so long to fire him. She should have listened to her gut and kicked him to the curb after his first week.

On-screen, Ike stumbled around to the corner of the building by the alley.

"Frank," Janet muttered darkly, knowing her obnoxious bouncer had likely kicked Ike out early just to be rid of him. That move might have cost Ike his life. "Is he—"

"Yup," Mel said with a grimace, "he's taking a leak." They couldn't be sure—the camera was far away and the image wasn't crisp—but Ike stood facing the wall, his back to the camera, thankfully, for almost a minute without moving.

Then, headlights swept over the scene.

"Well, there's his taxi," Janet said, and they watched Ike move away from the building, "but why didn't he take it?"

Another customer with perfect timing came out of the bar and hopped into the taxi.

Ike realized around the same moment Janet did that his ride was leaving without him. He hurried after the departing taillights, only to reach down for a handful of rocks to throw at the taxi as it disappeared around the corner. A sudden gust of wind must have blown back some of the gravel and dust, because he doubled over and turned away, scratching at his face.

So there was Ike, drunk and stuck in her parking lot without a way to get home. "Why didn't he just go back into the bar?" she asked.

Mel shrugged.

Back on-screen, Ike meandered over to his car, opened the door, and sat behind the wheel. Apparently, the car had been unlocked, and maybe Ike had planned to sit there until he'd sobered up before going back inside to ask for his keys.

Minutes passed, and Ike didn't move from behind the wheel.

"That fool passed out in his own damn car," Mel said.

Janet grunted and then tapped a few keys. The video zoomed

forward and the final customers seemed to race out of the bar. When Janet pressed the space bar again, the video slowed to real time, and Elizabeth, Frank, and Cindy Lou left the building, locked the door, and drove away.

Soon, the only car left in the lot was Ike's. It was easy to see how the staff, assuming he had taken the taxi home, wouldn't have given his car a second glance. Janet sent the video forward again, until headlights whipped across the scene.

When she hit play, the time stamp in the lower-right corner of the screen said it was just after three a.m.

Another vehicle, a beat-up SUV, slowly pulled into the lot and parked next to Ike. The driver got out and walked around Ike's car. It looked like the person knocked on the driver's-side window. After a moment, Ike climbed unsteadily out of the car and they faced each other.

It was frustrating to watch, not knowing what was really happening on-screen. Was Ike arguing with the other person? Did he know them? Were they trading recipes? Without audio, there was no way to know.

"Oh, whoa! Did you see that?" Mel exclaimed, watching the mystery driver jab at Ike. Ike struck back, and soon his arms swung around in wild circles.

"Holy—is that—"

"A knife? Yeah." Mel's hand snaked out and hit the space bar. "Didn't the cops say that Ike carried some kind of army knife?"

"Yes," Janet said. "He used the bottle opener a time or two at the bar when our service wasn't speedy enough. But O'Dell told me Ike's own knife killed him. That knife kills him."

She started the video back up. One of Ike's wild swings landed a blow, and the other person dropped to the ground like a keg pushed off a shelf. Ike continued to stumble around, finally falling in a heap next to the other person. Janet stared, unblinking, at the screen for several minutes, but nothing else happened.

She turned to her new bouncer, who looked as confused as she felt, and took her hand away from her mouth. "This is crazy!" She jumped out of her chair, too wired to sit still. "Are the police missing both Ike's car and a second body?"

# CHAPTER TWENTY-THREE

"Wait, wait." Mel held her hand out toward Janet. "Didn't you tell me that you found Ike's body by the Dumpster?"

"You're right. Of course," Janet said. "Something else has to happen here." She sat back down and fast-forwarded the video. "What, though?" she asked quietly as the scene flickered past. "What else happens?"

She and Mel watched things unfold with mounting incredulity.

At 3:34, the stranger lying on the ground stood unsteadily, then got into their car and drove away. Just minutes later, yet *another* stranger meandered over to the remaining body lying on the ground. Ike came to and wobbled to his feet, but his arm swung wild circles, and the two moved across the lot and disappeared into the alley, out of view of the camera. Before long, a car pulled into Old Ben's lot. The driver left the car in the side lot and walked to the alley. After about ten minutes, Ike's car started to move.

Janet spluttered, "What—who—"

Mel leaned toward the screen and squinted. "What in the hell?"

Ike's car drove away, but who was behind the wheel? They rewound the video for another look.

"There!" Mel slowed the video. Someone streaked around the

front of the building and ran under the eaves until they were even with Ike's car. They'd missed it the first time through because their eyes had been glued to the other side of the screen. The mystery person looked both ways, then dashed to Ike's car. Within seconds, the vehicle—no lights on, merely a dark splotch on the screen—backed out of the lot.

Janet paused the video and turned to her bouncer. "They either hot-wired that car in record time or had the key." Mel gave her a significant look and she started up the video again.

Another ten minutes passed, and then, at 3:56, *two* people emerged from the alley. They paused in the parking lot and one of them flailed their arms, alternately pointing between the bar and where Ike's car had been just minutes earlier. After another minute, they climbed into the waiting car and drove away.

"What just happened?" Janet turned to Mel. The other woman's hand pushed her hair back from her face, pulling her expression unnaturally tight.

"The last person to fight with Ike called for a ride away from the crime, and left his body by the Dumpster."

"But then who took Ike's car?"

Mel shrugged.

Janet turned to squint at the screen. "There are clearly several people with information on what happened that night. I can't believe no one has come forward!"

"The deck is always stacked against the police, but this time . . . maybe more than usual, huh?" Mel said. "Do you think Jason left this out for you—on purpose?"

Janet scoffed. "He probably just forgot it was on the screen. He hasn't been any help in this case from day one."

Mel looked around the kitchen, which was spotless—empty, really, except for the two monitors, hard drive, and keyboard.

"I don't know. Looks to me like he wanted you to watch it."

"If that's true, then why isn't he here with me? Why is he having me do it on my own?"

Mel didn't answer, because there was no answer. The truth was Jason had abandoned her at the worst time possible.

Finally, Mel said, "Well, we just learned a lot about *what* happened, but we can't really tell who all the players are—the camera was just too far away."

Janet scrutinized the screen. Mel was right.

"Maybe my dad will come up with something," she said, and pushed up from the stool.

"Your dad? Does he live here in town?"

"No, but his reach is impressive," Janet said. Mel looked confused, but Janet plowed on. "I'll give him one more day. If he doesn't find anything, then I'll call O'Dell."

"Why wait?" Mel asked. "Why not give this to the police now —let them figure it out?"

"Like you said, the video isn't exactly crisp." Janet paced behind the bar stools. "They might try and make the case that one of the people in the lot was Jason. They've been reckless with facts from the beginning. No way am I giving them evidence they might use against us."

"Yeah, but maybe they can make sense of it all," Mel said, then, when Janet looked doubtfully back she added, "I counted three people in the parking lot between the time the staff left and dawn. That's three people who knew about the body and didn't call the police."

"You're right. I need to track them down."

Mel looked at her like she'd announced a new, all-craft-beer menu for the bar. "You shouldn't be tracking anybody down— those people are involved in a murder. Besides, you don't have time. You need to find Elizabeth."

"Elizabeth?" Janet said doubtfully.

"She must have seen something—that's why she took off. Let's operate under the assumption that she's okay—but in hiding."

"Well how the hell would *I* know where to find her?"

"Put your head into this one, Janet. You've worked with her for two years. Where would she go in a crisis?"

Mel got up to leave.

"Where are you going?" Janet asked, shocked that Mel, too, was abandoning her.

"I have to go help with Hazel," Mel said, looking at her watch. "I told Kat she could nap through the lunchtime wake-eat-nap rotation. But I can't help you now anyway—I've never even met Elizabeth. Use your head. Find Elizabeth and I bet things might start making sense."

After Mel left, Janet sat in silence for over an hour, replaying everything she'd heard, said, or done since she found Ike's body behind her bar.

She thought about Larsa feeling the pull of family obligation after Ike died, and how she was leaning on her father now to help dig up some information.

It would stand to reason that Elizabeth might turn to family if she felt like she was in trouble, and in her case, turning to family was as easy as going to them, where they were: the cemetery.

———

Janet's breath hummed out her lips, and the sound echoed in the deserted room.

The first five cemeteries she'd tried all had automated menus and she couldn't get a live voice on the phone, no matter which buttons she pressed. If only one could search online for gravestone locations. She groaned—it would take days to drive to every cemetery and search for Elizabeth.

*Put your head into this one, Janet.*

"Goddaaa—" Janet stopped the curse mid-syllable. *God.* In a land of Southern Baptists, Elizabeth was Catholic. Her mother would be buried in the Catholic cemetery in town. The only one.

She looked up the address and grabbed her keys. The oppressive heat hardly registered, because when her finger pressed against the key to unlock her car door, there wasn't a corresponding thump of pain. Hallelujah! She nearly giggled at the normalcy of the movement. Saved by the doctor, and all it cost her was half a beer and his raving lunatic wife shouting at her—not a bad trade, really. Hardly different from any other night at the bar.

Her car was scalding, so she dropped the windows, and the wind whipped her hair around her face as she drove through town. She needed breakfast—and coffee, and, frankly, a toothbrush—but first, she was going to find Elizabeth.

Calvary Catholic Cemetery had been serving the Knoxville area since 1869. Looking at the graffiti-covered sign at the entrance, it wasn't hard to imagine kids from the middle school nearby accepting dares to deface the sign—or worse. The grounds were close to downtown, and though the area was large, it had a city feel to it. She came to a stop at the entrance and looked over the posted map to get the lay of the land.

She had no idea where Elizabeth's mother might be buried, but with the engine off and the heat seeping into her car, the idea that Elizabeth might have been camping out at the cemetery for the last few days suddenly seemed ludicrous.

Okay, so if not outside where her mother was buried, why not *inside* a church?

A quick Internet search on her phone told her that Elizabeth's mother's funeral mass had been held nearby at Holy Ghost Catholic Church.

Janet cranked the engine again and did a U-turn back onto the main road. Within minutes, she spotted the church, but just before she turned the wheel, a cyclist passed her on the right. She slammed on her brakes, fishtailing to a stop on the road, narrowly avoiding the rear wheel of the bike. The cyclist shouted out some curse words and pedaled away. Janet, her heart beating fast, cursed right back.

"Don't pass a car that's turning! I had my signal on, you asshole!"

The curse word echoed out of her window around the church lot and Janet sucked on her lower lip. What an entrance.

She parked and stared at the stained-glass windows, gleaming in the early-morning sunshine. She hadn't been to a church since her own mother died several years earlier. After another minute of uncertainty, she climbed out of the car and walked up to the structure before she could change her mind.

With a deep breath, she pushed open the door and went in.

# CHAPTER TWENTY-FOUR

The church was dark and cool, lit only by candles and the sunlight that managed to eke past the colored glass windows. After the initial *whoosh* of cold air hit her in the face, she breathed in the familiar combination of incense and wood polish. It took a moment for Janet's eyes to adjust, but when they did, she wasn't any closer to knowing where to go.

Several people sat in pews, sprinkled throughout the enormous nave, and Janet eyed each of them as she crept down the side aisle. One head of glossy, golden hair stood out among the bluish-white tresses. As Janet got closer, the woman's long hair looked darker than usual, and Janet stopped, suddenly unsure. But when the woman tossed her twisty braid over her shoulder with a familiar flip, she knew it was Elizabeth. She'd been watching her do that hair flip for two years.

Janet crept into the row just behind her and lowered the kneeler. Elizabeth's back stiffened when she became aware that someone was near, but she relaxed a fraction when Janet spoke.

"Feels like the world has been looking for you these last few days, E."

"I've been here the whole time. Go figure, huh?"

"No one's seen you—not even your neighbor."

"Well, that's what I told him to say. He's a good egg—been nice to me since my mom died." Elizabeth's hair was greasy, as if it hadn't been washed in days. When she turned to the side, her face, usually young and fresh, appeared haggard, with dark circles under her eyes. Her skin was pale and drawn. "He even offered to take care of Bitsy until I could come back."

"Bitsy, that little brown ball of hair? She's your dog?" Elizabeth nodded.

Old Paul had played her like a fiddle. She'd have to remember his deaf-and-don't-like-anyone game and use it in the future.

"Why are you here?" Janet finally asked. "What happened the night Ike was killed, Elizabeth?"

"It's . . . I don't even . . ." She shook her head and finally turned in the pew to look at Janet. "I think I'm in real trouble, and there's no one who can help me."

"I'm here—I can help you. I'm on your side, no matter what."

"What about all those messages?" She held up her cell phone and fixed Janet with an unblinking stare. "Why were you calling me?"

"The—the messages?" Janet asked, stalling for time. Now was not the best time to bring up her suspicion that Elizabeth was the one who'd been stealing from her.

"Yes, like this one." Elizabeth tapped a few buttons on her phone and added, "It's from the morning after Ike was killed."

Janet's peeved voice piped out of the phone's tiny speakers, causing an old man two rows away to look over and frown. "Elizabeth, it's Janet. We need to talk, and I'm not jumping to any conclusions, but there's a situation here and I guess you need to come in."

"Oh, that." Janet blanched, scrambling for an excuse. "It was just . . . it was about Ike being dead. I mean, if that's not a situation, I don't know what—"

Elizabeth held up a hand. "The message isn't over."

Sure enough, after a long pause, her voice continued. Janet

apparently hadn't properly disconnected the call. She was now speaking to Jason on the landline in the office, her voice still recorded by Elizabeth's voicemail.

"Well, Jay, I called her, and we'll see if she has the balls to come in or if she just never shows her face here again. Shit. Either way, I guess the stealing will stop, so I don't care which way it goes."

Janet winced as the curse word echoed off the vaulted ceiling, and she realized with striking finality that everyone was right: the cursing had to stop. She sounded like an angry preteen trying out foul language for the first time.

She cleared her throat, stalling. Elizabeth turned back to the altar, letting Janet fumble.

"Elizabeth, I don't care about that now. I care about what happened outside the Spot Wednesday night—or Thursday morning—and why you've been on the run ever since."

Elizabeth nodded grimly. "That's what I thought. You don't care about me, just your business. I figured as much. It's why I've been here. Father Andrew said I could stay as long as I like."

"You want to stay here?" Janet asked, stung by the insinuation, and by the fact that Elizabeth had seen through her so easily.

"No, but I'm not going to trust anyone to help, because what's going down is big and ugly, and it's not going to turn out all right just because I want it to. There are more things at play here than you could possibly imagine, and I'm not sure how all this ends up with me okay—with me . . . not . . . dead."

"Okay, let's not be dramatic—"

"Dramatic? There's a cop out there willing to help cover up a crime—a murder! He's actively keeping a killer safe, and you think I'm being dramatic? I saw him, okay? I saw him."

Janet leaned forward, glad they were finally getting to the heart of the matter. "A cop? What did you see, Elizabeth?"

"Nope." Elizabeth shook her head and moved a few feet down the pew, away from Janet. "See, that's just what I didn't want to say. I don't know anything, because nothing I say is going to make a difference."

"Elizabeth, Jason found some video of the crime. I sort of know what happened—just not who did what."

The young woman turned around and looked back at Janet through narrowed eyes. "Then it sounds like you don't know anything."

Janet grimaced; it did sound like that. "Elizabeth, we have surveillance video from the night Ike was killed. The police don't know about it yet, but the video quality isn't the best. We can see there were more people involved than the police know, but you're the missing link. If you know something, combined with the video, we can give the police a better idea of what happened—of who killed Ike."

"That's just it, Janet. Don't you see? The police are involved. They killed Ike—or at least helped cover it up—and that means it's only a matter of time before I wind up in jail. Or dead."

# CHAPTER TWENTY-FIVE

Elizabeth hadn't spoken since they got to Janet's house, save a low groan that had escaped when she stepped under the shower spray. Now Janet listened through the wall to the sound of rushing water as she paced her bedroom just outside the bathroom door. She had to make some big decisions in the next few hours, and she wasn't sure who she could trust.

She walked toward the kitchen to cue up the video for Elizabeth but stopped just short of the doorway. The computer, keyboard, and monitors were gone.

"What the . . ."

Jason was hiding something. She scrutinized the space on the plywood where the computer had been just an hour earlier. Suddenly, his assertion that he needed space didn't add up. He'd left the video out for her to watch, she was sure of it, then he'd taken it away. But why? The fact that he didn't want to watch it with her was telling. She didn't know what it meant, but she knew it meant something.

She raced down to Jason's office in the basement, but it was empty. Where was he?

She leaned back against the wall and raked a hand through her hair, then plodded back up the steps to her room to wait out Elizabeth's epic shower. The longer she stood there, the more jittery she felt.

According to Elizabeth, someone at the police department was on the wrong side of a murder. Janet herself had more information than she wanted about the crime, and it was only a matter of time before the truth came out. She needed to make sure it all went down on the record, in front of an audience, so no one at KPD could claim they didn't know something important or illegal later.

As Elizabeth's shower entered its fifteenth minute, Janet's cell phone rang.

"It's your father."

"Yes, I know. That's why I said, 'Hi, Dad,'" Janet said. "The name Sampson Foster comes up on my screen, it's not a surprise—"

"It doesn't say 'Dad'?"

"Oh, ah . . ." She scrambled for an excuse. "I guess I put it in there a while ago, before we really knew . . ." She'd been about to say before they knew each other, but they still didn't really know each other.

After a moment, Sampson cleared his throat. "I have some information for you. It's not much, but it's a start. I made some quiet inquiries with an old law clerk who works there in Knoxville, and she says someone was researching Ike Freeman's history recently. A lawyer was at the clerks' office just last week, asking for copies of Freeman's arrest warrant dated July nineteenth, which includes things like his home address and license plate information."

"Who? You got a name?"

"Nope. But I'm waiting on a call from one other friend. I'll be in touch by close of business today."

They disconnected. Ten minutes later the bathroom door finally opened and Elizabeth, her skin red from the long, hot shower, emerged.

"Thanks," she said, toweling off her hair. "I needed that. The church had a lot of things, but not a shower." She dug a comb out of her bag and worked it through the tangles in her hair.

No one else was home, but Janet stood reflexively and closed the bedroom door. She'd filled Elizabeth in on what she'd been up to since Ike's death, but Elizabeth hadn't been quite as forthcoming. In fact, she hadn't said a word about what happened the night Ike was killed. "I need to know what happened, Elizabeth. It might just be you and me together on this. I can't even trust Jason right now—he's telling me not to—so I need to know everything if we're to have any chance of figuring a way out of this."

Elizabeth stared at Janet through the mirror, her expression calculating. She put the comb down and dug around in her bag for a moment before she turned to face Janet, something clutched in her fist. "I left with Frank and Cindy Lou that night—our usual time, probably half past two in the morning. After I got home and changed, though, I realized I still had Ike's car key in my pocket." She shook her head, and Janet could imagine that she was still irritated that forgetting one small detail that night had so irrevocably changed her life. "He left in such a hail of fury that I'd put his key in my pocket, so he wouldn't try to grab it from the basket."

Janet nodded, remembering one recent night during which that very scenario had unfolded, resulting in Frank's tackling Ike and a worker's comp case being filed. She was still paying off the claim.

"I didn't want to come in early the next morning to return the key, so I drove back right after I found the damn thing. It must have been after three—maybe three thirty."

Janet nodded again. So far, her story lined up with the timeline from Old Ben's video system.

Elizabeth continued, "When I got close to the parking lot, though, I could see . . . something. I didn't know what, but there were people there who shouldn't have been. Now, Janet, you know the Spot's not in the best neighborhood. I wasn't going to walk in on a drug deal or a hooker doing her job, okay? So, I circled the block, parked on the street, and crept along the storefronts. I was thinking I'd just sneak in the back door, put the key in the basket, and get on my way."

"Why didn't you just go home?" Janet asked, shooting a suspicious look at Elizabeth. The bartender she'd known only peripherally for nearly two years had never struck her as someone who'd go out of her way to do *anything*, let alone something dangerous in the middle of the night.

"I should have—believe me, I've asked myself that every hour since—but I was already there and had already wasted so much time. So, I was unlocking the back door to get in when I heard what they were saying."

"Who?"

"Well, that's just it: I still didn't know, did I? I saw two people, but I only heard the one. He shouted, 'You killed him! *Ike's dead!* He's dead, and it doesn't matter what you meant to do,' and it . . . it just turned my stomach.

"The man was swearing up a storm, and I was backing up— believe me, I was heading straight back to my car, but then I heard him say, 'This will be my badge, for sure,' and, 'We'll have to burn the body.' Janet, I froze. I—I felt so guilty. Here I'd been the one to take Ike's keys! If he'd had them, he might not be dead!

"I felt this . . . I don't know, sense of responsibility to make sure no one got away with anything. So, when the people were debating what to do with Ike's body, I . . . I hopped in Ike's car and drove away."

"Jesus," Janet whispered.

"I know! What was I thinking? I didn't have a plan—I just thought whatever was happening out there wasn't good—it-it wasn't right—and I wanted to . . . keep them from covering up whatever had happened."

"Where did you go?"

"Well, I called you! Fat lot of good that did me."

Janet blanched. She remembered getting the delayed notification of Elizabeth's call the next day at the Spot, but if she was honest with herself, she probably wouldn't have answered an after-hours call from Elizabeth, anyway.

The young woman continued, her tone fevered as she reached the crux of what had sent her into hiding that night. "I flew out of the lot, I didn't know if they were going to chase me, so I drove hard all the way home and didn't stop for a single red light. I knew I couldn't go to the police—one of them was involved! I was going to just park the car at the downtown courthouse that morning, make an anonymous call or something, and be done with it—but then I was so out of sorts that I nearly rolled over the parking block at my apartment and this fell off." She plunked a small electronic device down on the bed between them.

"What is it?" Janet asked, holding it up to eye level. It was smaller than a belt buckle, and had a smooth front and rounded edges. Or at least, it used to. One side was smashed in, a crack spidered out from the center of the device, and the whole thing looked like it had been melted.

"I researched it when I got inside, and that's when I started running." She looked at the device with mistrust. "It's a GPS tracker. A really powerful one." She passed something else to Janet. It was about the same size but had a hinge on one side and a powerful magnet on the smooth back. "The tracker was inside this case—someone put it under Ike's car. It must have scraped loose when I hit the block."

"So, you were worried someone would know where Ike's car was—where you were!"

"Exactly. So, I dropped it in a bowl of water, microwaved it, and smashed it with a hammer." She grinned at Janet's bewildered expression. "I wanted to be absolutely sure it didn't work, but at the same time, I knew my house had been trackable. I mean, who'd put a GPS tracker on Ike's car?"

Janet didn't answer.

"I'm not sure it makes sense now in the light of day, but then, I was worried it was whoever killed him. So, I dropped my dog off at

Paul's next door and took Ike's car to the church. I've been in and out of churches and parks ever since."

Janet felt a gut punch of guilt. This poor girl, all of twenty-five or twenty-six, was all alone with no one to turn to. She certainly wouldn't have thought to turn to her boss, who'd been leaving her angry messages, accusing her of theft.

"Why didn't you come into the bar the next day? We could have sorted it all out together."

"I did."

"What?"

"I came in—walked straight into the office—and I was going to talk to the detectives, but then I heard the voice from the night before—the one who'd been making such a ruckus about moving the body. So, whoever was in on Ike's death is a major player. That's when I knew I had to hide."

Janet sucked in a breath and tried to clear her head. She'd thought she'd heard something in the office when O'Dell was interviewing her. Finch had been nearby, too. So, which cop knew about the murder—or did they both?

They had work to do.

"I think we need to gather all the players tonight—get them all in the same room and start asking questions. We've got the place wired up—"

"Because someone was stealing from the register? Janet, I wanted to say—"

"It's not important now—we have other things to worry about," she said over Elizabeth. "The Spot is wired from top to bottom, though, and if we get people talking, we might shake some information loose. If it's all caught on camera, no one can deny it after the fact.

"I'll invite Benji and Abe to the bar to talk with Larsa, Ike's daughter," she went on. "Abe wanted to discuss something with her the other night, but she wasn't there," she added when Elizabeth raised her eyebrows. "We'll have Detectives Finch and O'Dell sitting on the other side of the bar, listening in."

Elizabeth jumped up, nodding with a spark of something other than fear for the first time that day. "They'll think they're there to witness a confession—"

"But we'll really be finding out which of them was involved. If we're lucky, we'll also find out who delivered the fatal blow. A bar is like a confessional—you never know what might come out when people have a beer in front of them. We can use the TV screens to our advantage, if anybody clams up."

Elizabeth dropped the destroyed GPS tracker back into her bag. "How do we get them all there, though? Abe and Benji won't come if they know what we're planning."

"True, but I have some ideas about that," Janet said.

"Well, what do you want me to do?" Elizabeth asked.

"Head back to the church and keep a low profile. We'll need you in place in the office before we open. Seeing you will be such a surprise that it might help shake some tongues loose." Elizabeth gave her a look and Janet shrugged. "We'll clue in Cindy Lou and Mel, but that's it."

"What about Jason?"

Janet blew out a breath and sat down with a thump. She stared at the door before finally shaking her head. "I have an idea about why Jason's backed out of this one, but I don't know exactly where his loyalties lie. He can't know what we're doing."

Elizabeth frowned. "I guess I have one last question: who's Mel?"

"She's our new bouncer."

"What happened to Frank?"

"He got reassigned . . . to another job."

Elizabeth nodded grimly. "I never liked him."

"Me neither."

"Okay," the young woman said, now pacing the same stretch of floor Janet had trod just a few minutes earlier. "It's going to happen tonight. The Spot opens in just a few hours. Is there enough time?"

"It will be close," Janet said. "But I think we'll make it."

"What about Larsa? Where are you going to find her? You said she was acting odd last night?"

"I have an idea of where to find her, too. Come to the Spot before five. Make sure to park Ike's car around back, so nobody sees it."

Janet sent a text to Jason, telling him what she needed him to do but leaving out the other details. She had to get moving—there were phone calls to make and people to see. She drove away from her house feeling hopeful for the first time in days. She didn't know everything about Ike's murder yet, but she was finally on the right track to finding out.

Would Larsa agree to help her—if Janet could even find her? She had to at least try. But first, she was going to the Spot. She had to get organized for the day ahead.

# CHAPTER TWENTY-SIX

The bar was dark when she pulled up, and the building gave off an unexpected abandoned feeling that matched Old Ben's place next door. Cindy Lou was scheduled to open, but not for a couple of hours, so Janet knew she'd have a quiet place where she could make some phone calls to put that evening's plan into motion before going in search of Larsa.

Anxiety crept up her spine as she pulled out her key ring, and when she turned the key, the dead bolt didn't make a sound, because the door was already unlocked.

A quick look behind her confirmed that hers was the only car in the lot. She could taste the tension in the air.

She hesitated at the threshold and pulled the door open wide. It was dark inside, so dark she could barely make out the tables and chairs sitting mere feet away. She glanced to her right and saw that the blinds—which she'd opened and pulled up last night—were closed and lowered. She gulped. Someone had been here.

"Hello?" she called, her voice weak and warbly. She cleared her throat and in a stronger voice said, "Who's here?"

Janet felt around the wall for the baseball bat that always rested right by the door. When her fingers closed around the neck she swung it around, then stalked into the bar—*her* bar. She held her head cocked to the side, ready to pick up any noise that didn't belong, as she made her way to the light panel on the opposite side of the room. Her body betrayed her brain, though, and all she could hear was her own heartbeat thundering in her ears.

Reaching out a hand, she flipped the switches up. Nothing happened. "What the—" Had vandals broken in and cut the power, or was something more sinister at play?

Pressing her back against the wall, she stood frozen until her eyes adjusted to the dark. Still on high alert, she looked slowly over the room, then shuffled along the back wall to the office door. She tried the handle—it gave without resistance. She pushed the door open, then, with a small gasp, gripped the bat and rushed toward the stranger inside with a banshee yell.

Just before she swung, though, Frank said, "Jesus, Janet, what the hell?"

She skidded to a stop and took a few steadying breaths before her shock turned to anger. She swung the bat down to her side. "Frank! What are you doing here? Did you break in?"

He dug a key out of his pocket. "It's not breaking in when you have a key."

She tapped the bat against the concrete floor. "It *is* breaking in when you're no longer authorized to use that key," she said. "And obviously you know that; you lowered the blinds out there to hide the fact that you're in here messing around. I'm calling the cops!" She stalked past Frank to the phone and picked up the receiver.

"Hey, wait a minute. I didn't do anything to the blinds. I'm just here to get a few things I left behind. It's not my fault you left the office unlocked!"

"Unlocked? I didn't leave any of these doors unlocked. And what'd you do to the power?"

"I'd guess you didn't pay the electric bill," Frank answered with a smirk.

"No, you pr—" When she'd turned back to Frank she noticed something was wrong with the door. She set the phone down and tracked back across the small room. In the dark bar she hadn't noticed, but now, with light streaming in through the office window, she saw that the lock had been broken. A large dent bowed in the metal door near the dead bolt. Parts of the lock were flat-out missing.

"What did you do?" she asked. "It was you, wasn't it? Stealing from the register? Here I've been thinking it was Elizabeth, but it was you all along!"

"I wouldn't steal from this hole-in-the-wall bar any more than I'd be caught dead working here. Please. You're not even worth my time." He turned back to the storage cabinet and pulled some items off a shelf. "I just came to get my things."

"What things?"

He held out a small mirror and a comb, and when he shook out a folded jacket, a piece of paper fluttered to the ground. "Ah, sweet," he said, bending down to retrieve it. "I forgot about that."

"What is it?" Janet looked at the scrap of paper. "You broke in to get a shopping list?"

"No. It's the phone number of a girl from the other night. I told her I'd call her, and right now that might be the only thing I've got going for me. The phone number for a pretty girl." He smiled at the paper and tucked it into the breast pocket of his button-down shirt.

Janet looked incredulously at her former employee. "If you think of anything else you left behind, come back during normal business hours, okay? I'll walk you out." She led the way back to the bar.

Coming from the sunlit office, the bar felt darker than it had before. From her new vantage point, she saw that a table by the door was tilted at an odd angle. Two chairs lay on the floor, clearly knocked off the tables in a path directly to the gap in the countertop that employees used to get behind the bar.

"Did you do this?" she asked.

"Of course not," Frank answered. "I swear, I came straight through to the office."

A tiny flare of sunlight from the open office door glinted off the cash register. "You didn't stop to check behind the counter for this precious note? Wait right there. I'm not sure I believe you." Still gripping the bat, she headed straight for the bar, keeping Frank in her sights. She skirted around the counter to the opening. With a relieved sigh, she saw that the cash drawer was in place, locked just as she'd left it. "Do you have any other keys, Frank?" He shook his head and she pivoted slowly again. That's when she saw it.

The circular shelves to the Beerador leaned heavily against the other drink coolers. Her brow furrowed and she crept closer to the appliance, noting as she passed the trash can that it was full—full of whole and broken bottles that used to sit on the shelves inside the sturdy old unit.

"What did you do, Frank?"

He wasn't paying attention, though; he was too busy folding the jacket back into a neat square to hear what Janet had said.

From the side of the Beerador, she gripped the handle and pulled, but the door didn't budge. She blew out a frustrated sigh. All the doors in the bar that were *supposed* to be locked that day had swung easily open, and the one door that was supposed to be *open* was now, inexplicably, locked.

She stepped closer to get a more direct handle on the door latch and turned her focus from Frank to the Beerador, then sucked in a loud breath. "Jesus H. Christ," she breathed, stepping away from the unit.

Detective Finch stared out from the Beerador, unblinking, unseeing. His face was smashed against the glass; a lone streak of blood marred the blue-white skin of his face.

"F-f-Frank!" she stuttered, calling to her former employee. She stumbled back and almost fell when she bumped into the cooler drawers behind her.

A clash of noise at the front of the bar made her jump.

"Janet?"

She turned, but with bright sunlight streaming in behind him, she could only make out the outline of a man standing in the open doorway.

Suddenly feeling vulnerable, she held the bat aloft.

"Who's there?"

"Janet, it's me, Patrick." She squinted, finally recognizing O'Dell's voice. "I got a text to meet Finch here. Have you seen him?"

She lowered the bat and pointed to the Beerador. "Yeah. Yeah, I think he's been here for a while."

# CHAPTER TWENTY-SEVEN

For the second time in as many weeks, crime scene tape surrounded the Spot. However, this time, with a dead active-duty cop in the mix, there were more police brass inside and outside than at the station downtown. Beyond the sea of blue, on the other side of the tape, the press circled the crime scene like hungry dogs.

Janet kept a wary watch across the bar as Frank and a homicide detective huddled in a booth. She didn't trust anything about her old bouncer, and while she couldn't imagine him killing Finch, she also couldn't imagine that he would be completely forthcoming with the police when he was in the middle of a homicide investigation.

"Where's Jason?"

O'Dell towered over her, his fingertips white where they pressed into her table.

She didn't answer, she only had the strength to rest her forehead against her hands. Through her splayed fingers, she saw medics gather on either side of the gurney holding Finch's body. They raised him up to hip height and pushed him out of the bar.

She looked up and found O'Dell staring at her. He rubbed a

hand over his face and sat down across from her. "I talked to Haverfield."

She nodded, barely remembering the cop who'd interviewed her an hour ago. Instead, burned in her mind, was O'Dell rushing into the bar and trying to pull the Beerador open. He'd yelled Finch's name over and over, and had nearly wrenched his arm off pulling at the handle. Janet had finally pushed him away from the cooler and yelled at Frank, frozen by the office door, to call 911. It had eventually taken four firefighters and two steel crowbars to pry the door free, they learned later that the door had been jammed by a metal button on Finch's sleeve. After another conference session, emergency responders finally figured out how to get Finch's cold, stiff body out of the cramped space.

Janet felt sick to her stomach, but she looked across the table at O'Dell and said, "Finch was here this morning. I was rude, maybe even slammed the door in his face."

"And he came here to tell you that the investigation had stalled?" O'Dell looked up from the notebook but couldn't hide his skepticism.

"I know, it sounds like something I just made up, but that's what he said. He asked me if I had any more surprises, and I told him I didn't. And then he accused me of not caring about Ike's death, and said that the case was going to fade away like so many others." She looked down at her hands. "I don't know why he would have come back to the bar. I watched him drive away, and then I left. I'd just come back when I found the bar door unlocked, and Frank in the office."

"Where did you go?"

"Hmm?" she asked, stalling for time. She'd told the first cop that she ran some errands, and he hadn't pressed, but she knew O'Dell would, and she still hadn't decided what her story was going to be. Elizabeth's concerns for her safety now seemed well founded, indeed, and while O'Dell's shock at finding Finch's body earlier had seemed genuine, she truly didn't know who to trust.

"I said, where did you go? What errands did you run today?"

She took a slow, steady breath and made a choice. "I guess they weren't really errands. I . . . I went to the cemetery and then to church."

"Really?" O'Dell said, his surprise evident. "You went to church?"

"Is that so surprising? Doesn't everyone in Knoxville go to church?"

"Yeah, but . . ." He squinted at her and then asked, "Which church?"

"Holy Ghost."

His skepticism turned to disbelief. "I've never seen you there."

"You're Catholic?" she asked, remembering too late that O'Dell wasn't from Knoxville. She should have known the New York transplant wouldn't be Southern Baptist.

"Mmm-hmm. And I go every week."

"Well," Janet said, her poker face back, "I don't. My mom died a few years ago and I've been spinning my wheels for a while. But today I felt . . . called to visit."

"A confession?"

"No," she said, disgruntled at his insinuation. "Just to sit."

O'Dell chewed on that silently for a while, then said, "I had a squad car stop by your house."

"You did?" Her brow furrowed, and she wondered what O'Dell was going to throw at her next. Elizabeth was waiting at the church for their planned showdown. Janet was going to have to get in touch with her somehow—as the plan would have to be delayed, if not outright canceled, because of this murderous turn of events.

"No one answered, and Jason's car isn't there." O'Dell leaned closer. "Where is he?"

"I don't know."

"When did you see him last?"

She gulped, not liking how her answer was going to sound. "Uh . . ."

"Janet. We have a dead cop. Don't play games, just answer the question."

"I'm not playing games, I just don't see how—"

"When did you last see Jason? It's a simple question. What are you hiding?"

"I'm not hiding anything! I saw him last night. Here, at the Spot."

He sat back, looking triumphant. "He didn't come home last night? Or this morning? Where has he been?"

"No—I mean, I don't know for sure, because I didn't go home last night."

That information pulled O'Dell up short. "Where did you go?"

"I . . . I slept here, in the office. We had a fight. Just a dumb fight, but I didn't feel like going home, so I didn't."

"What did you fight about?"

"Me being a bitch."

"Sorry?"

"You asked what we fought about, and that's the answer. We fought about me being mean and rude."

O'Dell nodded but his face was tight. "Excuse me." He walked across away with his cell phone pressed into his ear.

Janet sat there for another ten minutes before she felt too antsy to be still. She stood up and started walking toward the office, thinking she could try Jason's cell phone again, but a hand reached out and landed on her shoulder.

"Miss Black? You'll need to have a seat right there, please."

Janet turned to find a woman in a white uniform shirt with several bars and stars pins surrounding a name tag. "Captain Wiggins, is it? I don't feel like sitting."

"I don't care," the woman answered. Janet stood mutinously for a moment, and the captain said, "You can sit in cuffs or on your own. The choice is yours for the next fifteen seconds. Then the choice is mine."

She lowered herself to the chair with as much dignity as possible and turned her face away from the captain. Several words came to mind, but she bit her tongue, realizing that pissing off the highest-ranking cop on the scene wouldn't do her any good. Plus, this woman's colleague had just been brutally murdered. She likely had more on her mind that Janet's feelings.

She smothered a bitter laugh: she was feeling *compassionate* toward the captain. Not that it mattered, but Jason would have been proud.

"We're going in," O'Dell said, nodding at the captain as he took a seat. She walked away and he leaned toward Janet. "We're going into your house. Judge just signed a probable cause warrant to see if Jason's hiding in the basement."

"What?" Janet said, and a tiny tick of annoyance in the back of her head said, *See, this is where compassion gets you*, but she tried to focus on O'Dell. "Jason's not there! I was home this morning, and no one was there!"

"But that doesn't mean he's not there now," O'Dell said with a superior smile. "And we're not taking any chances. My guys are going in with a battering ram. I just gave them the okay."

"Will you let it rest? Jason had nothing to do with this murder!"

O'Dell frowned. "Then why did we find his pen inside the Beerador with Finch's body?"

# CHAPTER TWENTY-EIGHT

Janet sat in mutinous silence across from O'Dell, forcing herself to stay calm. She was surrounded by the enemy, and they all had guns.

"What pen?" she finally managed to ask.

O'Dell shook out a zip-top evidence bag. Sure enough, Jason's customized, obnoxious, neon blue and yellow pen was inside. But she snorted when she saw it.

"Are you kidding me? That's not evidence in a murder. That just shows that your department took all of Jason's stuff yesterday, and Finch apparently wanted to use the pen!" Her temper finally got the better of her. "You call this off right now, O'Dell, I'm serious!"

"Janet, this is happening. Jason was angry, a cop is dead, and we have evidence that he was here at the time of the murder. Or at least right after. That's enough for me."

His words only enraged her more. "That's your probable cause? That Jason was angry and had a *pen*? That's not even true, you asshole, he was *disappointed* in me, okay? Which is worse for me but has nothing to do with you, Finch, or the fact that someone killed him!" O'Dell was maddeningly calm as he sat opposite her, unfazed by her emotion. "O'Dell—call off your people! Just—" She stopped talking and jumped up when an idea struck. "My tenant has a key! You don't have to break down the door! They don't know it's there, but it's hanging on a hook in the cabinet over the oven. Just use the key to get in, okay! A new door is going to cost me five hundred bucks!"

"You don't care if we go in?"

"No. Knock yourselves out—just don't knock the damn door out!"

"You're upset about the cost of the door?"

"Yes—I'm not made of money, and I won't be able to open the bar again tonight. Give me a break!"

"You're not worried we'll find Jason inside your house?"

"No. He told me he needed a break. From me. And since you took all his computer equipment, there's no reason for him to go home."

O'Dell studied her for a moment before speaking again. "I can't get a read on you, Janet, and it's starting to piss me off."

"Yeah, well, it's part of my charm." She leaned over the table. "Will you call your guys? Tell them to knock on the other half of my house—and carefully! They've got a baby over there and don't need you people waking it up if it's finally sleeping."

"It?" He cocked one eyebrow at her.

"The baby." She wrinkled her nose. "It's a *her*, okay?"

O'Dell signaled to another officer and they conferenced for a moment before O'Dell said, "It's done. They'll get the key and search the house. They gonna find anything else I should know about now?"

"No," Janet answered mulishly, though her heartbeat accelerated, thinking about the computer that had sat on the kitchen "island" only hours ago.

"Janet?" he pressed.

"What? I'm worried about Jason is all. It's not like him to disappear like this."

"I'm worried about Jason, too. I think he's involved in this,

Janet, and if I were you, I'd start thinking about how to protect myself."

"I may not know where Jason is, but I know he'd never hurt me. Not in a million years."

"He already has!" O'Dell gestured around them. "He's involved in this murder and in Ike's death, too!"

"That's ridiculous, and if it were true, you'd have already arrested him. Finch was right about one thing: you guys are floundering on the investigation into Ike's murder, and now you've got nowhere to go on this one, either. Don't try casting out random lines just to see what you can catch."

"You have no idea what we've got on Jason, no idea."

She sat back in her chair, frustrated into silence. She crossed her arms and looked over toward the bar when she heard a deafening crash.

Two burly men with hand carts flanked the Beerador. Their white jumpsuits were already marred with dirt and dust, and their hands and feet were covered in plastic gloves and boot covers.

"Again," one of the men said. His partner tried to tilt the Beerador to the right so the other could shimmy his hand cart underneath, but he lost his grip, and the heavy refrigerator slammed to the ground with another crash.

"Ugh!" Janet cringed at the noise.

"I got it," the second guy called triumphantly. He'd managed to slide the lip of the cart under the Beerador, and his partner rushed to his side, ready to help stabilize the huge appliance. With an almighty heave, the cart operator tried to tilt the hand cart back. Nothing happened. His partner reached over and pressed down on the cart. For a moment, the bar fell silent as everyone watching held their collective breath. Instead of succumbing to the attempt to move it out of the bar, however, the Beerador seemed to bear down. The metal hand cart snapped in half, sending the two men tumbling to the ground.

In the shocked silence that followed, Janet looked over to

O'Dell to find him staring, not at the scene in front of them, but at her.

"Are you seriously worried about the Beerador when another man is dead—*dead*—at your business?" Any vestige of friendliness was gone, and O'Dell looked at Janet like she was the enemy. The sight filled her with anger.

"There's so much you don't know about this case it could fill that damn Beerador," she said. O'Dell winced, and Janet flushed, realizing what she'd just said. "That's not what I—" She sighed. "I'm sorry," she said quietly, "but you're all wrong about this case, O'Dell. All wrong."

O'Dell grabbed her arm roughly and led her to a booth in the corner, away from the pack of officers watching the Beerador removal process. "What do you know? Start talking, Black. Now."

She pulled out of his grip. "I'm not telling you anything. Not yet. You're so focused on my boyfriend that you're not in a place to see anything else now anyway. I won't waste my breath."

"Why are you so certain Jason is innocent? Ike Freeman was a nuisance who, according to many of your customers, loved to talk trash to you, specifically, when he was drunk! Maybe your boyfriend decided he'd messed with you one too many times. Mark Finch was screwing with Jason's business, making accusations, and now he's out of the picture. Pretty convenient for your boyfriend."

"You're so wrong it's painful, O'Dell. Painful."

"Listen, Black, you wanna open for business? Then start talking. Otherwise, it might take us weeks to get all the evidence we need out of here. Weeks. It's up to you."

"Unbelievable!" Janet rubbed the spot on her arm where he'd grabbed her. "You do what you have to do, O'Dell. But leave me out of it."

"I wish I could, Janet," he said, looking at her with surprising concern. "I wish I could leave you out of all of this. But you keep turning up right in the damn middle of things."

She sank down into the booth and looked around the room. "What is Frank saying?"

O'Dell lowered himself into the seat across from Janet. "Exactly what you said he told you. That he came in for some things he'd left here and didn't touch anything else."

"Do you believe him?"

"I do," he said.

"Of course you do," Janet scoffed. "You guys always stick together—that's the problem, isn't it?"

"What do you know, Janet? I can't help if you don't let me."

She stared at a tiny nick in the table, torn about what to do. Elizabeth had said that a cop was there the night of Ike's murder, and that cop helped cover up the crime. Was Finch the helper that night, and Ike's killer had decided to tie up loose ends? Or did Finch start asking too many questions and the killer got nervous? And if so, who was the killer? Another cop, or someone else?

"You can trust me, Janet."

She almost opened up—almost told him everything she knew. But something stopped her. She couldn't put her trust in the wrong person, and the only way to know for sure was to continue on with the plan she and Elizabeth had come up with—God, was it only a few hours ago?

She looked up from the table. "How much longer is this going to take?"

He broke the eye contact first and frowned. "Could be hours, could be all night, Janet. It'll depend on those guys." He gestured to the men—now numbered at four—who surrounded the Beerador.

"Go," one yelled, and two men together pushed against the side of the heavy appliance, with the other two bracing it from the opposite side. They finally tipped it up enough so that one could slide the edge of a fortified, heavy-duty rolling hand cart under the bottom edge. With a crash they let go, and then with one dragging the cart and the other three surrounding the Beerador, supporting it with their arms, they pulled the refrigerator out from behind the bar.

A flurry of detectives and patrol officers flung tables and chairs out of the way, clearing a path to the door.

"Now what?" Janet asked, watching them drag her property off like a prize. With a pang, she realized she was going to miss that giant steel and aluminum bottle.

"Now they take it apart and see what evidence is hiding inside." He leaned in, forcing Janet to turn and face him. "You can trust me, Janet. I'm here for you."

His eyes were clear and convincing, but he seemed to be looking for something from her that she couldn't give him. At least not yet.

"We'll see, O'Dell." She stood and headed for the door.

## CHAPTER TWENTY-NINE

Janet's joy at finally being allowed to leave the Spot was quickly overshadowed by the wall of sound that hit her when she stepped foot in the parking lot. She looked over the crime scene tape that circled the lot in shock. A bevy of reporters, some standing next to the unblinking eye of news cameras, others holding out tape recorders, lined up and pressed in, yelling questions they couldn't possibly have expected her to answer.

"What did you do?"

"Did you kill Detective Finch?"

"Who else is in there?"

"Are you guilty?"

"Are your customers all targets?"

Exasperated, she'd just opened her mouth to answer that last one when a nearby officer standing guard at the perimeter shook her head.

Janet realized with a start it was Officer Davis—the same cop who had been there when she'd found Ike's body.

"Where are you headed?" the officer asked.

"Home, I guess. Looks like we won't be able to open tonight."

"No, I'd say not," Davis agreed. "You be careful. Someone's angry. Hard to guess who."

Janet nodded slowly and climbed into her car without a word, chewing over the policewoman's words. *Someone's angry.* Until a couple of hours ago, she'd have said *Finch* was angry. Now he was dead.

But the list of angry people seemed long and noxious. Frank was angry about getting fired from his last two jobs. Abe's wife, Vanessa, was angry, convinced her husband was cheating. Benji the lawyer was angry that Ike had gotten away with murder so many years ago. Ollie's parents were angry that the police were complicit in protecting their son's killer. Was Jason angry? She started up the engine, mulling that over. If she was being honest with herself, sure, Jason was angry with the cops for messing with his business. But she'd have guessed he was more angry at O'Dell for serving the subpoena than Finch.

Of course, she couldn't know until she spoke to Jason. She picked up her phone and dialed his number using the keypad, instead of tapping his name, as if the process of pressing each number might make him more likely to answer. But once again, the call went straight to voicemail. She left Elizabeth a message, only advising her that the plan had changed, and that she should stay put at the church for now.

She stared out the windshield, barely noticing her route as she wondered why her boyfriend wasn't answering his phone. What was he hiding?

Ten minutes later she pulled up to her house in time to see the SWAT team loading up their trucks, ready to depart.

"You Janet?" one asked, swaggering up to her car.

"Yes."

"Here's your key. It wasn't as much fun as the battering ram, but I guess they can't all be fun."

"So no one was inside?"

"Nope."

"Did you guys take anything?" Janet checked the trucks behind him, wondering if they were going to call her TV evidence and haul it away.

He pinched his lips together. "We're not thieves, we're law enforcement."

She nodded. "Mm-hmm. Right. So, did you take anything?"

"No," he said, before turning with a sneer.

The engines growled to life and all three SWAT trucks pulled away.

Janet stared uncomfortably at her house. It hardly seemed like home just then. Her boyfriend was gone and the police had been there more than she had in the last two days. Before she could shake the feeling of discomfort, Mel waved from the porch.

"Everyone okay?" Janet called, glad to have a reason not to go in her half of the duplex. "I hope they didn't scare the baby!"

"Not as much as they would have if they'd rammed in your front door! What were they looking for?"

"Jason," she answered, then said in a low voice, "Aren't we all looking for Jason."

She filled Mel in on the latest from the Spot, and the other woman whistled under her breath. "So . . . Now what?"

"Now we wait for the police to finish their investigation, I guess." They stared at each other for a moment before Janet turned toward her half of the structure.

"You wanna stay here tonight?" Mel asked, and Janet felt a sudden urge to cry at the offer. But before she could even consider it, Hazel let out an almighty yell that shook the entire first floor. Mel chuckled. "I'm not saying you'll get any rest, but you won't be alone at least."

"Thanks, Mel. I'll be fine."

"Don't—" Mel cut herself off. After a moment she said, "Just be careful." She shook her head as Janet turned to walk back to her car.

Maybe Mel knew that she wasn't going to wait on the police. After all, they'd been wrong about just about everything so far. So she was going to get to work.

Finch's murder felt personal, and Janet was determined to get to the bottom of things, even if that meant starting back at the beginning.

Margaret, Vanessa and Abe, and Benji—she wanted to talk to all of them again, but on her own this time, and she'd start, she decided on the fly, with the doctor and his wife.

———

Abe's house looked much the same this time as the last, and Janet felt just as out of place as before.

Curtains fluttered at the house across the street and Janet knew she was on display as she walked up the path to the front door. She raised her finger to the buzzer, but before she pressed it, Vanessa flung the door open from within.

"What?" Gone was the matching athleisure wear from before. Instead, Vanessa wore designer jeans, a form-fitting sweater, and high-heeled booties.

"I'm sorry, are you headed out?" Janet asked, stepping aside to let her pass.

"No," she snapped, her face twisted in dislike as she stared at Janet.

"Oh." She'd never met anyone who dressed so meticulously to sit at home.

"What do you want?" Vanessa narrowed her eyes. "If you're looking for Abe—and you shouldn't be, if anything you were a small, disposable distraction for him—but anyway, he's not home." She stepped back and made to move the door.

Janet stepped across the threshold, blocking the other woman. "I actually wanted to talk to you."

Abe's wife was so surprised, she stopped pushing against the door. "About what?"

"About the other night. In my bar." Janet used her most superior tone, and it worked. The manners bred so strongly into Vanessa came out, and she looked abashed at the memory.

She leaned against the wooden door frame. "Oh, that. Abe insists I got everything wrong that night."

"Not everything," Janet said, hoping to shock Vanessa into letting her in. No one in this kind of neighborhood wanted an ugly scene outside. "Can I come in?"

Vanessa frowned but pulled the door all the way open.

Janet stepped into a massive entryway, about the size of her entire house. An actual crystal chandelier hung from the vaulted ceiling, and a curved staircase wound its way up to the second floor. She followed Vanessa through to the kitchen, a room so immaculate she was convinced they did as much home cooking there as she and Jason did at their place.

"Wow," Janet said when they were both sitting at a claw-foot, round cherry table surrounded by a wall of windows. "Great place."

"Cut to the chase. Did you come here to tell me that you are, in fact, sleeping with my husband?"

"No! I've only met Abe twice. Once here, and again at my bar. He wasn't there looking for me, though. He was looking for another woman."

"Oh, well now I feel completely at ease," Vanessa said with a scowl. "Thanks for coming." She pushed up from her chair and made to move past Janet.

"Sit down, Vanessa. After I've had my say, then you can act shocked, or appalled, or whatever emotion comes to mind in your designer booties. Until then, shut up."

Vanessa's mouth opened and closed twice before she finally sank back into her seat. She had the impression Abe's wife was grappling with how to deal with a rude person in her own house. Her every instinct must have been telling her to offer Janet a drink or hors d'oeuvres. She was trying hard to ignore those feelings and settled on looking over Janet's head at the far wall of cabinetry.

Now that she had Vanessa's attention, Janet took her time. "Did you know that Abe's college roommate was hit and killed by a drunk driver?"

Vanessa didn't answer, and Janet waited. Finally, she blew out a sigh and said, "Yes."

"Did you also know that that man, Ike Freeman, was recently murdered behind my bar?"

A flicker of unease in Vanessa's eyes put Janet on high alert.

"Yes, I—Abe did tell me that, yes."

"What did he say?" Janet asked, curious as to what was making Vanessa so uncomfortable.

"He said that Ike Freeman was dead, that's all."

"Did you know that the murder happened the same night that Abe wasn't here at home, and wasn't at work like he'd told you?"

"No, I'm sure that's not—"

"The very same night. You told him at the Spot yesterday that his administrative assistant didn't know how to code the receipt from that twenty-four-hour diner. I did some digging, and it turns out there's only one twenty-four-hour diner in town. It's not by the hospital." Vanessa fiddled with her hair, her eyes now magnetically attached to Janet. "Do you know where it is?"

She shook her head.

"It's about two blocks away from the Spot."

No response from Vanessa, save a line that formed between her drawn eyebrows.

"Why would Abe have been near the Spot the night that Ike Freeman was killed?"

"He . . . he took a shower right when he got home. That morning?" Vanessa stared over Janet's head again. It was almost like she was talking to herself, except that her eyes occasionally flicked over to her guest. "And I found his clothes from that night in the outside trash can the next day. Not the kitchen trash can or the bathroom trash can. He'd taken them all the way outside. So I wouldn't find them. I thought it was because—because he'd been with another woman."

They sat in silence for a few minutes and Vanessa's countenance seemed to improve with each passing second. She finally looked over at Janet with a victorious smile. "So, you're telling me there's not another woman?"

"Well, no—not another woman, but a *murder*, Vanessa—"

"But not another woman! All right. I can work with that." Vanessa clapped her hands and stood up with markedly more spring in her step than when Janet had first arrived. "You've got to go. I've got things to do!"

"What things? You do realize that I'm telling you your husband may have been involved in another man's—"

"Oh please. Even if that's true, which I don't think it is," she added hastily as she steered Janet to the door, "I'm still not worried. All the lives Abe has saved in his career? And some old drunk who killed someone is dead now? My husband's karma is just fine."

Before Janet could think of a counterargument, she was alone on the front porch, her only company the echo of the front door slamming.

"Rich people are strange," she said out loud as she headed to her car. *She* wasn't ready to cross Abe off her list; in fact, he sounded more guilty than ever based on what his wife had said.

She circled his name on the list she'd made earlier and pointed her car across town. Time to check in with Ollie's parents. It had occurred to her this morning that Detective O'Dell hadn't asked them where they'd been the night Ike was killed. They had the strongest motive of anyone she'd met so far. Time to get some answers.

# CHAPTER THIRTY

Though Janet had been there only days ago, she was surprised to find the house looked the same. So much had happened over the last week, it felt like months, maybe even years, had passed. But the flowering shrub by the door had the same endless number of blooms, and she admired the plant as the door opened and Margaret walked out.

"Crepe myrtle. Dan loves them, he just planted two more out back. They never stop blooming."

Janet reached out to touch the nearest flower. "The red is stunning."

"Blood red." Margaret walked down the steps to join Janet. "They're hearty, and the blooms last. It's a great combination. Janet, right?"

"Yes," she said, startled that the other woman almost seemed to have been expecting her. "I wanted to ask you a few questions. Do you have a minute?"

"More than a minute. Why don't you come in for some tea?" She turned and walked into the house without waiting for Janet to answer.

With only a cursory concern about walking into the house of a woman she hadn't yet crossed off her suspect list in two murders, Janet followed her in.

The house was still and quiet. "Is Dan home?" she asked as they made their way into the kitchen.

Margaret put the kettle on the stove and went through the same methodical process of preparing the mugs. By the time the teakettle whistled, she still hadn't answered Janet's question.

"Dan always likes milk and sugar in his tea, but I think that masks the real flavor. You might as well just have chocolate milk at that point." She looked up from the mugs. "How do you take it, Janet?"

"Plain," she answered, the first prickle of unease touching her stomach. She took the steaming mug from Margaret and set it down on a coaster in front of her. It was just shy of one hundred degrees outside. She wanted a hot cup of tea like she wanted another dead body on her property.

Margaret blew on the surface of her tea and took a small sip before placing her cup on the table, too. "Perfect. What did you ask?"

"Ten minutes ago?" Janet stared at Ollie's mother over the curls of steam between them. "I asked where your husband is."

"Ah. Yes, Dan. Where is Dan. You're not the only one asking that question."

"What do you mean?"

"Well, I haven't seen him since yesterday."

"What are you saying? He's missing?"

"No, not missing. He left a note. Says exactly where he is going."

"Which is where?" Janet asked, perplexed by Margaret's demeanor. The woman was edgy and nervous, and kept looking out the window to the backyard.

"Well, it's not that specific. He just says he needs a break and is taking some time for his health." Margaret picked up her mug again and cradled it in both hands, like she was cold and needed the warmth. "It's not the first time it's happened. Dan doesn't deal with things as well as he used to. This business about Ike Freeman, it just ate away at him after you and that handsome detective were here. He needed an escape, and I understand that, I really do!" She ended with such force that tea slopped over the side of her mug and she set it down without taking a sip. "This house has been an absolute hive of activity these last days. Reminded me for a moment of having a teenager at home."

"What do you mean?"

"Just so many visitors. On Sunday it was Larsa."

Janet leaned forward. Now she knew where Larsa had gone after she'd left the Spot. "What did she want?"

"What she did was make my poor husband upset. What she wanted? Who knows. She was a rambling, incoherent mess."

"And it upset Dan?"

"Just all the talk, all the discussion about that day—the day Ollie died. You think you've forgiven everyone involved, and you spend a lot of time praying about the right thing to do, and you think you're there! You think you've made it to this kind of holier-than-anyone-can-imagine space, where you still miss your son but you've done what you're supposed to do. You've forgiven his killer. And then you realize, quite simply, Janet, that you haven't. You haven't forgiven the man who took your son, you haven't forgiven the ones who helped him get away with it, and you're in fact as angry as you were the day it happened."

"So . . . *Dan* was upset?" Janet asked, taking stock of Margaret's heavy breathing, red face, and glistening eyes.

Ollie's mother pulled a wadded-up tissue from her sleeve and dabbed at her eyes. "Fair enough. We were both upset."

"At Ike?"

Margaret agreed.

"At the police?"

Another grim nod.

"At Larsa?"

Margaret froze. "No. That poor girl is worse off than us. We, at least, had each other to lean on. She had no one. Nothing."

"How did she leave? Did she say anything?"

"Well, that's just it, that's what got Dan so upset. Her visit was difficult enough—but then she . . . Well, she must have been drunk is all I can guess. A rambling apology turned rude and confusing and we finally asked her to leave. She grabbed a branch of the crepe myrtle on her way out the door and snapped it clear off. Dan spent the next two hours working on the shrub, pruning it, cutting it, cleaning it up." Janet raised her eyebrows. "We planted it to memorialize Ollie. It's a very special plant to us. The blooms remind us that Ollie's love will live on through us, even if he's not here physically." She teared up again, and Janet looked down at her tea, unsure what to say. In the backyard, she saw two more flowering crepe myrtles. Mounds of dirt at their bases made her think they'd only been planted recently.

After a few moments, Margaret seemed to compose herself. She sniffed, and the tissue came out of her sleeve again. She got up and threw it in the trash, tucking a clean one into her sleeve before leaning against the counter by the sink.

"Well, I've taken up enough of your time," Janet said. "Thanks for the tea."

"If you can apologize to your friend—tell him I just wasn't in a space to chat earlier," Margaret said absently as they walked to the front door.

"What—what friend?"

"Your friend with all the tattoos? He was here earlier, said the two of you were working on something and he had some questions. But I just—I was just a mess earlier," Margaret said. "He said you'd be by later and it was no problem. Very nice gentleman. Very friendly for all those tattoos."

"Jason?" Janet asked, looking back at Margaret and then losing her footing on the last two steps down to the front walk. She managed to catch herself just before falling, face-first, onto the concrete.

"Yes, that's it!" Margaret said, tenderly touching a bloom on Ollie's plant. She hadn't noticed Janet flailing and turned back into the house before Janet's mouth had closed from the surprise of Margaret's last revelation.

She climbed back into her car. What an eventful twenty minutes. Larsa was possibly off the wagon, making rambling, confusing statements to Ollie's parents. Dan had been so upset with the police yesterday that he'd disappeared, mere hours before Detective Finch was murdered, and Jason was asking the same questions she was—had told Margaret they were "working together."

Funny, it didn't feel that way.

She took one last look at the crepe myrtle as she drove away, and a startling thought entered her mind. If they'd planted it after Ollie died, were they memorializing two other deaths with the new plants behind their house?

# CHAPTER THIRTY-ONE

At a red light, Janet drummed her fingertips on the steering wheel, thinking. A cruiser drove by, going the opposite direction, and she instinctively turned her face away. She hadn't felt this on the run since she'd left Montana several years ago after her mother had died.

A horn blared and she took her foot off the brake, easing through the intersection and giving a single-finger salute right back to the driver behind her.

She needed to think about Benji, Ollie's old college roommate turned bicycle-rights lawyer. She was headed toward his downtown condo, but she suspected that he'd be much harder to press for information than anyone else on her list. As a lawyer, he would likely be adept at keeping interesting things to himself.

But instead of focusing on how she could get Benji to open up, all she could think about was Jason. What was he hiding? And was he trying to help Janet now or make her job more difficult?

Her stomach growled. It was after five, and she realized with a pang that she hadn't eaten anything all day.

Benji's brick building was an imposing structure—an old candy factory from the 1920s, with high windows and weathered brick.

She drove slowly past, her eyes trained on the entrance. The main door was in an alcove, set back several feet from the street. It looked dark and dangerous. Despite the sun still shining down outside, Benji's building resembled the opening scene from a movie where you'd yell at the stupid girl for going in anyway.

She wanted to talk to Benji, but her gut was telling her to keep driving. So that's what she did. She needed to get Elizabeth. She had to break the news about yet another homicide.

———

Janet saw Ike's car parked by the Dumpster at the church. She parked nearby and then headed up the stairs and pulled the door handle. It didn't budge.

She stepped back for a moment, unsure of the proper protocol. Should she knock at the house of the lord? Sounded like the title to a song you'd find in the hymnal. Before she could take action, though, the clunky lock turned over and Elizabeth pushed open the door.

"We watched you pull in." She stepped back to let Janet enter, then locked the door behind her and led Janet up the aisle, to the side of the altar, and through a door to a surprisingly normal-looking office space.

"I thought churches were always unlocked," Janet said once they were sitting at a small table by the door.

"Strange times, huh?" Elizabeth's eyes darted back to the exit. "Father Andrew thought we should be careful tonight." Janet nodded, and Elizabeth turned her worried brown eyes to her. "What happened? Why aren't we going through with the plan?"

"There was an . . . an accident." Janet looked down at her hands. "And I can't open the Spot tonight while police investigate."

"Why are police investigating an accident?" Elizabeth's focus on Janet was now razor sharp.

"Well, it wasn't exactly an accident. It was . . . ah, hell. Detective Finch is dead. Murdered, by the look of things."

"What? Killed at the bar?" Elizabeth fell back against her seat and all the color drained from her face.

"Yes. I'm not sure how it happened, but I—I found his body. It was shoved into the Beerador."

"Oh my God!"

"Who is calling for God?"

A young man walked into the room. By his dress, jeans and a T-shirt featuring some rock band she'd never heard of, she guessed he was an older altar server. "I'm sorry, sweetie, we'll just need a few more minutes here, okay? Or did you need the phone to call your mom or something?"

Elizabeth continued to stare blankly at Janet, but the altar server grinned and pointed to himself. "Me? Call my mom? She'd probably appreciate that, but we usually talk on Wednesday nights. I'm Father Andrew. You must be Elizabeth's friend Janet."

"Father?" Janet stared at the boy in shock, and before she could stop herself she said, "You look like you're fifteen!"

"Well, I'm not."

"I'm so sorry, I—I've never, I mean, I guess I've only ever seen old-man priests. Gray hair, potbelly, the whole bit. You look like you should still be in school—and I'm not talking about college. I mean high school or something." Then she added under her breath, "Maybe even middle school!"

"Long out, I'm afraid. Well, I graduated the seminary several years ago, but I guess in reality you never stop learning in the school of life, right?" She raised her eyebrows and he smiled again.

He held out a hand and she looked at it like it was an alien.

"You can touch me, you won't burn in a fury of hellfire, I promise."

"I'm sorry—I just never . . . it's strange to say it, but I've never actually talked to a priest before. I mean, except for confession, which is so painful, and you're not actually looking at each other, you know?" She reached out her hand and they shook.

"How was it?" he asked, dimples forming.

Janet smiled back. "Just like anyone else."

"Well, good. Now that we've established that I'm human, and not fifteen, let's check on Elizabeth." He turned. "You don't look so good."

Elizabeth shook her head and blinked a few times. "This is—it's just what I was worried about. I don't think it's safe here. I should go, but I don't know where . . ."

"You're coming home with me. That's why I'm here. We'll stay together and figure out what to do next. Come on." She stood and nodded at Father Andrew. "Thanks for your help, Father."

"You don't have to go, Elizabeth. This is a safe space, and we've made it even more so tonight for you, by locking the doors and keeping this monitor of the parking lot and entrances here for you to watch." He motioned to a small TV set on the desk nearby. "And I don't think you have to worry about visitors, anyway. Monday nights are very slow. Sometimes old Mr. Jones comes to light a candle for his wife, but that's not every week."

They all looked at the monitor as he spoke, and Elizabeth let out a moan when a pair of headlights swept across the lot.

A car pulled up to the main entrance and Janet moved closer to the TV, drawn to the monitor when she recognized the make of the car. "That's a Crown Vic," she breathed, wishing the screen was bigger. "Is that—" She bit down on her cheek to keep from gasping. She didn't want to alarm Elizabeth, but she grabbed her arm and pulled her up. "It's time to go. Let's go."

"Oh," Father Andrew said with a smile. "Well this is a nice surprise. It's one of our Eucharistic ministers. This is an unusual time for a visit, but I'll go let him in."

"Wait!" Janet blocked his path. "Patrick O'Dell can't know that we're here, okay, Father Andrew? Just keep him busy out front, and we'll head out the back door."

"I think that's a mistake. Patrick might actually be just what we need tonight. You know, he's a very highly regarded detective with the Knoxville Police Department. Maybe he'll know what to do."

"Or he'll try to kill us," Janet said, and Father Andrew snorted, then sobered quickly at her expression.

"I just came from my bar, where I found his partner dead. Elizabeth knows that a cop was involved somehow in Ike Freeman's death last week. I'm not saying Patrick is involved, but he's coming down mighty hard on my boyfriend with no evidence, his partner's dead, and now he shows up at the very church where the only woman who can tie a cop to Ike's murder is hiding out?" Janet glared at Father Andrew. "I'm not taking any chances. Now, we need to get out of here, and you don't have to help us, but you'd better get out of my way."

She grabbed Elizabeth's arm and pushed her out the door in front of her.

"Janet, Elizabeth, wait!" Father Andrew called. "You're going the wrong way. I'll hold O'Dell off by the sacristy. You head out the Epistle side and get directly into your car." At her blank stare he pointed. "That way. Wait until you hear me unlock the door." Janet nodded and he said, "Godspeed," then disappeared.

She would have laughed at the absurdity of the conversation if it didn't feel like their lives were on the line.

# CHAPTER THIRTY-TWO

"Was he coming for us?" Elizabeth's voice shook as they made their way through town. The heat was still oppressive, and the long summer days meant the sky was still bright at quarter to seven at night. "Should we have left Father Andrew alone with O'Dell? Oh my God, if anything happens to him, I'll never forgive myself!"

Janet felt shaky for another reason entirely. "I know this is bad timing, but I need to eat." She pulled into a drive-through. "Do you want anything?"

"N-n-no," Elizabeth answered, "I can't eat now! I can't even think, to be honest."

Janet ordered a double cheeseburger, fries, a large soda, and a cookie. "You sure? I'm buying," she clarified, remembering that Elizabeth might have been stealing from the till at the Spot because of money trouble. Her bartender shook her head again, and Janet shrugged. "Suit yourself." When the drive-through employee handed over a bag of food, Janet dove straight into the bag of fries, shoving four into her mouth at once and reaching right away for more. Meanwhile, Elizabeth covered her face.

"Erf gow be aw-ight," Janet said around a mouthful of food. She glanced over and slowed her chewing. Elizabeth was more than pale. Her face had taken on a greenish hue.

"Pull over! I think I'm gonna be—"

The rest of her words were cut off by a screech of tires. Janet wrenched the wheel over, and Elizabeth just got the door open in time. After two more heaves, she sat up and wiped her sleeve across her mouth. "The smell of that food—it just turned my stomach."

"I know the feeling," Janet said, chewing what now felt like a wad of wet concrete. She rolled the top of the full bag of food and tossed it into the backseat. Hard to keep your appetite with the smell of vomit in the air.

"I'm sorry."

"Let's go back to my house so you can clean up. It's going to be okay, Elizabeth. We're going to get through this."

"How can you say that? If that O'Dell guy *is* behind everything —he's got a badge. He can do whatever he wants and we can't stop him." She crossed her arms over her stomach and slumped against the door frame.

"I don't—I don't know who's behind this, but no one has that kind of power, Elizabeth. And eventually, the killer's going to screw up. Hell, they probably already did, we just don't know about it yet. They need to start laying low. I mean, you can't get away with too many crimes in a row. So at least we have that going for us." Janet smiled, realizing her words were true. They were only a block from home now, and she relaxed her grip on the wheel. "You mark my words, Elizabeth. I think we've turned a corner, here, and everything's going to be all right."

She pulled up to the curb, not realizing there was a problem until Elizabeth said, "Oh my God."

"Wha—" She saw it as soon as she turned toward the other woman. A message was spray-painted across the front of Janet's house.

*Mind your business. Stay home.*

"Well how can I stay home if you're targeting my house?" Janet asked, trying to break the increasing tension in the car, but Elizabeth didn't smile.

"This was the killer, Janet. They're telling you that you're next!"

———

"I didn't see anything," Mel said. She frowned as she patted Hazel's back and adjusted the baby's head so it was squarely over a burp cloth lying across her shoulder. "I've been home all night. Kat's asleep, so we've just been sitting on the floor, talking about life." Janet shot a disbelieving look at her bouncer. "You have no idea what happens when you're alone with a baby for too long. You really do start talking about life. It's crazy."

"But didn't you hear anything unusual?" Elizabeth pressed, looking past Mel to Janet's front door.

"Nothing. I mean, what would I have heard, though? Someone pressing the nozzle on a can of spray paint? Graffiti's not exactly noisy, is it?"

"Pretty brazen, wasn't it? I mean, it's not even dark yet. Anyone driving or walking by would have seen them do it." Janet inspected the graffiti up close. Paint dripped down from each letter, as if the person was using spray paint for the first time that night and didn't know how far away to hold the can from the house.

"Do you think it was O'Dell?" Elizabeth asked. "He could have stopped by here on his way to the church."

Janet shook her head. "Graffiti seems pretty childish to me. Not something I'd expect from a cop."

"Then who?"

"Could have been a random teen," Janet said. Though she was still staring at the letters, she heard Elizabeth's irritated sigh.

"It's not a coincidence. Who did you talk to today? Who's angry?"

Janet barked out a laugh. "Who isn't angry is probably the shorter list." She turned to find Mel and Elizabeth staring at her.

"Oh, okay, let's see, I spoke to Abe's wife, Vanessa; Ollie's mother, Margaret; and then a bunch of cops at the Spot—"

"Including O'Dell!" Elizabeth interjected.

"Yes, including O'Dell."

"Anyone else?" Mel asked.

"No, but I tried to talk to Benji." She felt her face flush at the semi-lie. She'd driven right past his apartment without stopping, which wasn't much of an effort if she was being honest. "He wasn't, uh, he wasn't home. And I *need* to talk to Larsa," she hastily added, trying to cover her embarrassment. "Still no sign of Jason?" she asked, looking at her neighbor.

Mel shook her head. "Sorry, Janet. I haven't seen him, either."

Janet turned away to hide her frustration. She and Jason hadn't spent more than a day apart since they'd met. This behavior was unusual and, if she thought too hard about it, worrisome.

"Do you think he's on the run from the police?" Elizabeth asked. "They sure are putting the screws on pretty tight." Janet shrugged. "You don't think . . . you don't think he did anything, do you?"

"Oh, please," Janet said, glaring at Elizabeth and Mel. "There's no way. Like I told the cops on day one, Jason and I were here the night Ike was killed."

"Kat and I were loading up the moving truck that night." Mel eased into the lone chair on the porch. Hazel stirred sleepily, then fell quiet again. "Hard to believe how much life has changed, huh? New house, new job, new baby."

Janet tried to smile at Mel, but she felt the blood drain from her face at a sudden memory. She and Jason had been watching a new TV show the night before she'd found Ike's body. It was a remake of the old show *This Is Your Life*. Janet had fallen asleep on the couch right after it started and hadn't woken until the next morning. She'd slept for thirteen hours.

But now, with two dead bodies and a missing boyfriend, she had to face facts, at least to herself: who was she to say where Jason had been all night?

"But what about Finch?" Elizabeth asked in a small voice. "I mean, you don't know where Jason was this morning, right?"

"But he wouldn't have needed to break the locks at the Spot!" Janet shouted triumphantly. Both women jumped, and Mel shot her a dirty look when Hazel let out a cry, but she hardly noticed. "Right? He wouldn't have needed to break the locks, he'd have just used his key. Jason is innocent." *Of killing Finch, at least*, she added silently.

# CHAPTER THIRTY-THREE

"What is this place?" Elizabeth asked, gingerly stepping out of Janet's car and looking at the building in front of them.

Mel climbed out cautiously, too, but for another reason. "There's something gross on your car over here," she called, using her elbow to slam the door. "It's kind of smelly. And chunky. You don't think the spray-painter got your car, too, do you?"

"Oh, yeah, sorry about that," Elizabeth said, looking back at the door with a grimace.

"Onward," Janet said, walking forward with purpose. "The Wheelbarrow is the closest competitor to the Spot. And I mean in distance, not quality," she clarified as she pulled open the door. It was like walking into a smelly barn.

"The Wheelbarrow? Oh, I get it, Wheel-*bar*-row. I guess it's clever?" Elizabeth said, staring at the sign.

"It's more like trying to be clever and failing," Mel said. "If your goal is to get the word 'bar' into your name, surely there are better choices?"

"Like *Bar*bershop?" Elizabeth offered. "It's already known as a good place to meet up for dudes."

"Or *Bar*racuda?" Janet said. "Angry, fast fish you don't want to mess with."

"What about Em*bar*go?" Mel said, and Janet and Elizabeth nodded appreciatively.

"I like that," Elizabeth said. "You get both 'bar' and 'go' into the name. It's almost like some kind of sneaky mind-control thing."

"How did you end up with 'the Spot' as the name of your bar?" Mel asked, leading the way to three open seats at the counter.

"Oh, we didn't pick it. That's what it was called when we bought it, and it was too expensive to order a new sign. First round's on me, ladies." She motioned for the bartender.

The Wheelbarrow was as dimly lit as the Spot but had fewer tables, more shady characters, and not as many friendly faces— although that likely had more to do with the fact that they were surrounded by strangers, and were, perhaps, on the run from a killer.

They ordered their drinks, and then Mel lowered her voice.

"Assuming Jason is innocent of both murders—"

"He is!" Janet said.

"Then what are we going to do to prove it?" Mel asked.

The bartender slid drinks in front of the women and Janet downed half of hers in one sip. "The morning Ike died—"

"Ike Freeman?" the bartender asked, leaning against the counter. "I heard about that. Sad business, huh?"

Janet wrinkled her nose and took another sip, smaller this time, before looking up. "Who're you?"

The first rule of being a bartender is stay out of the conversation unless you're asked to be a part of it, but this guy seemed to be settling in for the long haul. He picked up a glass of beer from a lower shelf in front of him and took a sip. "I'm Carl. Longest-serving bartender here at the Wheelbarrow."

Mel rolled her eyes and leaned toward Janet and Elizabeth, attempting to cut Carl out of their conversation. "What happened that morning, Janet?"

"I remember it well." Carl rested both elbows on the bar top, and leaned closer still to the group of women. "His daughter had been in here just the night before. We haven't seen her since. I'm sure she's right torn up over it all."

Elizabeth rolled her eyes, but Janet's stomach rolled over at his words and she leaned toward him. "Ike Freeman's daughter was here the night he was killed?"

"Well, yeah, I guess that's right. She used to come every night, though, so that's nothing newsworthy."

"Larsa Freeman?" Janet asked, just to make sure Ike didn't have another daughter she'd never heard about before.

"Yeah, you know her?"

"Sure," Janet answered. "Long, flowing hair? Drinks hot water with lemon?"

"Nah—well, she's earthy, sure, I'd even say kind of granola-y if you know what I mean, but she drinks straight-up gin. Sometimes with a squeeze of lemon. Mean as a snake, but a good tipper, which is more than I can say about most," Carl said, looking darkly around the room. "That guy, in particular." He pointed at a bearded man lurking at a corner booth. "I'm lucky if he leaves the penny behind on a five-ninety-nine drink special!"

Elizabeth stared at Carl in shock, but before any of the women could speak, a whiny voice rose from the far end of the bar.

"Can I getta beer over here or what? Carl? Can I getta—"

"Sorry, ladies, duty calls," Carl said, excusing himself and heading down the bar.

The three women put their heads together.

"Have you ever heard a bartender flap his lips like that before? Like a bird taking flight?" Elizabeth shook her head. "How is he still a bartender?"

"I don't care about that," Janet said. "Do you believe him?"

"No reason for him to lie," Mel said.

"So why did *Larsa* lie?" Janet asked. "She told the police she'd been home praying the night Ike was killed. She's also said, over the last week, that she's been sober for anywhere from one to three thousand days." She looked at Carl, who was now pulling a pint of beer for the other customer. "But she was here the night Ike was murdered."

"Drinking," Elizabeth added.

"Drinking very close to the Spot," Mel said. "What do you think? Four blocks?"

"Three," Janet said.

"Much closer than *your* home, at any rate," Elizabeth said.

Janet turned toward her bartender. "Did you see or hear *anything* at all from the other person that night? The one the cop was helping to move Ike's body?"

Elizabeth shook her head. "Not a thing. I guess I should have stuck around, tried to see who else was there—"

"Don't be ridiculous. You might be dead now if you'd done that!" Mel interrupted.

"And you did enough. You got Ike's car and got yourself out of there. There's nothing to feel bad about!" Janet added.

"Who's your money on?" Mel asked.

"For the killer? It seems murkier now than ever before!" Janet stared broodingly into her drink. "Abe, Benji, even Ollie's father all seem like possibilities. Now you add Larsa to the mix? Ugh."

"What about O'Dell?" Elizabeth asked after taking a fortifying sip of her beer. "He's so committed to proving Jason guilty. Isn't that suspicious? What if he's the one I heard, and Finch started asking too many questions?"

"I don't know. You didn't see his face this morning when he saw Finch's body. I'm not sure anyone, even in Hollywood, is that good of an actor," Janet said with a shudder.

"Suspicious, or just choosing the most likely suspect," Mel answered, stirring her cosmopolitan with a tiny red straw. "Sometimes cops just get stuck in a groove and can't see the forest for the trees, ya know?"

Janet looked at Mel. "What does that mean?"

Mel looked up. "Tell me this: does Jason have a record?"

"A what?"

"A criminal record," Mel said. "Of any kind."

Now it was Janet's turn to stir her drink. She finally heaved out a sigh. "Yes. A hacking conviction. He got a five-year suspended sentence when he was a teen. It was juvie court, and it was ages ago. He's been off probation for years."

Mel nodded sagely. "And that's all it takes, sometimes, for a cop to turn their focus on someone. He's probably the only one at the Spot with a criminal record, and that's what made him a suspect in O'Dell's eyes."

"Even Ike didn't have one!" Janet said with a bitter laugh. "Where did you work before the Spot, Mel?" she asked. Elizabeth looked over with interest.

"Nowhere," Mel answered, taking a small sip of her pink drink. "Nowhere worth mentioning."

Janet narrowed her eyes, but she dropped it. She didn't have time for another mystery just then.

"We're going to go ahead with our original plan, Elizabeth," she said, sitting up straighter on the stool. "It happens tomorrow night at the Spot. We'll call it a memorial for Finch and we'll see what shakes loose when we have all the players—all together."

# CHAPTER THIRTY-FOUR

After a restless night of sleep at her graffiti-covered home, where every noise made her pick up her baseball bat and rush the door, Janet padded through the kitchen to the makeshift coffee station parked just outside the bathroom door. She caught sight of herself in the mirror—dark circles under her eyes, frizzled hair, pale skin —and decided an extra-strong brew might help her feel human again. She reached for the pot and grabbed air. Looking down she muttered, "Those assholes."

"Which assholes?" Elizabeth asked, coming from the guest room on the other side of the bath.

"Cops must have taken my coffeepot along with Jason's computers as evidence on Sunday." She shook her head at the injustice. What kind of unlawful activity could happen with a coffeepot? She was going to reread that subpoena. Just as soon as she was awake.

"That's just mean," Elizabeth said, opening the refrigerator. "When's this renovation supposed to wrap up?" she asked, motioning to the empty room behind them that used to be the kitchen.

"When will it *start* seems to be the more appropriate question."

"Juice?"

Janet sighed but took the cup Elizabeth offered.

After a shower and another quick conference with Elizabeth and Mel, Janet set out to find Larsa, but not before sending a text to Jason with a very specific request. She didn't know why he had taken himself out of the mix, but the fact that he'd been to Ollie's parents' house reassured her. If he wasn't on her side anymore, he'd have been long gone. Instead, he was lurking, asking questions, just like she was. That meant something. It meant she could trust him.

She drove directly away from civilization for fifteen minutes, from bright highways to shaded, two-lane country roads. She hadn't passed another car for five minutes when she finally slowed to make a sharp turn onto a small driveway. The contrast between this cemetery and the one downtown was sharp. Though marked only with a plastic banner stuck into the ground like a For Sale sign, the Descendants of Valor Cemetery was naturally beautiful this time of year. Wildflowers burst from the ground, not yet wilted with the afternoon heat.

She didn't know exactly where Ike was buried, so she slowly drove down paths in a haphazard manner, meandering this way and that. She passed old tombstones and newer graves still mounded with fresh dirt. The parklike setting was peaceful and quiet.

When she rounded the fourth or fifth bend in the road, she saw a lone figure among the grave markers and slowed to a crawl. The woman's arms were raised, scarves circled her neck, and rosary beads swung from one hand; with the window down, Janet could hear strange, organ-heavy monk-chanting music rise above the sounds of nature.

She parked her car and cut the engine, then raised her hand in greeting when Larsa looked over.

The other woman pulled her scarves closer around her neck before reaching for the bottle of water at her feet.

"How are you?" Janet called, not sure she wanted to get out of the car. The cemetery was deserted, and who knew what Larsa had in that big bag of hers?

Larsa looked down at the speakers and reached over to lower the volume. Without the music, the sound of twittering birds and chirping crickets swelled like an orchestral crescendo.

"I'm finding it far more peaceful here than at your bar," Larsa said with a small smile. "Leaving that sin-soaked, booze-infested structure was probably the best thing I've done since my father died."

Janet stepped out of the car and stopped a few feet away from Larsa. "Are you okay?"

"I'll be fine. I always manage to be just fine."

Larsa attempted to regain some of her serenity and raised her face back up to the sky.

Janet bit her lip and considered the best way to approach what she'd come here to say. She needed Larsa's help to pull off her plan that evening. Silence extended between them, with Larsa raising her hands skyward again and Janet trying to figure out how to proceed.

"There are . . . new developments in your father's murder."

Larsa's eyes slowly opened and she lowered her hands. "What kind of developments?"

Janet filled her in on Finch's death.

"Do they have any suspects?" she asked, studying Janet intently.

Was that true concern, or something more sinister behind her eyes? Janet didn't know—she didn't trust her own impression of Larsa anymore. "No," she answered. "As far as I know they're still collecting evidence."

"Well, you know what the police say about that," she said, almost to herself. "Evidence will only get you so far."

"What does that mean?" Janet asked sharply.

Larsa smiled slightly and turned her music back up. "It just means evidence is amazingly accurate. As long as the police have something in their system to match it to. And I certainly hope they do this time. That's all." She looked quizzically back at Janet. "Is there anything else?"

"I've invited some people to the bar tonight." Larsa raised her eyebrows and she continued. "I was trying to figure out a way to help bring you closure," Janet said, skating close to the truth so she could really sell the story. "I called some of the people you said you wanted to talk to—to apologize to—for your father's actions. They want to talk to you, too. Maybe you could finally set down this burden your father left you with. Cross it off your list, you know? Ike's problems shouldn't follow you for your whole life."

Larsa closed her eyes. Janet was slightly downhill from the other woman, and the sunshine shimmering off her hair created a halo effect, a stark contrast to the tension Janet felt emanating from her.

"I'm not sure I'm strong enough," Larsa said after a long pause. Janet didn't disagree. It would have been a difficult encounter for anyone, but Larsa's hands shook slightly, and despite the cooler morning air, her temple was wet with sweat.

"It might be uncomfortable, that's true," Janet agreed, "but I think it's the best way to finally get peace. You don't have to come tonight, but it might help . . . lighten the load."

Larsa was quiet for a while before finally nodding. "What time should I get there?"

"Around eight o'clock."

She didn't answer. After a few moments, Janet backed away and climbed into her car.

One down, two to go.

She had an idea of how to get Abe to the bar, but she wasn't sure how she was going to entice Benji—if she could even find him.

There was no time to worry about what-ifs, though. She had a lot of work to do, and the clock was marching steadily toward eight.

# CHAPTER THIRTY-FIVE

Janet swiped a dishrag across a pint glass as she stood behind the bar, staring at the door. She felt jittery again but shot Cindy Lou a dirty look when her bartender muttered, "It ain't gettin' drier than dry." Janet set the clean—and dry—glass on the shelf and took another off the drying rack while Cindy Lou handed two bottles of beer over the counter to a customer.

"That'll be nine—" Janet started before the customer cut her off.

"I just paid!" He shot a confused look at Cindy Lou, who nodded in agreement, and then turned to take his drinks back to his table.

"You'd better just settle right down, boss," Cindy Lou said before walking to the other side of the bar to help another customer.

Janet knew she was right, but it was nearing nine fifteen; Larsa was supposed to have shown up at eight, and Abe and Benji shortly after.

Mel caught Janet's eye from the door and shrugged before she turned back to check an ID.

"Is this happening or not?" O'Dell asked from a corner seat at the bar right across from Janet.

"I know Larsa wants to pay her respects," she said, glancing over at the detective. Earlier that day, after speaking with Larsa, Janet had called O'Dell. He'd reluctantly agreed to come to the bar for the memorial candle lighting but clearly wasn't happy to be kept waiting.

Dressed in plain clothes, he hunched over a glass of sweet tea, looking hulking and out of place at the bar. Not only did he take up enough real estate for two people, but he was dressed more formally than her other patrons, and his sports coat hung open, revealing an underarm-holstered gun and handcuffs hanging from his belt loops.

Janet couldn't decide whether she was relieved that the other people she'd invited appeared to be no-shows. It was one thing to *talk* about getting all the kindling together and hoping for a spark. It was another to wait for the fire.

"Any news on the . . . on the case?" she asked, and they both looked at the empty spot where the Beerador had stood. Janet rubbed some lingering fingerprint dust off the liquor shelves nearby with a bar towel.

O'Dell grunted and took another sip of his tea.

"Excuse me," Nell said. O'Dell had to shift sideways to make room, and the older woman brushed against his arm as she squeezed into her regular seat at the bar. Her eyes lit up at the contact.

Janet bit back a grin, then turned away to fill an order from a persistent customer. Business wasn't booming as it had right after Ike's murder, but it was busier than a usual Tuesday night.

She lost track of time busing tables, keeping on top of dirty glassware, and filling drink orders. Eventually her phone vibrated on her hip.

She reached down and read the incoming text from her father. Her breath caught in her throat. It was a lot of information—

mostly screenshots of heavily redacted files from the old Knox County courthouse.

*My source went down to the file room personally and pulled the case file. You're welcome.*

It wasn't a smoking gun, but it was close.

It was certainly enough to change everything.

She tucked the phone guiltily into her pocket when O'Dell spoke.

"So much for a memorial. Makes me more depressed than I was before. Does no one care?" He nodded when she motioned to his glass and she refilled his tea. "How late are you open?"

"Supposed to be two a.m., but I'm going to call it early." She felt the weight of O'Dell's disappointment added to her own, that her plan, however tenuous it had been, was a complete failure. Janet rang the cowbell hanging above the cash register and Nell groaned.

"Last call!" she shouted, then rang the bell one last time, just to make sure no one could claim not to have heard it later.

Nell put two fingers out, so Janet lined up two drinks in front of her, then helped a customer cash out before her impatient fingers ran out of things to do. Just as Cindy Lou started to run dirty glasses through the washer, Mel made a funny "hup-hup-hup" sound at the door.

Janet looked up to see a long, blond, frizzy head of hair sail past the bouncer. Larsa's eyes scanned the space before locking onto Janet, and she headed, unsmiling, toward the bar.

"I almost didn't come, but in the end, I thought, *I want to hear what Abe has to say,*" Larsa said. "Do you know I've decided he must be guilty of something? I'd like to have the chance to ask him some questions."

"I . . . I would, too," Janet said, taking a deep breath, hoping O'Dell didn't jump up from his seat too quickly.

"Uh, yeah, we'll take two frozen margaritas and some kind of loaded fries basket." A man wearing jean shorts and a bright orange tank top had scooted right in front of Larsa and plopped down in the seat Janet had been saving for her.

With a frown of distaste on her face, Janet said, "We don't serve frozen drinks—or food. Do you want it on the rocks? Cindy Lou?" She motioned for the bartender to take over.

"Hon? On the rocks?" he called back to his date. What ensued was a loud and lengthy back-and-forth conversation on whether a bar could choose to not serve frozen drinks.

"Sir, if I can have you move away from the bar until you're ready to place your order—now," she said with a look that brooked no argument. Larsa stepped up to the empty seat and smiled when Janet placed a glass of fizzy water in front of her and slammed a lime wedge onto the rim. "They should be here any moment."

"They?"

"He, I mean—Abe."

"Okay, what about a frozen spritzer?" Orange Tank Top Guy was back.

"Oh, a frozen spritzer? Let me check." She stared at the man without moving. "Nope, we're fresh out of frozen spritzer." She sent him scurrying back to his date with a glare and Larsa sat down. Before she could say anything, though, the front door opened again, and this time a tall, lanky man walked in, waving off Mel's attempt to card him. He stalked directly to Janet at the bar as if he'd spotted her from outside and knew just where to go. He stopped behind the row of chairs, towering over Larsa.

"Don't do that again, Janet. People at the office are starting to talk—asking questions that I can't exactly explain to Vanessa."

*I'll bet*, Janet thought, a grim smile on her face. "You wanted to talk to Larsa, Abe. Here she is," she said, motioning to the woman just below him.

He froze and stared at Janet for a moment before his eyes traveled down to Larsa's golden crown of hair. "Oh. I, uh . . . oh."

"Have a seat, Abe." Janet pulled a pint of beer for him and plunked it down next to Larsa. His face was still slightly stunned as he picked up the beer without taking his eyes off Ike's daughter and gulped half the glass down. He finally tore his gaze away and looked reproachfully at Janet.

"I'm serious. You don't know what my office is like. You can't go in there telling my receptionist to have me stop by 'late night' to discuss things. It sounds dodgy. She'll tell Vanessa, and I'll never be able to explain things, especially lately, she's off her rocker, you saw her—"

"I don't plan on visiting you again, so I think we're all set on that front," Janet said drily.

Abe nodded and took another bracing sip of beer.

"Janet told me you wanted to talk. About what?" Larsa asked in her dreamy way.

On the other side of the bar, O'Dell fidgeted with his wristwatch.

"Just wait," she muttered, and plunked a bowl of trail mix down in front of him.

She hoped he would stay put. No one had noticed him yet, and she wanted to keep it that way for as long as possible.

"What's—"

"Just wait. And listen." She tuned back into Abe and Larsa's conversation.

"I—well, I just wanted to say I'm sorry for your loss. Sorry about your dad, I mean," Abe said.

"You are?" Larsa fixed her large, bulging eyes on him.

"I am. He changed my life. I don't thank him for it, but at the same time, I guess I do."

"Hmm." Larsa turned back to her drink, stirring it with the tiny black straw before taking a sip. "I think you brought nothing but heartache to my dad—especially at the end."

"I brought heart—what? What do you mean?" Abe asked, incensed.

"Were you there at the end?" Larsa asked.

"No—that's not what I—I just came here—I wanted to talk to you because I know what you must be going through, and I . . . I . . ."

Larsa ignored his stuttered excuses. "Did he say anything—at the end, I mean?"

Janet stole a look at Detective O'Dell. Larsa was a better interrogator than he was. O'Dell had pushed his drink aside and stared, captivated, at Abe and Larsa.

Meanwhile, Abe's face had turned ashen. His mouth opened and snapped shut wordlessly before opening again. It was another voice that spoke, though.

"As a lawyer, I recommend you not say anything else, Abe."

Janet had been so focused on Abe and Larsa that she hadn't even noticed Benji sit down on Abe's other side.

"Benji," Abe said, but not with relief—more like accusation. "I think it's fair—it's right for her to know—"

"There's been nothing fair about this family since they first crashed into our lives, Abe. Like I said, I think it's time for you to shut up and for us to walk out of this bar and never look back—not at the bar or at that family." He spat the last word out as if it were a curse. His face was twisted in dislike as he looked at Larsa.

Larsa blanched at his tone, but Janet, sensing a pivotal moment in the evening, jumped in. "It's not fair to bleed out alone on the asphalt," she said. Larsa cringed and Abe looked down at his beer. She held up a hand to cut off Benji's response. "What happened to your friend Ollie wasn't fair, either." She fixed Benji with a stare. "Wouldn't you agree?"

"It's not that I don't agree," he answered in a measured tone. "But sometimes, when shit happens, it happens for a reason."

Janet looked reflexively at the swear jar before saying, "Did it happen for a reason anyone here can say?" She looked pointedly at Abe, who was now staring at his drink as if it were an escape potion.

"I—look, I don't know what happened, but I was there—here —at the end," Abe said. "I don't know who killed your father, though, Larsa."

Larsa didn't say anything, so Janet leaned in to cut Benji out of the discussion. "What do you mean you don't know? You just said you were here—*that night*! Who else would know?" Abe shook his head, and Benji stood, trying to pull Abe up by the elbow. "Why were you here, Abe?" Janet demanded. "And more importantly, why did you put this GPS tracker on Ike's car?"

Abe gasped when she placed the small, magnetized device onto the bar in front of him. "How did you—where did that . . .Wait, what happened to it?"

Janet was ready with a follow-up question, but before she could get it out, Benji said, "Okay, folks, I think that's enough for the night." He put his hand on Abe's shoulder. "Time to go. As your friend, I'm telling you to get a lawyer before you do or say anything else."

# CHAPTER THIRTY-SIX

"I don't need a lawyer." Abe shook his friend's hand off and drained the last of his beer. "At least, I don't think so."

"As a lawyer, I can tell you that everyone here needs a lawyer." Benji motioned to the group of people listening raptly and then in an undertone, he said, "And if you think you don't, I'm almost certain that you really, really do." But despite his own plea for silence, Benji seemed unable to stop himself from adding, "It's tearing you up, isn't it?"

Abe nodded sharply and then held his glass out to Janet. She pulled him another pint. After he took a slow, steady sip, he carefully placed the glass down in front of him.

"I think about the accident a lot. Did you know that?" Abe looked up from his glass to meet Larsa's gaze. "Not just in the last week, either. I mean, I think about it all the time, ever since . . . ever since Ollie died." He looked away when a tear rolled down her cheek. "I don't say that to make you feel bad—it's just how it is. I think about the squeal of the tires, hear the crunch of metal as Ollie went down, and the sound of his head—God, the sound of his head hitting the pavement." His breath stuttered and he took another drink before looking back to Larsa. "You don't know how the nurses make fun of me—I tell everyone to wear bicycle helmets. A patient will come into the office asking about a blister on their ass, and I make sure to tell them to wear their helmet next time they ride anywhere before they leave my office. I just can't stop thinking of that awful sound."

He took another shaky breath. "I was always so surprised that I never saw your dad again after Ollie died. One minute, he was there, asking in a slurred voice what he'd hit, and the next, he was gone—ferreted away to safety while I waited with Ollie for an ambulance.

"Knoxville's small, you know?" he said to Janet. "It's a small, big city. Odds were I'd run into him again at some point. I always knew what I'd say—worked on my speech of forgiveness all the time." He turned back to Ike's daughter. "It's not that I wanted him to suffer, but he never apologized, you know? And not just to me! Not to Ollie's own family, either."

When he lapsed into silence, Janet prompted him. "But then you did see him?"

Abe barked out a laugh. "I didn't just see him—he hit me with his damn car!"

Janet sucked in a breath. "What? When?"

"A few weeks ago. I was coming home from a late shift at the hospital—I fill in sometimes in the emergency department. I was tired as hell, just trying to get home to sleep, when a car came out of nowhere and sideswiped me. I was able to keep control of the wheel, but the other car went careening off the road and slammed into a pole." Abe ran a hand over his forehead and said, "Of course, I stopped right away to check on the other driver—had the phone to my ear to call 911 when I recognized him. He must have recognized me, too, and started ranting about ghosts from his past. Well, once I realized he wasn't seriously injured, I—well, I read him the riot act and told him to get off the roads and stop drinking —or at least stop drinking and driving." His voice had risen over the din of the crowd, and some patrons nearby looked over to see what the fuss was about.

"You were angry," Janet said.

"No, no, no," he laughed, but the sound wasn't happy. "'Angry' doesn't begin to describe it. I was livid! He killed my roommate ten years ago and could have killed me that night if I hadn't moved my car at the right time. Did he learn nothing from Ollie's death?"

Janet looked over to see how Benji was reacting. His face was closed off, but he said, "So, you called 911 like any good citizen would have done. Abe, I think that's enough."

Abe shook his head, though. "Don't you see? It wasn't enough. He was out there, drinking and driving again! When I saw the ambulance in the distance, I left—didn't want to stick around and watch him act the victim. I scoured the papers for the next few days and couldn't believe there was no sign he'd been arrested—or at least charged with DUI."

"That's why you had Benji call and check his record?" Janet asked, remembering her father had told her a lawyer was recently digging into Ike's history. She was desperate to keep the conversation going.

"Yes! I don't understand why he was able to keep wriggling out of being held responsible!"

Larsa finally spoke. "What did you find out?"

Benji shook his head. "Abe, I think that's enough. We don't owe anyone here anything, and that includes this woman."

Janet held the GPS tracker out to reclaim Abe's attention. "So you took matters into your own hands and contacted the best security expert you could find." Janet almost smacked herself in the head when she realized what was going on. Jason must have recognized Abe when the doctor came into the Spot and fixed Janet's finger. Abe hadn't spared Jason a second glance, he'd been so worried about Vanessa's assumption he was cheating on her, but Jason must have known at once that Abe was somehow involved in Ike's death, and that was why he'd disappeared. "Is your car damaged?"

"Hell yes it's damaged! The whole driver's side is smashed in."

Janet nodded. Jason's absence finally made sense—Abe was his client, and Jason was doing his best to protect him. But Abe was nothing to Janet, and she wasn't about to let him off the hook now, so she pressed on with another question. "You wanted to keep track of Ike at all times. Why? What were you planning?"

"I thought I could keep him from drinking and driving—or at least make sure he was arrested if he did it again! I figured if his car was at a bar for longer than an hour and then started moving again, that meant that he was drunk and shouldn't be on the road. I was just going to keep track of him, so I could tip off the police. He shouldn't have gotten another chance to kill someone! Why am I the only one who seems to feel that way? He was dangerous—and you know what? I'm not sorry he's dead. Now I can sleep easy at night, knowing the rest of us are safer for it."

Janet looked at Larsa. Ike's daughter stared into her sparkling water, her eyes sparkled with unshed tears. Janet reached out to touch her hand, but Larsa pulled away, shaking her head violently. "No," she said, finally looking up at Abe. "That's not true!" She banged her hand down on the bar to emphasize her anger, but then she clamped her lips and fell silent.

It was Janet who spoke next. "That's a nice story, Abe, but it doesn't explain why you were here in the dark, deserted parking lot of the Spot on the night Ike was murdered."

"There's a lot I can't explain," Abe said, staring over Janet's head at the back wall of the bar.

Larsa wiped away a stray tear that had streaked down her cheek. She mumbled something, and when no one answered, she cleared her throat and said it louder. "Try. You'd better try to explain why you were here the night my father was killed."

Abe fell quiet, though. When Janet looked to Benji, she was surprised to see him looking at Abe with a mixture of surprise and concern.

"Abe, I agree with Larsa. Try."

# CHAPTER THIRTY-SEVEN

Abe lifted his glass to his lips and then looked surprised to find that it was empty again. He started to hold it out to Janet, but seemed to think better of it and instead set it down carefully on the coaster in front of him.

"I can only tell you what I know—and things get hazy at a certain point."

"Hazy when you killed my father?" Larsa's voice was oddly triumphant, and O'Dell sat forward in his seat, staring not at Abe, but at Ike's daughter.

"No, hazy when he nearly killed me—again." Abe swirled the foam around at the bottom of his glass and then slammed it down on the counter. "God dang it. *Again!*" He picked up the GPS tracker. "Yes, I bought this from a security expert here in town and slapped it under Ike's car one morning. I was on my way to work and made a quick detour to his house—figured he'd be sleeping off whatever hangover he had from the night before and no one would notice.

"I was mad—just furious—that Ike kept getting away with things. He killed Ollie and suffered zero repercussions, and then he ran me off the road and somehow, instead of getting booked into jail, got a ride home—again. When Benji told me there weren't any subpoenas or arrest warrants in the system for him, I decided to track him at night, and tip off police when he was at a bar."

"That's not an easy job," Janet interjected, thinking about how Jason could track someone with all of his specialized equipment and how different it would be for an average joe.

"Yes, I realized that the first time I tried to see where Ike was. That's why Vanessa thinks I'm cheating—I'm online all the time, looking up GPS coordinates, trying to see if there's a bar nearby."

"Why didn't you tell her, man?" Benji asked. "She'd understand."

"No, she'd tell me to move on, and I just—I couldn't. I needed to see justice served *just once* when it came to this guy."

Benji rubbed a hand across his jaw, but he finally nodded.

"So, last Wednesday night, I was working late but checked to see where Ike's car was before I left the hospital for home. It was after two in the morning, and there it was, parked right in the lot of a bar. The bar was closed and his car was there—I figured he must have drunk too much and left his car. I thought maybe he had finally learned something." He looked up. "And I also realized I was being stupid. A GPS tracker on his car? What had I been thinking?"

He looked at Benji, who shrugged, but Janet nodded. She got it. If someone in authority lets you down—in Abe's case, the police had, time and again—then you take care of it yourself.

"I decided to take the tracker off his car. I mean, it was an extreme idea in the first place, and Vanessa was getting hysterical about things . . . it just wasn't practical. But when I got there—got here," he corrected himself, "I found Ike, passed out in his car, drunk. I just . . . I couldn't believe it."

O'Dell, who'd been leaning forward with increasing interest since Abe started talking, was unable to stay out of the conversation. Only Janet heard the scrape of his bar stool as he pushed out of his seat, but when he approached, Benji sucked in a breath, clearly recognizing him from an earlier interview.

"So, you stabbed him—decided to exact your own street justice? Is that what happened?" O'Dell said, towering over the group of suspects.

"No!" Abe said, clearly upset. "Well, I don't know exactly what happened next."

"Because you blacked out in a fit of rage," Larsa said with conviction, "after you stabbed my dad."

"No, that's not what happened. I mean, I don't think . . ."

Benji left his own bar stool and wedged himself between Abe and O'Dell. "You're in it now, friend. Tell us everything you know. Now is not the time to leave anything out."

Abe took a deep breath and turned to Janet, the only one not staring at him with contempt or judgment.

"I confronted him, yes. He was passed out behind the wheel—why wasn't he in the backseat, for God's sake? So, I knocked on the window until he came to. I was just going to talk some sense into him, I swear, but he came up swinging. He thought I was some kind of ghost—someone there to punish him—"

"Weren't you?" Larsa said combatively with a strange look on her face.

"No. Well, yes, but not like that. I wanted him to stop drinking and driving, and I was angry, yes, but then he took out a knife and came after me. I barely dodged his first swipe, but then he dropped the blade. We both dove for it, and that's the last thing I remember."

"What a load of crap," Larsa said, glaring at Abe. "You're going to claim you blacked out and don't remember killing my father? Officer, arrest this man. He as good as confessed to murder."

O'Dell didn't move, but Benji did. He turned to Abe and said urgently, "What's the next thing you remember?"

"I came to maybe an hour later. Ike was lying next to me, but he was breathing—he was alive, I swear—and the knife was still in his hand. I didn't want to risk getting hurt even more, so I took off. I just got in my car and drove to a twenty-four-hour café to clean up, get some coffee, try and recover my wits. Then I went home. I swear, he was alive when I left!"

"Were you safe to drive with what I'm guessing was a fresh concussion? Doesn't sound like someone who should've been behind the wheel!" Larsa snarled.

Abe blanched but nodded slowly. "I agree. I wasn't thinking clearly—fear drove me from that lot. I didn't know what had happened."

"Why didn't you call the police?" O'Dell asked.

"I was going to! I got home, fixed myself up as best I could, and was going to call and report the crime—I mean, Ike had assaulted me! But then I saw on the news that he'd been killed, and I knew it didn't look good."

"Of course it didn't look good! It still doesn't! It looks like you're the one who killed him!" Larsa raged.

"Wait just a moment," O'Dell said before Abe could respond. Janet had been so engrossed in hearing Abe's version of events that she'd almost forgotten the homicide detective was standing right there. He turned his piercing gaze on her and said, "Janet, you've been holding out on me, but that stops now. I need to know how you got that GPS tracker. Where is Ike's car?"

# CHAPTER THIRTY-EIGHT

The room seemed to contract, to heat up, and Janet felt cramped behind the bar. She hadn't been planning on revealing any of her secrets—at least not yet—but with O'Dell staring her down, she decided to put phase one of her plan into action.

"Cindy Lou?" she called. Her assistant manager scurried back to the office. "Hold on," Janet said, looking up at the TV monitor closest to her. The replay of a favorite UT Knoxville football game cut off mid-down and the screen went to black. Several customers shouted out in protest. "Oh, please," she muttered, "Y'all have seen that game a dozen times. Spoiler: UT wins!"

"Janet?" O'Dell's fingers tapped against the handcuffs clipped to his belt. His impatience was palpable.

"Just wait," she said, crossing her arms over her chest. "Ah, here it is." Cindy Lou had changed the TV input from cable to Janet's computer system. Old Ben's surveillance video played on every television set in the bar. Earlier that day, Janet had asked Jason to cue it up to the struggle over the knife between Ike and Abe.

"Ooh, I bet that really hurt. Did you need stitches?" Cindy Lou asked when she walked out of the office just as Abe went down hard on-screen.

"Probably should have gotten two or three, but I didn't," he answered darkly.

"What the hell is this, Janet?" O'Dell asked. "You said there wasn't any surveillance video. We subpoenaed your boyfriend and he said that it was gone. Plus, we took all of his computers. So where'd you get this?"

"This is from our neighbor's camera." Janet explained about the abandoned building next door, and O'Dell swore loudly.

Larsa's eyes were locked in on the screen, and one hand covered her open mouth. O'Dell's laserlike focus shifted and he assessed her with new eyes. Janet felt a surge of hope that O'Dell wasn't in on the crimes.

"Larsa," Janet rested her elbows on the bar top and leaned forward, "why don't you tell us what happened that night—before you called your uncle in for help." She hated to admit it, but this evening would likely have gone off the rails just then if not for her father's text.

"Uncle?" Benji asked, shifting his gaze from Larsa to Janet. "Who's her uncle?" In that moment, Janet could easily picture him in the courtroom, both his tone and stance demanding answers.

"Step-uncle," Janet clarified, "but same thing, really. You knew Finch practically your whole life."

"And he failed me every step of the way, just like my father did," Larsa whispered. "It's his fault—all his fault."

"Finch? What's going on?" O'Dell's eyebrows knitted together, his frown equal parts disbelief and anger.

"Why do you think it was me?" Larsa asked Janet, ignoring O'Dell completely.

"It was something you said last week. You were telling me about that last conversation you had with your dad on the phone. Only, what you said wasn't something you'd say to someone still alive—it was something you'd say to someone already dead."

Larsa looked confused for a moment, but then her face cleared. "I was so relieved he couldn't hurt anyone else. I did say that to him . . . after. Does that make me an awful person? I felt no remorse that he was dead—only that I'd killed him by accident."

She looked furtively around the room, her eyes finally landing on the tap in front of her. She held her glass out for Janet. "Fill me up first, okay?"

"You don't drink!" Janet said, refusing to take the cup.

"I . . . I only quit last week—Thursday morning, as a matter of fact—but it's not going so well." Her hand shook. What Janet had mistaken for overwhelming emotion last week now looked more like withdrawal symptoms.

Janet still didn't move, but Elizabeth, drawn from the office by the spectacle unfolding, reached past her and took the glass. Larsa's brow furrowed for a moment, and then she licked her lips in anticipation as the alcohol flowed. When the glass was in her hand, she took a long, slow sip before speaking again.

"It wasn't supposed to happen, you know. I just came here to talk. I knew this was Ike's hangout—he'd been coming here for years."

"You just happened to be in the neighborhood after the bar closed?" O'Dell asked. "Where were you coming from?"

She took another slow sip, then she and Janet said together, "The Wheelbarrow."

"Where?" Abe asked.

"The dodgy bar down the street," Janet answered.

"That's a bit rich, coming from you," Benji said, looking around the Spot with a frown.

Janet bit back a retort and tried to focus. She wanted Larsa to share everything.

"I've been battling demons for a while now," Larsa said, swirling the cheap draft beer like it was a fine wine.

"So you were drunk and came to talk to your drunk dad?" Abe interjected. "What a great plan. What did you want to tell him that couldn't wait?"

"My uncle had told me about Ike's recent accident, and I was upset. Dad ruined our family when he killed Ollie. I know you think he got off easy by not facing charges," she said, turning to Abe and Benji, "but it was the worst thing, in the end. If he'd have gone to jail, he would have been forced to sober up. He might have come out a new man. Instead, he drank more. The guilt nearly killed him, and it did take my mother. Without her, I was lost. In the end, I turned to the same thing that ruined my father." She took a drink of the very thing she professed to despise.

"Need another?" Janet asked angrily, motioning to her empty pint glass.

"God, yes," she said, holding the glass out.

Benji smashed it out of her hand, and Larsa flinched at the crash of breaking glass. In the silence that followed, Janet looked up, shocked to see that the bar was empty, save for the people involved in the investigation. Mel was ushering the last patron, Nell, out the door. Then her bouncer turned back, her stance wide, her eyes narrowed as her gaze swept the room.

"Enough!" Abe shouted. "Just tell us what happened, Larsa. Stop blaming other people and tell us what you did."

Larsa was startled for a moment, then another tear streaked down her cheek. She roughly wiped it away. "I got here too late—the bar was closed and the parking lot was empty. I was going to head back to my car—I mean, walk home," she corrected herself when Benji gasped in anger, "when I saw Ike lying on the ground. He was alone, so you must have already left," she said to Abe. "I tried to wake him up—I—I was angry. I mean, who passes out on the ground? Jesus. He woke up swinging that damn knife of his, though. I shouted at him—told him he was an embarrassment to our family for his behavior. He didn't disagree, but then I fell back against the curb and he tripped over my feet and landed on the knife right by the Dumpster. I rolled him over . . . it was too late. I called my uncle, but by the time he got there, Ike was dead."

"Why didn't you call 911?" Janet asked, not sure she could buy Larsa's story completely.

"Uncle Mark said it didn't look good for me. He... he didn't want me to take the blame. He'd risked so much for my family already."

"What does that mean?" O'Dell asked, staring intently at Larsa.

"He was the first on the scene when . . . after . . . when Ollie died. He drove Ike home that morning and didn't pick him back up for a Breathalyzer for the whole shift. He was trying to protect us," she said, her eyes filled with pain as she looked at O'Dell. "But he only made it worse for us."

"W-worse for you? You p-people still don't get it! You never think about anyone else," Abe stammered. "Ollie's family was broken by his death and again when Ike wasn't charged. Didn't Finch know that? How could he have done that to them—to us?"

"Family," Elizabeth said with a shrug, as if that explained everything. Maybe it did.

"That certainly explains why the paperwork for Ike's recent DUI didn't get filed," Benji said, sitting down slowly. "Finch buried the report so Ike wouldn't get charged."

"Sounds like something he'd do," Larsa agreed.

"You tell a nice story, Larsa," Janet said, "but let's not forget there's another dead body to discuss. And Mark Finch's death was no accident. So what happened?"

# CHAPTER THIRTY-NINE

An uncomfortable silence fell over the group. Larsa took small, savoring sips of her beer. O'Dell's piercing gaze moved down the line of people. Abe shifted uncomfortably in his seat. But no one spoke.

After a few more minutes Janet cleared her throat. "Cindy Lou, do you know how our security system works?"

The bartender looked up from the glass she was wiping, her face blank. "Huh?"

But Abe snapped to attention. So did Benji.

"I asked if you know how our security system is set up. How the actual cameras work."

"Oh, uh . . . no, boss. I have no idea."

"Well, it turns out a few weeks ago, I started to suspect that someone was stealing money from the cash drawer." She locked the drawer, then pulled the key out, tucking it into her pocket for safekeeping. "I asked Jason Brooks—my security-expert boyfriend," she added, talking over Abe's gasp of recognition, "to wire the place from top to bottom. Top," she said again, pointing to a tiny disc embedded in the ceiling above the cash register, "to bottom." This time she pointed to the bottom edge of the front door.

Mel, surprised to suddenly be in everyone's line of sight, stepped away from the door.

Silence fell again while the group looked at the door, perplexed.

"In the cooling register cover?" Mel said, inspecting the brass plate.

"Yup," Janet said. "Right there in the corner. It's practically invisible. But the camera is all-seeing. Gets a great shot of anyone who's leaving the bar through the front door. Then a camera right over . . . there"—she pointed to the space above the office door —"can capture anyone walking toward the back of the bar. So," she said, looking back at the group, "coming, going, and being here"— she pointed back up to the ceiling—"all recorded. And the best part is, it's not on a timer, it's motion activated. So *whenever* someone's moving around in the bar, it starts recording."

"That must take up a lot of computer space," Benji said. "How many hours can you keep at a time?"

"I have terabytes of storage."

"Terabytes? That's—that's enough for—"

"Days—no, weeks of video. It's got 1080p high-def resolution, night vision, a huge field of view—" She noticed that Cindy Lou looked lost and said, "It means the camera captures a wide shot of the room, doesn't miss anything. Oh, yeah, and it records sound, too."

"Wow," Abe said.

"My man is thorough," Janet said with a shrug. "What can I say?"

O'Dell stood up, his face red again. "Are you saying you have video evidence of the murder of a police officer and haven't yet offered it up?" He breathed in and out noisily a few times, like he was trying to control his temper. "Janet Black, I should arrest you right now for obstruction of justice. That was my partner who was shot and shoved into a damn refrigerator like a piece of meat yesterday, killed in cold blood"—the group cringed at the expression, but O'Dell plowed on—"and you couldn't bother yourself to let anyone know?"

"What I'm saying, O'Dell, is that the person who killed Finch has nothing to gain by remaining quiet. In fact, they'd better come forward now. There's no hiding anything here." She looked darkly at the group. "Not when every little step and sound you make is being recorded."

She narrowed her eyes at Abe. Just behind him, a police officer slipped into the room, then another. A third led Mel outside. Janet started to lose focus. What was going on?

"Abe?" she said, watching the other man fidget with his watch. "Now's the time."

"Time for what?" he said, looking up. "I didn't kill anyone. I—I mean, yes, I should have called 911 when I found Ike drunk and passed out behind the wheel, but I don't think those are technically crimes, isn't that right, Benji?"

Janet looked to his old college roommate and friend for confirmation, but he was staring at the camera above the cash register with barely concealed rage.

"I can't believe it's going to come down to this," Benji said, shaking his head.

"Down to what?" O'Dell asked, carefully putting some space between himself and the rest of the group. Janet heard soft muttering, maybe from a walkie-talkie, and O'Dell seemed to be readying himself for something.

"Ending in a bar. I just can't—I can't believe it. You know, I never meant for this to happen. I came here to talk to *you* yesterday!" He pointed accusingly at Janet. "I wanted to let you know about Ike slipping through justice's fingers *again*. But you weren't here. Finch was. And we got to talking, because frankly, I wanted to know why the police continued to let this guy get away with shit. Even though Ike was dead, I wanted someone to be held accountable, you know? Someone let him off the hook twice— twice that *we* know of—when he was alive, and even though he's dead now, they shouldn't get away with that.

"Finch starts giving me a song and dance about how Ike Freeman needed a second chance. Well that's bullshit!" he exploded, leaping up from his seat. "He got too many second chances. That guy deserved a second chance like Ollie deserved to die!

"And I don't know, maybe he was feeling guilty or sorry, because then he told me that he and Ike were brothers. Stepbrothers. Had grown up in an awful house together, and Finch just wanted to protect him, he was the big brother, it was his job. But instead of calming me down, it just pissed me off more.

"I asked him, I said, 'Did you let Ike off—did you help him get away with murder all those years ago?' And do you know, he just nodded his head and said, 'Yes, that's what family does.'" Benji shook his head, still in disbelief a day later. "No remorse at all— and in fact, said he'd do it again if he had to."

"And you snapped," Janet said.

Unnoticed by Benji, O'Dell and the patrol officers behind him moved into place. Sweat rings bloomed out from under Cindy Lou's arms and Larsa reached over the bar and refilled her own beer.

"Damn straight I snapped," Benji said. "I—I keep this gun for safety when I ride," he said, whipping a tiny, purse-size gun from his pocket and setting it on the bar top. Abe gasped and Cindy Lou stumbled back into the liquor shelf, sending at least two bottles clanking loudly to the floor.

"When you ride your bicycle?" Janet asked. "How does that work?"

"I bought it after I got run off the road the last time. These cars, they think they own the space—that I shouldn't even be allowed on it! Do you know how many times I've been nearly killed? Last time was close—a car pushed me into a fire hydrant. I nearly broke my arm! I decided if they have a deadly weapon— their car," he clarified when he saw Janet's confused expression, "then I should, too. I carry this now when I ride, so I'm ready. Just in case.

"And you were ready yesterday. Did Finch try to run you off the road?"

"No, but he railroaded the justice system ten years ago, and then again just a few weeks ago, when he made sure Ike didn't face charges for sideswiping Abe. *He was enabling a killer*, don't you see? I couldn't stand for it. He was getting back in his car, trying to leave the scene of the crime. So I—I shot him."

A cop grabbed Benji's arms from behind. A second officer took the gun off the countertop and dropped it carefully into an evidence bag.

"But why the Beerador, Benji? Why go to all that trouble?" Janet asked, even though he was being led away in handcuffs. O'Dell stepped closer and Janet frowned, not liking his expression.

Larsa finished her beer. "Now what?"

"Now I take you downtown," O'Dell said to Larsa. He turned and pointed at Janet. "You too."

# CHAPTER FORTY

Janet's foot tapped out an uneven beat against the concrete floor of the interview room. She wasn't nervous; she *was*, however, tired, hungry, and a little chilly, if she was being completely honest. She was glad to be wearing a boxy black T-shirt instead of a tank top, at least.

"Coffee?" O'Dell asked when he stepped into the room.

"You know, when we first met, I had you pegged as the good cop. But after sitting here for two hours, I'm not so sure anymore."

He took a sip of the very coffee he'd just offered her. "I wasn't going to give you the coffee, even if you'd said yes. So I guess I am the bad cop." He sat down opposite Janet. "You pulled a very risky move back there, Janet. And if I could have my way, I'd charge you with so many offenses your head would spin."

Janet scoffed. "I don't have the video of Finch's murder! I made that whole thing up to get *Abe* to confess! I had no idea Benji was the killer."

"You don't have the video?" O'Dell said skeptically.

"No, god—*bless* it, Jason didn't give me a fifty-thousand-dollar security system! We were trying to catch an employee who'd stolen a couple thousand bucks! Plus, his system really has been down since before Ike died. He's finally getting it back up and running, but his priority was his paid clients—not me."

"I doubt that," O'Dell said.

Janet grinned despite her circumstances. "Okay, fine, you're probably right, but regardless, my system isn't back up yet."

"Actually, it is. Why do you think all those officers showed up tonight?"

"Didn't you call them?"

"No," O'Dell said with a rueful sigh. "I've been blind when it came to this case from day one. I've gotten everything wrong, pinned the blame on the wrong people, didn't trust the right ones," he said, staring at Janet. "But Jason called 911 as soon as Larsa confessed. He was watching the whole thing go down from a computer at a 'secure location,'" he added with a sour expression.

"What secure location?"

"Wouldn't I love to know."

"You don't?" Janet asked, now thoroughly confused.

"No. He won't tell me. I just finished talking to him in the next room."

"What?" Janet leapt up from her chair and took a step toward the door. Then she remembered she was stuck in this room for now.

"He came in on his own—wanted to tell us what he recorded and what he didn't."

"What did he record?" Janet asked, crossing her arms and staring at O'Dell, incensed.

"He recorded everything tonight, from the moment Larsa walked into the bar. He said he knew that you were going to get to the bottom of things, and he wanted to make sure that he captured any confession that came out on camera. That's why he had Mel empty the bar."

"Jason had Mel—wait, what?" She suddenly felt like Cindy Lou: totally clueless.

"She says he called her cell phone and asked her to get everybody out so the microphones would pick up anything important, and to keep the customers safe. He wasn't sure what might go down when the killer was cornered."

Janet flinched. Why hadn't she thought of that?

"Does that mean that you have the whole thing on tape? Larsa's claims, Abe's involvement, Benji's confession—all of that is on camera? Is it admissible?"

O'Dell steepled his fingers under his chin. "I think so. We'll let our prosecutor have the final say, obviously, but Benji's already claiming coercion."

"Bah," Janet muttered.

"Exactly. A regular citizen can't coerce someone to confess to a crime. He's grasping at straws."

"What about Larsa? What's going to happen to her?"

O'Dell took a long, slow sip of his coffee and Janet licked her lips, wishing she'd grabbed the cup from him when he walked in. Now that she thought about it, she was parched.

"I'd like to book her on murder two," he said, "but I know the prosecutor's not going to try for a court conviction. There's no one to counter her claim that it was an accident. Patricide is pretty rare, hard to get a conviction when you consider her sad story. Jury'll be very compassionate toward an orphan with an unhappy childhood."

"Do *you* think it was an accident?" she asked.

He swatted the question away with an irritated hand. "I don't want to think about it. It doesn't make a difference what I think, anyway. Prosecutor does what she wants to do."

"Huh," Janet said, slowly sitting back down. "Kind of like homicide detectives, then."

He looked up sharply, then nodded. "Fair enough. I zeroed in on Jason on day one. I didn't like his attitude, and he had that juvie conviction. Not hard to see him snapping at an obnoxious customer. I was wrong."

"So how did Jason's pen get into the Beerador with Finch's body?"

O'Dell's face flushed, and he looked uncomfortable for the first time that night. "Rebecca, one of our evidence techs, says she remembers Finch using the pen yesterday. He must have picked it up from the evidence we gathered at your house by mistake."

Mistake? She'd file that one away with *Where the hell is my coffeepot?* and move on. Now that she knew Jason had been watching over her for the past twenty-four hours, she felt warmer and fuzzier toward him than ever. "Any idea who spray-painted my house?"

"Someone graffitied your house?"

Janet shook her head. "Never mind. Can I go?"

"I just need to ask you a few questions and then we'll get you on your way. Your boyfriend is in a barely concealed rage in the waiting room; be sure to tell him we treated you nice."

Her eyebrows drew together. "Jason's still here? Why?"

"I knew you'd need a ride home—and, contrary to popular opinion, I *am* the good cop." He smiled lightly and then looked down at his notebook. "Did you ever consider telling me anything you knew when you knew it?"

"No." He grimaced and she said, "I answered one, now it's your turn. Why was Larsa so involved after Ike died? You'd think she'd have had a better chance of getting away with an 'accident' she had her uncle help cover up if she'd just laid low and stayed out of the way."

"Maybe she knew he didn't end up knocked out on the gravel by himself that night. Maybe she wanted to get to the bottom of who put him there. I think she blamed them for his death as much as anyone else."

"That's grim," Janet said, quoting O'Dell from what felt like a lifetime ago.

He shrugged. "But true." He blew out a breath before looking back up at Janet. "I would have helped you. I would have helped Elizabeth."

"Before or after charging my boyfriend with murder?"

He didn't say anything for a moment, just nodded slowly. "How'd you find her, anyway? It seems like she was the missing link to figuring everything out."

"Family," Janet said. "It always comes down to family."

O'Dell frowned. "You'll need to write it all down in a witness statement." He pushed a pad of yellow legal paper toward her and motioned to the pen on top.

She crossed her arms and leaned back in the uncomfortable metal chair. "My dad told me not to say anything until he gets here."

"No, no, you don't need a lawyer. This is just your chance to—"

"I have knowledge of a police cover-up of a debatably 'accidental' homicide," Janet said, staring stonily across the table at O'Dell. "I'm pretty sure I'm going to need a lawyer."

"Larsa has already confessed—to her version of events. And Benji will. It's only a matter of time."

"Sure, and you have to tell me the complete truth in this room, don't you? Cops *never* lie in the interview room." Janet looked suspiciously in the corners for hidden cameras. "No way. I'm waiting for my dad."

O'Dell made a face. "I guess you can wait at home, then. Come back when he gets here," he said, "and we'll get you sorted."

They both stood, and he opened the door for her to leave. "Hey, you did good," he said, all the flip attitude gone from his voice. "This would have taken years to get to the bottom of without your help—your boyfriend's help, too. I was wrong about him and you."

"Gee, thanks," Janet said drily. "It's always great to hear someone assumed you were crap until you proved them wrong."

"That's not—you know what? Fine. You're welcome."

She smiled to herself as she walked down the hall. He was fun to tease—she'd miss that.

O'Dell pointed to the exit, then continued walking down the

hall with a wave. "As soon as your father gets here, Janet. Don't make me come find you."

Her lips flattened. How could he still be issuing her orders after the night they'd just had?

When she pushed open the door to the lobby, she stumbled right into the one person she wasn't yet prepared to see.

# CHAPTER FORTY-ONE

"Janet!" Jason rushed forward, his expression a mixture of relief and concern. "God, what took so long in there?"

"Power," she said, knowing it was true. The powerful could take as long as they wanted.

Jason pulled her into a hug. "I'm sorry," he said, rocking her back and forth, not letting go. "I'm so sorry. You know why I couldn't be involved, but it was tearing me up inside. I knew you'd figure it all out; that's why I left Old Ben's video out. You're so good at reading people, I knew I didn't have to worry about you, but man, I worried about you!"

She breathed him in, getting scents of mint and vanilla as usual before steeling her nerves and pushing away. "Mmm-hmm, I can imagine. So very worried that you cut off all contact with me."

He flinched. "Don't be like that—it was a client! You know I couldn't help police investigate a client."

"Right, and now I know that in a time of crisis, I can lean on Cindy Lou, Elizabeth, and Mel, but not my boyfriend if his job happens to get in the way!" She turned her back to him. "I don't even know Mel, but she was there for me tonight and you weren't."

She wanted to make him sweat, just like he'd made her do.

"How about some new intel I got tonight?"

"Nice try. I know everything that happened tonight. I was there—you weren't—and O'Dell filled me in on the loose ends."

"I'm not talking about the murder or the confessions. Yes, yes, I saw all of that—and you were great." He stopped to look admiringly at her. "I'm talking about something else."

"What *else* could possibly have been going on at the Spot tonight?"

"While you were yammering on and on about Ike and Ollie, Larsa and Finch, the bar thief struck again, right under your nose. You were so busy, though, that you didn't notice."

"What?" Janet swore loudly. "Elizabeth is back one day and she's taking more money from me? Unbeliev—"

"Not Elizabeth."

"Not Eliz—" Janet dropped her facade of anger at Jason and popped a hand on her hip. "Then who?"

———

Nell took a sip of her screwdriver and carefully placed the highball glass on a cocktail napkin.

"Can I get you anything else?" Janet asked sweetly, making a note on a nearby pad of paper with Jason's god-awful, ugly pen that they needed more cocktail straws. When Nell shook her head, she loaded up a tray and walked around the bar to a table in the back.

"Don't forget about us, here!" she said, putting a sweet tea in front of Chip and handing the other to Cindy Lou. Janet's eyes twinkled as she added, "When you're away at school, we'll be thinking of you."

Chip's eyebrows knitted together and he looked at his mother. Cindy Lou laughed, swatting Janet's arm with good humor. "Oh, stop. I know I've been a mess lately. You just have no idea how fast it all goes," she said, motioning to the space around her son. "Watching you grow up has been the longest and the shortest stretch of time I could imagine. Yes, at the same time—it's true," she added when Chip shook his head.

"Mom, I'll be down the street. Seriously, my biology lab is less than a mile from here." The deep timbre of his voice didn't match his young face and scrawny arms.

"Did you ever find out who spray-painted your house?" Cindy Lou asked, taking a handful of trail mix from the basket Janet had just plunked down between them.

Janet chuckled. "Can you believe it was Jason?" When Cindy Lou gave her a blank look, she explained. "He's never liked the color of the house and saw this as his chance to force a paint job ahead of the kitchen remodel."

"With all that was going on, he thought it was a good time to—"

"I'm pretty sure with all that was going on, he thought he could slip one by me," Janet interrupted.

"Not a chance," Cindy Lou said.

"Nope, not a chance," Janet repeated under her breath as she walked back to the bar. Nell motioned for another lime wedge, and Janet—her finger both bandage- and pain-free—happily took one from the container.

"So, right after Mel hustled me out of the bar—very unceremoniously, by the way—the lawyer confessed to killing Detective Finch?" Nell asked.

Janet nodded. "Just two seats away from where you are right now."

"Can you imagine carrying that kind of anger around for so long? That kind of rage? Mmm." Nell dug around in her small clutch. A moment later, a tube of lipstick was in her hand, and her ruby-red lips got a touch-up. "I can't believe I missed the grand finale. Sounds like Elizabeth really saved the day by taking Ike's car."

Janet nodded. "And to think I almost fired her!"

"Why? She makes the best vodka-soda—gets the ratio just right." Nell looked up quickly and added, "No offense."

Janet shrugged. "None taken." She leaned in closer. "I thought she'd been stealing from the register. Money's been missing." Nell's back stiffened and Janet lowered her voice as she said, "And I can't have that, now, can I?"

The older woman pursed her lips and kept her eyes trained on her drink. "Well, she has to go, then. No second chances, that's what I say."

"What if there was a good reason, though? I don't want to throw someone out if they're just in a bad fix. I'd want to help them," Janet said, keeping close tabs on Nell's face.

"She's too old—she should have known better," Nell said, and Janet knew the other woman wasn't talking about Elizabeth. She drained the last of her drink and pushed her chair back with finality. "Goodbye, Janet. Thank you for—"

"No."

Nell primly fixed a flyaway hair, her face impassive. "What?"

"No, you're not walking out of here. You owe me at least two thousand four hundred twenty-nine dollars, and that's just from the last three weeks. What gives, Nell? Why have you been stealing from me? I thought we were . . . friends?"

Nell straightened her shoulders defiantly before sinking back down onto the bar stool. "I don't honestly know why. I've got a problem. I, uh, I take things that aren't mine. I just can't stop myself."

She opened her purse and took out a fat wallet stuffed with cash. "I didn't need the money—didn't spend a dime. I just like knowing I can do it." She unfolded her wallet and turned it upside down. The money was so jammed in that nothing fell out. She huffed out an irritated sigh and then forced her fingers around the edge of the wallet, freeing the wad of bills.

"It's just under one thousand. There's some change, too, but it was too heavy for my clutch. The rest of it is back at home."

Janet stared in disbelief at the mound of money between them. Her eyes flicked to Nell's open purse. "Is that my pen?"

"Oh." Nell's cheeks colored and she took Jason's pen out and handed it over.

"How long has this been going on?" Janet asked. She obviously needed a new accounting program.

"About a year."

Janet's jaw dropped, but she shut it quickly when Nell finally looked up.

"You don't have to say it—I'll go. I've lost a lot of people over my lifetime because of it, but I just can't . . . I can't make myself stop." She slid a smooth piece of sea glass across the bar. "This is Cindy Lou's. I just took it from her back pocket twenty minutes ago."

Janet stared at the aqua glass in surprise.

The older woman stood once again, slower this time, and took a step toward the door.

"Nell, you're still welcome here. You're just not allowed to sit by the cash register anymore."

The other woman looked uncertainly at Janet before smiling. "Really?"

"Like, far from the register, okay?"

Nell glided over to the opposite side of the bar and settled onto a new stool, her old smile back in place.

Janet wiped down the counter and looked at the clock; Elizabeth would be in for her shift any minute. Janet would have to rearrange the schedule soon to accommodate Elizabeth's new semester of classes at the community college. Mel had the day off so she and Kat could attend an adoption hearing, but Janet wasn't expecting any trouble at the door that night, and if there was, Jason was in the office, ready to spring into service if needed.

Her father, as much as she wasn't looking forward to it, was due at the airport first thing the following morning. He was going to help her write out a statement for the police, and—if she knew him at all—give O'Dell one hell of a talking-to.

She hummed to herself as she worked, giving the cutting board and lemon knife a wide berth. Not long ago, Janet had been all alone. Now she'd reconnected with a father she once didn't know existed, her boyfriend had her back, and the truth was that everyone at the Spot was a part of her family, too.

"Another one, sweetie?" Nell asked, pointing to her empty glass.

Janet nodded and pulled a glass from the shelf. Sure, they were a bunch of nut jobs and kleptos, but they were hers, and that's all that mattered.

<<<<>>>>

(Turn the page for a preview of Last Minute, available now for pre-order!

# ALSO BY LIBBY KIRSCH

**The Stella Reynolds Mystery Series**

The Big Lead

The Big Interview

The Big Overnight

The Big Weekend

The Big Job

**The Janet Black Mystery Series**

Last Call

Last Minute

Last Chance

For updates on new releases or to connect with the author, go to
www.LibbyKirschBooks.com

# ABOUT THE AUTHOR

Libby Kirsch is an Emmy award winning journalist with over ten years of experience working in television newsrooms of all sizes. She draws on her rich history of making embarrassing mistakes on live TV, and is happy to finally indulge her creative writing side, instead of always having to stick to the facts.
Libby lives in Michigan with her husband, three young children, and Sam the dog.

*Connect with Libby*
www.LibbyKirschBooks.com
Libby@LibbyKirschBooks.com

facebook.com/LibbyKirschBooks

twitter.com/LibbyKirsch

amazon.com/author/libbykirsch

bookbub.com/authors/libby-kirsch

goodreads.com/libbykirsch

A JANET BLACK MYSTERY

# LAST
# MINUTE

## LIBBY
## KIRSCH

# LAST MINUTE—SPECIAL PREVIEW

## Chapter One

Janet Black stood back and looked at a spot on the floor near the bed critically for a long moment, then finally nodded at her boyfriend. "You know what? I think you're right."

Jason Brooks raised his eyebrows. "Well, darlin', let the record reflect that on September fourteenth, at three forty-seven in the afternoon—"

"Oh, shut up and get a stool! That should take care of the problem."

Jason's eyes lingered on her before he turned and left the room. Janet adjusted her garter belt and tapped the heel of her stiletto against the wood floor. *Ta-ta-tap. Ta-ta-tap. Ta-ta—*

"Something like this?" Jason was back, his expression betraying his opinion that it would never work.

"Yes!" Janet grabbed the stool and then eyed the bed before placing it on the floor about two and a half feet away from the edge of the mattress. "If I stand on the stool and then do a back-bend to the mattress, everything should line right up—"

"What kind of tread do those heels have?" Jason's eyes

narrowed and he nudged the stool closer to the bed by a few inches with his toe. "I don't know . . . if your hands slip, you'll fall to the floor." Jason crept toward her, despite his objection.

"Well, you won't just be standing there, will you? You'll be holding on to my hips!" Janet tossed her shoulder-length light brown hair back and pushed her chest out while batting her hazel eyes at her boyfriend. At five foot six, she was too short for her original idea—but the step stool and heels combined more than made up for the height difference. "I know you won't let me fall."

The colorful ink on Jason's arms rippled as he crossed them and considered Janet's plan. He'd shed his shirt earlier and the top button on his jeans was undone. Janet licked her lips as she watched him, picturing him doing what she wanted him to do.

She wiggled her hips and he finally reached for her.

*Ring, ring.*

"The phone," Jason murmured, stepping close. His day-old whiskers tickled her neck.

"Let's ignore it," she sighed, and ran her hands down his arms.

The phone went quiet, and his lips moved across her neck and up her jaw until he finally parted her lips with his tongue. Heat licked up from her core. Her legs felt like jelly.

*Ring, ring.*

"Damn it," she moaned, reaching back blindly for the receiver on the nightstand. "What?" She sucked in a gasp when Jason knelt in front of her, nibbling at sensitive skin.

"Uh, boss?" The woman's twangy, uncertain tone made it clear who was on the other end.

"What is it, Cindy Lou?" Janet focused on not moaning as she shifted her body to the right. Jason grinned and kept working his way up her leg.

"I think you better come in," the bartender said. "We've got—well, cops are here, and I don't know what to do."

Janet pushed back from Jason and thumped down on the bed, worry edging away all other emotions. "What do you—wait, never mind. I'll be right in."

She dropped the phone back onto the receiver. "Cops are at the Spot! I've got to go."

Her boyfriend's eyebrows knitted together. "I'll come, too."

"That's sweet, but you don't have to—"

"Janet! Of course I'm coming." He hopped up with a scowl and snagged his shirt off the ground as he stalked out of the room.

She blew out a sigh. Somehow he'd taken her offer for him to stay home as an insult.

She slipped out of the lingerie and got dressed in her usual bar "uniform" of jeans and a T-shirt. So much for being spontaneous. She picked up an envelope off the dresser and left the room. Jason's dad's mail had inadvertently been mixed in with hers, and she tossed it on the hall table on her way to the front door.

William Brooks had moved in with them over the summer, after he and Jason's mom argued their way through a messy divorce. The situation was not ideal, but Jason felt bad; his dad had nowhere else to go, so they'd been making the best of it.

On the plus side, William had been working on their kitchen remodeling project. In the minus column, he spent a lot of time moping around the house. Janet struggled to feel empathy for the man; after all, you can't cheat on a woman and then be mad when she leaves you!

"Ready?" she called to Jason.

"Let's go." He swept past her and she frowned. Every time she tried to do something nice, Jason took it as dismissive. William Brooks had brought his bad mojo from Memphis and Janet couldn't wait for him to leave.

"Bye, William. We'll be home later."

"Everything okay, Janet?" He stuck his head through the open kitchen door; drywall dust covered his hair. "I forgot to tell you I called an arborist to come to the Spot. Those ash trees need to come down—they're being devoured by emerald ash borers—"

"Fine, William, thanks so much." She turned and walked out of the house, a stiff smile plastered on her face. He needed to get his own home and business to worry over, and leave hers alone.

———

Janet stood frozen in the parking lot. The bar's Beerador, a massive seven-foot-tall, bottle-shaped refrigerator, stood guard by the door. The unusual appliance had come with the bar when Janet and Jason had bought it years ago, but it had been taken during a murder investigation several months earlier. Why was it back?

She shuddered slightly, remembering the body she'd found, staring lifelessly out the Beerador's window. A quick look behind her confirmed that Jason was still on the phone call that had just come in when he parked. She waved when he looked up, then turned and strode into the Spot. It took a moment for her eyes to adjust to the low lighting inside.

Her bar looked like it had been ransacked.

Someone had cleared a path from the door to the center of the room, forcing tables and chairs aside in an uneven mess.

Janet made her way behind the bar to Cindy Lou.

Her assistant manager, and most faithful bartender, was channeling Rosie the Riveter that day; her bleached-blond hair was tied back in a red bandana, and a short denim jumper with a plunging neckline replaced the blue jumpsuit from the poster.

"What's going on?"

Cindy Lou stared pointedly across the bar but didn't speak, only continued to prep a pile of lemons for the night ahead, her knife making *click, clack, clack* sounds against the cutting board.

"I should charge you extra for the door-to-door delivery, but I won't." The deep voice came from Janet's left. Detective Patrick O'Dell grinned from a bar stool, his green eyes sparkling mischievously. A sports coat hung off the back of his chair, and his white shirtsleeves were rolled up to the elbow. One of her regulars, Nell, an older woman with silvery-gray hair, waved, but Janet could only stare at the cop, her mouth open.

His resulting chuckle shook her tongue loose. "You're giving it back? I mean, shouldn't it go to . . . I just assumed it would be disposed of, or something—I . . ."

Janet eyed the Beerador suspiciously. She'd thought—hoped—she'd never see it again.

"Would have cost the city too much to bring it to the dump with the fees and everything," O'Dell said. "Where do you want my guys to put it?"

"Ahhh . . ." Janet grimaced. "Has it been cleaned or anything?"

"Nope."

"Son of a—"

"Biscuit!" Cindy Lou interrupted with a sharp elbow in Janet's side. "It can be just as satisfying if you say it right," she added out of the side of her mouth.

Janet snorted. Nothing could be as satisfying as a real curse word, but she bit back the one that had been on her lips, crossed her arms, and glared at the refrigerator. She'd once considered the Beerador fun—campy, almost—but now . . . Now it was a tainted vessel of death. "What am I supposed to do with it?"

"Clean it out, I guess, hon." Cindy Lou wiped her forehead with the back of her hand, then pointed at the offending appliance with her chef's knife. "I'm gettin' dirty just looking at all that fingerprint dust! I bet if we use a mixture of bleach and baking soda—"

"We'll blow up the building?" Janet popped a hand on her hip and scowled at the Beerador.

"Everything okay?" Jason edged past the Beerador at the front entrance, then stopped short when he saw O'Dell. "Oh." He crossed his arms over his chest and came to a stop several feet away from the bar.

O'Dell forced a grin. "Jason. Good to see you, man."

Just beyond O'Dell, Nell leaned in, her eyes flicking from O'Dell's wallet to his hand resting just inches away. Nell's dark, quick eyes—magnified through the enormous lenses of her bold, black eyeglass frames—were even then calculating the distance between his wallet and her handbag.

Janet stifled a groan; the last thing she needed just then was for their resident klepto to strike against Knoxville's lead homicide investigator. She cleared her throat. "Nell, did you need another round?"

Nell dropped her chin to her chest and tucked a stray gray hair back into her tidy, low bun. "All good here, Janet."

Janet smiled to herself, then racked her brain for how to solve the larger problem in the room. "I think . . . we should . . . turn the Beerador into a coat closet."

Cindy Lou's nose wrinkled, and her head tilted to one side. "I don't know. It wouldn't hold that many coats, would it?"

Jason didn't smile. With a scowl still etched firmly on his face, he said to O'Dell, "Now that it's here, I guess you'll be on your way."

O'Dell slid off his bar stool and laid a few bills from his wallet on the bar for Cindy Lou, then all six foot one of him tried to move past Nell. The older woman closed her eyes and leaned into the empty space between them with her puckered lips tilted up when he brushed past. Janet almost laughed out loud. Nell hated cops, but even she couldn't ignore O'Dell's broad, muscular frame and boyish good looks.

Janet met O'Dell on the other side of the countertop. "Can your guys move it out of the doorway, at least?"

"Sure." O'Dell grinned at Jason as he rested a hand on her shoulder and squeezed. "Anything for you, Janet."

Jason's chest puffed out and Janet stifled a groan. These two grown men were acting like possessive peacocks.

O'Dell tapped something into his cell phone and soon four burly men walked into the bar with a heavy-duty hand cart.

As they surrounded the Beerador, O'Dell asked, "Where do you want it, Janet?"

"Jason?" She turned to her boyfriend, but he was beyond being able to help. Waves of irritation rolled off his body like freshly applied aftershave.

She locked eyes with Cindy Lou. Her head bartender lifted one shoulder and dropped it back down, then motioned behind her. "I always did like having bottles in there."

Janet raked a hand over her face. "I guess back behind the bar, O'Dell. We'll deep-clean it and see if it still works." Could you get the smell of murder out of a refrigerator? Seemed like a Clorox wipe just wasn't going to be enough.

As the men navigated their way through the bar with the heavy load, the front door opened, and a beam of sunlight sparkled beautifully off the Beerador's curved glass door.

Cindy Lou gasped, and new emotion multiplied the twang in her voice when she said, "I think she's glad to be back home, y'all!"

Janet suppressed a snort and turned her attention to the newcomer. "Come on in, don't mind the mess. Can I get you a drink?"

But the man, wearing a herringbone sports coat over khakis and a blue button-down, beelined for O'Dell. A golden badge glinted at his waist. "O'Dell. What are you doing here?"

"I'm delivering that back to its rightful owners." He pointed to the Beerador, which came down off the dolly with a crash behind Cindy Lou. "I thought you were heading to a dead body call out, Rivera?"

"I did." Rivera scanned the bar. "Now I'm here to find Nell Anderson. Do you know her?"

Janet leaned in when O'Dell asked, "What's going on?"

Rivera blew out a sigh and lowered his voice. "I just came from her daughter's house. She's dead."

———

Pre-Order *Last Minute* today!

29831130R00154

Made in the USA
Middletown, DE
22 December 2018